LUKE

CORA ROSE

CREDITS

Editor: Angela O'Connell

To my readers who wanted this book to be written.
Without you, Luke wouldn't have had a story.
And who wants an unhappy ending (besides you, Ryan?)
Not me, that's who.

PREFACE

Initially, Luke wasn't going to have a book. But then, my editor and I discussed it and came up with this.

And it's perfect.

She dubbed this Whit 2.0, and I'm not even mad about it.

So, rest assured that this story is over the top and ridiculous. I cackled my way through it because it was Luke and Elliot, and they're hilarious together.

Once again, just suspend belief a bit and roll with it.

Life's too short to be upset about the little things.

Content warning: Brief mentions of transphobia.

CHAPTER ONE

LUKE

"Hey, man, you can't cut in line," I say to the guy who just waltzed his ass in front of me. He's wearing some fancy business clothes and is a few inches shorter and a bit leaner than me, but still, he turns and meets my glower with one of his own.

I could crush him in the palm of my hand, but he doesn't act afraid. Nah, he just glares up at me, narrowing his eyes, like he's looking down his nose at *me*.

Dark brown eyes meet my irritated stare. "You're bleeding," he says curtly. His voice is deep and crisp, and his forceful tone has me standing up a little taller. I haven't been talked to like this in...well, ever.

I roll my eyes. "So what? Still can't cut. Where you from, huh? Is this how you do it in the big city? Just cut your way through lines, take whatever you want? Where I come from, that gets you shot."

"Shocker. I assume missing teeth and banjos are involved too," he mutters, still eyeing my forehead. I swipe at it and see red smeared on my hand.

"Oh. Damn."

"I told you so," the man says and then sighs heavily, moving out of line and gesturing for me to follow him. Well, the joke's on him. I'm getting my damn coffee first.

Sucker.

I move to the counter and smile widely at the barista behind the register. She looks slightly horrified. Whatever. Getting my coffee is serious business. I don't mess around with this shit. I'd crawl in here with my legs blown off to get some of this sugary goodness.

"I'll have a large white mocha, extra whipped cream, with sprinkles on top. The red ones. *Please*," I tack on.

"You're...." She motions to my head, and I sigh.

"Yeah, I know. Everyone keeps talking about it, but I want to get my drink before I handle it. Do you mind? I've been craving this shit for *days. Days.*"

She swallows, eyeing the bloody mess on my head, and then nods. She takes my order, and I swipe my card. When that's done, I cross the small coffee shop toward the clearly annoyed man waiting for me near the napkins and straws. Hey, it's not my fault he lost his place in line. He has a terrible sense of priorities.

"What are you gonna do, patch me up? You a doctor?" I ask as he hands me a wad of napkins. I press it to my forehead and stare down at him. He's so serious-looking, with dark brown hair parted and combed neatly to the side. He sort of reminds me of that actor Nicholas Hoult from the *X-Men* movies with his long lashes, faint stubble, and full lips. He's a good-looking dude, in an uptight sort of way. His black-framed glasses are tucked into the pocket of his nicely pressed button-down shirt, and I resist the urge to touch the fabric. It looks soft.

"As a matter of fact, I *am* a doctor. And speaking with authority, you should really go to the urgent care clinic and have this stitched up," he says, peeling the wad of napkins from my forehead and peeking at the wound. "How did this happen?"

I run a hand along my jaw. "Uh, dunno."

His eyes narrow. "You don't know?"

"Nah. I mean, I have an idea, but I'm not sure."

"How can you not be sure?" the man asks, arching a stern eyebrow at me. Damn, he looks like Whit when he does that. Maybe they're related. If they are, they probably scowl at one another at family gatherings. I can only imagine what that Thanksgiving would be like.

I shrug. "This happens to me often. Just part of the job."

"It happens often..." He sighs. "Well, you can't just walk around with blood dripping down your face. This isn't a horror film. It's not okay. This is civilization."

I eyeball this guy and then lean toward him. "You gonna fix me up, Doc? Make me all respectable?"

He huffs and looks away from me. "This is so my luck," he mutters, and then those dark eyes meet mine again. "Before we continue this conversation, tell me, are you in the mafia?"

My head snaps back, and my eyebrows rise. "Why the fuck would I be in the mafia?"

He stares at me, deadpan. "You have a crazed look about you, and I don't want to be indebted to criminals."

I snort. "Indebted to criminals? What the hell are you even talking about?"

"We've all seen the TV shows. I help you now and then

the next thing I know, you'll show up on my doorstep with a gunshot wound, and I'll have to perform emergency surgery on my kitchen table before you bleed out. It never ends well for the doctor. I'm not cut out for a life of crime."

"Nah," I mutter. "I know gun safety. Now, a knife wound... that's more probable. The ones I have are sharp as fuck. Almost sliced my finger off last week. It was gnarly and scary as hell. Almost pissed myself."

The man just stares up at me like he can't believe I'm real, and then shakes his head.

"I don't have time for this. Come on. Outside. Now. I have butterfly bandages in my glovebox."

I hold a finger up. "Now, hold up. Not so fast, Doc. I need my drink first."

He lowers his eyebrows and taps his foot in annoyance as I walk to the front of the shop, grab my large white mocha, and take a long sip. Fuck, these are so good. The brilliant person who came up with this drink must be a billionaire. They're like sweet, frothy cups of magic. I'm pretty sure they're laced with drugs too, because I am fully addicted.

"Have you bled out yet? Because you floated across that floor slower than a manatee," the man says dryly. Well, fuck him. I don't want to rush. Life always moves so fast. Why the hell can't I just slow down and enjoy something once in a while?

"Nah, I don't float. I stride, or maybe saunter, but I don't float. What's with the attitude? Maybe you should get a coffee too, grumpy."

"I'm not grumpy, and I *was* getting a coffee before you interrupted me with this gory horror show on your face."

"You sure look like a grump, *Oscar the Grouch*. Where's

your garbage can, huh? That where you popped out of this morning?" I tease.

He narrows his eyes at me and then moves out the door toward the parking lot at the back of the building. I'm helpless to do anything but follow him because, damn, I'm intrigued.

"I'm right over here. I trust you won't murder me," he says and gestures toward a white Tesla Model X that nearly shines with how polished it is.

"Nah. I'm not a serial killer."

He eyeballs me like he doesn't quite believe it, but moves toward his car anyway and grabs onto the handle, pulling it open.

"Cool car," I say. "You must be rich, Mr. Moneybags."

"You going to rob me now, Mr. 'I'm not a serial killer'?"

"Nah. Money can't buy happiness..." I eye him and smirk. "Apparently."

A butterfly bandage appears in his hand, and then he pulls on a pair of blue latex gloves, snapping them loudly, before dousing a piece of gauze in some liquid and squishing it into my wound.

And fuck, that stings.

I hiss, and the man gives me a small, satisfied smirk.

I glare at him. "You're getting off on this, huh? Watching someone writhe in the pain you've caused. You're gonna jack off to thoughts of it later, aren't you?"

"You're assuming I have a dick I can jack off," he mutters, swiping the wet gauze over my wound again. My eyes instinctively move to his crotch and then back to his face, but he's not looking at me. He's working open the bandage and then sticking it to my head. "You should really go see someone about getting stitches. This is going to scar."

"Nah," I reply, eyeing him again, my mind reeling. "There are more important matters pending at the moment. Like, what did you mean by that?"

I'm fucking curious now. I'm like a cat sniffing around; gonna catch that mouse.

"Mean by what?"

"You said you don't have a dick."

He arches an eyebrow at me, and I meet his unwavering stare.

"You must be hearing things."

"Nah, man. I didn't. I have great hearing, like Superman."

He shrugs, peeling the gloves off, walking to the trashcan next to the brick wall, and tossing them away. I'm left standing near his car, watching him move back inside the coffee shop, and I can't fucking help myself. I follow him back inside, and stand right behind him in line, hovering over him like a gargoyle.

"What are you doing?" he hisses, elbowing me in the stomach.

I grunt at the contact and shuffle a half step farther away, but I'm still close enough that I can loom over him. "I'm in line."

"For what? You already got your coffee, if that sugar concoction you ordered actually passes for coffee."

"Getting another. I could drink like ten of those. Gives me the shits, but damn, it's worth it."

"That can't be good for your heart, or your bowels."

"Ah, worried about me, Doc?" Then I scoot closer to him, despite the threat of getting another elbow to my abs. They can handle it. I've dealt with *way* worse. Like that one time I flew off my ATV and broke most of my ribs. Or, the time my brother shot me point-blank in the stomach with a potato gun.

"What's your name?" I ask, leaning toward him and whispering it in his ear.

He sighs and folds his arms across his chest. "If I tell you, will you go away?"

I shrug, lingering like an idiot.

He turns to observe me and when I refuse to budge, he murmurs, "Elliot."

I beam at his acceptance that this is a thing. We are so friends now. "Elliot. I'm Luke."

He stares at my extended hand and then slowly places his in mine. I squeeze his palm gently, feeling his soft skin slide against mine. Damn, he has nice hands.

Suddenly, he tugs his hand away before turning to face the counter.

"Now," he says sternly. "Say 'thank you' and be on your way, Luke."

"Nah," I mutter, feeling defiant. "Doc Elliot. You've piqued my interest, and I need answers. I can't leave until I have them."

"Jesus. This was a mistake," he utters, pinching the bridge of his nose, and then steps forward to the counter to order his coffee. "Black. No room for cream."

My eyebrows meet in confusion. "Why don't you just make your own coffee at home with an order like that? Did you know they have sprinkles here, man? Red ones. And whipped cream that they make from scratch. Why would you order a black coffee?"

"I don't need to justify myself to you, Luke. Now go away."

Of course, I don't fucking listen. He's not my mom.

Instead, I follow him to the other side of the store and lean against the wall, watching him.

He pulls his phone out and pretends to fiddle with it, but I just stare at him steadily until he meets my gaze again. He groans loudly and then grabs his coffee from the counter.

He holds up two fingers as he walks outside, and I scramble after him, knocking into the garbage can as I go. "Fine. Two questions, and then I have to go back to work. You took up my entire break. I have patients waiting for me."

"Cool, cool," I say, lengthening my strides to keep up with him.

When we make it to his Tesla, he starts tapping his foot on the ground and glancing at his watch.

I run a finger over the smooth white paint on the roof of his car as he takes a slow sip of his coffee and glances at me warily.

"Why you lookin' at me like that?" I ask.

"Just ask your questions. I have to go."

"Fine. You told me you don't have a dick," I say, waving to his crotch. "Care to explain?"

"Not really, but since I'm pretty sure you won't leave me alone until I do..." he sighs and then meets my eyes. "I'm transgender."

My eyebrows hit my hairline as I let my gaze sweep over him. I did not see that coming. Not that I know what I'm looking for, but fuck. I had no clue.

"No kidding."

"Of course, I'm not kidding."

"So, you were born a...."

"Yes, I was assigned female at birth, but I'm a man."

"And you don't have a dick?"

"I do, but I opted against bottom surgery, so not in the traditional sense."

I rub a hand over my jaw and roll my lips between my teeth, trying to envision it.

I run my tongue over my teeth. "I kinda want to see that."

"Oh Jesus," Elliot mutters, opening the driver's side door. "You are insane. Certifiable. You should be committed. I have to go."

I rush toward him. "But wait, I get another question. You said I get two." I hold up a finger, and then another. "One, two. I can count."

"No. Teaching time is over. You're on your own now. It was *not* so nice to meet you, Luke. Goodbye."

I move to stop him, but he's locked the door and is already backing out of the parking space, running over my foot in the process.

"Fuck," I say, staring down at my throbbing toes.

But they don't matter, not really, because Elliot left me hanging. What the hell? Just when I finally go and meet someone interesting, they drive over my foot and leave me. He could have broken my toes for all he knows.

Hm, well, joke's on him. I'm a pro at online sleuthing. How many doctors named Elliot can there possibly be in this city?

I'll find him eventually.

Just give me a few days.

———

"I'm here to see Dr. Madden," I say, leaning over the small counter and grinning at the receptionist. She has pink hair and purple lipstick and looks like an anime character. *Amanda*, her nametag reads.

"Do you have an appointment?" she asks dryly, arching one bushy, sculpted eyebrow at me. It's impressive, really. It seems to have a mind of its own; I think it even scowls at me.

"Pfft, of course I do, Amanda. I made all the appointments."

I try to charm her with my eyes, but she just stares at me blankly. I sniff and then gesture to the bandage on my face. "He did this to me, busted my head right open. And then he ran over my foot with his car. He felt like shit about it, too. Told me to show up here so he could make sure I was feeling better. And hell, it hurts like a bitch. Could be broken. Could possibly fall off. It's starting to smell like cheese and not the good kind. Dr. Google told me I have gangrene."

She looks bored and unconvinced as she blows a large bubble with her pink gum. It pops loudly and she sucks the pieces back into her mouth, nodding to the seating area in front of her. "Take a seat, crazy."

I knew I could win her over. She's putty in my hands.

I lower myself into the chair next to an older, balding man and lean in close, eyeballing his *4-Wheel* magazine over his shoulder. He side-eyes me and then scoots three chairs over.

Asshole. No one likes to share anymore.

I glance up and see the anime receptionist watching me. She pops another bubble and then arches her other eyebrow at me. I'm convinced they're not actually attached to her face.

Two can play this game.

I waggle mine at her.

She crosses her eyes.

I stick out my tongue and fold it in half.

Fuck, I could do this all day. I have all sorts of tricks up my sleeve.

Two minutes later, I see Elliot enter the waiting room, his eyes narrowing as he takes me in. He's wearing fitted grey slacks, a tucked-in blue button-up, and a white lab coat. His hair is impeccably combed to the side, and his trendy glasses sit perched on his nose as he blinks at me in irritation.

"Luke," he mutters, and yeah, I notice that he remembers my name. How could he not? I'm memorable. I force my way into people's brains and stick like glue. "My worst nightmare, and yet here you are in the light of day. Amanda said it was urgent. Come on. Right this way."

I glance at Amanda, and she flips me off.

Elliot doesn't notice; he just holds open the door leading to the back of the office, and I push myself up.

I smirk at the receptionist one more time as I pass, and she narrows her eyes at me. It seems to be a thing in this place. Maybe it's in the job description.

Must be able to glower.

We enter a small examination room on the right, and Elliot closes the door. Quickly, I lower myself onto the table and lean back on my hands, taking in the small space. This whole building is so...quaint. This little private practice was not what I'd expected when I'd met Elliot. I thought he'd work in a busy ER, or maybe even a laboratory where he could scowl at Petri dishes all day. I glance around the room once more. It's clean, even if it's a little older. It could do with new floors and maybe even a coat of paint, but it's not bad.

I'd so be a patient here. Especially if Elliot was my doctor.

I wonder what kind of exams he specializes in.

Elliot clears his throat, folds his arms, and faces me. "What are you doing here, Luke?"

"Well, you stormed off without giving me your number, so I had to find you. It was a lot of work too. You should be impressed. I put in hours trying to find out where you worked. Even stood up a date to do some sleuthing. I'm like Scooby-Doo."

He blinks at me for a moment and then sighs, walking to a small sink in the room, and washes his hands. "You can't just show up at my place of work demanding to see me."

"Okay, well, that strange girl up front exaggerates. I asked nicely. I even smiled," I say, baring my teeth for him.

"Jesus," Elliot says under his breath and then dries his hands off. "Well, since you're here, I might as well take a look at this."

He gestures to the bandage on my forehead, so I lie back on the table and smirk as he pulls on gloves and examines the wound.

"It's healing well."

"I know. I'm like Wolverine. My skin just stitches back together naturally."

He meets my stare. "That's how all humans work."

I snort and sit up, rubbing a hand across my lightly stubbled jaw.

"Look, no more beating around the bush. I went through all this trouble, and I'm just gonna put this out there. I want to hang out."

"No, thank you," he says quickly, his eyes darting away from mine.

"Why not?" I ask. "You look like you need to have a good time. And I'm a good time."

"I'm sure you're something," he mutters. "And I have plenty of good times."

My eyebrows rise. "I guarantee that if you come out with

me and we hang, you'll realize your good times aren't that great. They're probably boring as fuck."

Elliot lets his gaze slide over me, and he deflates a little. "I am never getting rid of you, am I?"

I put my hands behind my head and stretch out a little. "Nope."

"I made a huge mistake engaging with you in the coffee shop."

"Apparently."

"Am I an oddity to you? Is that what this is?" he asks, and I cock my head.

"Why would you be?"

"Because I'm trans, and have you ever met someone like me before in your entire life?"

"Nah, but I like the unexpected. Makes life fun and interesting. And you definitely seem like you could use some fun. Besides, you can never have too many friends, right? Hey, what are your pronouns, by the way?"

Elliot eyes me like I've grown a hundred new heads. Whatever, I can be sensitive to this shit. I'm not an asshole or a bigot.

"He, him works just fine."

Elliot eyes me warily again and then rewashes his hands, drying them off quickly, like he's trying to run away.

Good thing I run really quick. Got chased by the police a few times, but they never caught me.

"Not so fast, dude. Can I have your number? Please?" I interject before he can slip from the room. "And I know all the tricks. So, I need to make sure you're not giving me some fake number, yeah?"

Elliot sighs, his shoulders slumping even farther. "If I give this to you, you will *not* be texting me at all hours. I have boundaries."

I sit up and rub my hands together. "Oh, fuck. I love boundaries."

Elliot stares at me. "Why don't I believe that?"

"I love trespassing," I add with a smirk. "Can't do that without boundaries."

"Jesus. Do not make me get a restraining order. Do you love those too?"

"Nah, that's serious shit. I don't mess with the law. Mostly. Sort of. Not really, if I'm being honest. But I don't hurt people and I certainly wouldn't run over someone's foot with my car and then not stop to see if they're okay," I say, trying for a pouty face.

Elliot blows out a breath and mumbles, "This is some psychological warfare shit." Looking resigned to his fate, he rattles off a series of numbers as I punch them into my phone and send him a text. His phone pings in his lab coat pocket.

He pulls it out and shows it to me. I see my number on the screen and beam at him.

"Put me in there as Bestie. BFF works too," I tease.

"No."

"Come on, Doc."

"I will put you in as Luke. Nothing more, nothing less," he mutters, punching the screen. Then he shows it to me. "Happy now?"

I glance at my name on the screen.

"Oh, Doc, you have no idea. You and I...we're going to be pals."

———

I stay away for two whole days before I crack. I never was very good at staying away from what I want. Self-control? Nah, that shit is boring. Who wants that?

Well, Elliot, maybe. He seems like the definition of self-control, all buttoned up and serious. I want to unbutton him, bit by bit. Not like that.

Well, maybe a little like that.

But mainly, I just want to watch that mouth of his turn up in a smile.

Or maybe even open for a laugh.

Yeah, I could go for that.

I pull out my phone as I turn my truck off and lean back in my seat.

Me: What are you doing?

Elliot's response is almost immediate, and I smile. That little fucker was probably waiting around for me to text him. He seems like the type, all fierce and grumpy on the outside, but a total marshmallow on the inside.

Doc: New phone. Who's this?
Me: Ha. Ha. Very funny, Doc. Want to hang out? You've been ignoring me. I didn't even get one single text these past two days.
Doc: NO. No hanging out.

I glance around at the quiet tree-lined street in this quaint suburb. It probably has an HOA, too. I look to my left and note the grey and white one-story house with the well-maintained front yard. Nothing seems out of place, even the hedges look tidy. Elliot probably stands out there in the mornings with clippers, cutting off individual wayward leaves.

I snort, envisioning it.

He probably has nice gardening gloves for those soft hands of his.

Me: Come on. Don't leave me hanging. I'm outside.
Doc: I'm calling the cops.

I slide out of the truck and slam the door. The sound echoes off the pavement, and I smile down at my phone.

Me: Just kidding.

Then I chuckle because I'm fucking hilarious.

Me: No, really. I'm not kidding. I'm outside your house. Come on. Let me in.
Me: I brought drinks.

I see the curtains in the house move, and I wave. Asshole thinks he can hide from me. He's not even being subtle about it. No, he wants me to see him looking.

Doc: Calling the cops now.
Doc: They're on their way. Better run.

Ten minutes later, I'm lying on the ground, the beers abandoned on the porch. My fingers fly over my screen, my mouth spread in a smile.

Me: I'm in the bushes. You fucking called the cops.

Me: You're an asshole.
Doc: Ha.

Oh fuck, did he just laugh? Maybe I made him laugh. I don't think he does that very often. I pull my bottom lip between my teeth and glance up at the window right above me. I shuffle around a bit in the dirt, trying to get comfortable. I think there's a twig in my lower back. It's bugging the shit out of me.

Me: I'm coming in your window. Try and stop me.
Doc: Front door is already open. Come on in.

I push myself up, emerging from the hedge like the Night Stalker, and then jog up the front steps to his house. I shuffle my feet around on his boring 'welcome' mat, grabbing the case of beers, and let myself in through his front door. I force myself to glower at Elliot, who is leaning against the kitchen island, but he doesn't seem bothered by my fake-angry stare. No, he just smirks up at me as I approach him and then reaches up to pull a leaf from my hair.

"You're an asshole," I mutter, but I don't mean it. He is halfway smiling, and I like it. I immediately want to make him smile again.

"You like to repeat yourself. Perhaps you need a diagnosis."

He grabs the beers from my hand and plops them onto the counter with a clink.

"Why'd you do that, though?" I ask, grabbing a beer and flicking the cap off. It tumbles onto the counter, and I take a long swig, letting myself look over his space. It's nice, really fucking nice, and new. Looks like he had it redone from top to bottom—real hardwood floors, custom-made cabinetry in the kitchen, granite countertops, and professionally painted walls.

Everything is grey and green and white. It's like living in a magazine.

In one corner of the living space is a large grand piano, and I wonder for a second if he plays. Fuck, I'd like to hear him play. He's probably good too. Those soft fingers floating across the keys.

"Do you mean, why did I call the cops? Oh, I don't know. Maybe because I never gave you my address, and yet you showed up here in the middle of the night...."

I glance at the microwave clock. "It's ten o'clock."

"On a Saturday."

I smirk at him. "And just like that, I knew you'd be home. Alone."

Elliot glances down at his pajama pants and his plaid button-up top. He looks like Bert from *Sesame Street*.

"What the fuck are you wearing?" I ask, flicking one of the buttons on his shirt.

"Pajamas. Let me guess, you sleep nude like the heathen you are?"

"Fuck yeah, I do. Freedom, baby. And you sleep like you're a fucking Muppet."

Elliot rolls his eyes, grabs a beer, and then takes a long swig. He coughs and then sets the beer down, muttering *disgusting* under his breath. I grab onto the discarded bottle and press it to my mouth. I kind of like that we're swappin' spit right about now.

Doesn't bother me in the least.

"I hate the Muppets," he adds, watching me gulp the liquid down.

"Me too," I shudder and give a small burp. "They are freaky little fuckers. It's not natural."

I eye the immaculate space again and run a fingertip across the sparkling countertops. He probably never cooks in here; probably has a chef come in once a week to prepare his meals. They're probably all healthy too.

"So, what are we going to do now?" I ask.

Elliot folds his arms across his chest. "Preferably, you'll leave, never to be seen again."

"Nah, you'd miss me if I disappeared. I've already wiggled my way into your heart. Let's watch a movie. I brought all the *Lethal Weapons*."

I reach into my satchel and pull out the DVDs.

Elliot stares at them for a long minute and then shakes his head. "Oh my god."

"Nah. Don't hate. They're so good. Have you seen them?"

He eyes the cases in my hand with despair. "There are *four* of them?"

"Fuck yeah, there are. Do you have popcorn? 'Cause I forgot that shit."

"We'll be up all night if we watch all four."

I chuckle at how mortified he looks and flick the button on his pajamas again. "That's the point. Live a little, Eli."

He arches his eyebrow at me, and I can't help but ask, "Are you related to Whit?"

His eyebrows rise a little higher. Damn, it's a gift.

"Who's that?"

"Never mind," I say, grabbing onto my third beer before moving toward the living room and putting the DVD into the player. I flop down on the leather couch with a loud squeak and spread my arms and legs. I glance back at Elliot and pat the cushion next to me.

"Come on, man. I'm lonely. Been a while since I cuddled."

Elliot huffs but moves toward me anyways. And when he sits a little too far away, I just scoot over until our sides are pressed together. He can't escape me.

I'm the best at hide and seek. Did that with the cops a few times too. Never was caught.

I turn my gaze to the television as Elliot fiddles with the controller. He's muttering under his breath, and I take a swig of my beer, biting back a smile.

Once the movie starts, I lean my head back on the headrest and eyeball my new friend. He's watching the beginning of the movie with slightly narrowed eyes like he's performing surgery. I wouldn't be surprised if he started taking notes.

He's intriguing and not at all what I'm used to.

Yeah, this dude is a keeper.

CHAPTER TWO

LUKE

Sun filtering in through the half-open window shade wakes me. I'm pressed against a warm body and blink through sleepy eyes at the man tucked underneath me. We're both fully clothed, lying lengthwise on the sofa, my left arm and leg wrapped around him, and his face tucked into my neck.

Damn.

It's been a while since I woke up next to someone. Usually, I fuck and run. I sure as hell didn't fuck Elliot. I would remember that in explicit detail.

I also don't feel much like running. I'm not sure I should analyze that too closely.

"Morning, sleepyhead," I say, my voice rough from sleep.

Elliot's eyes blink open and then widen when he sees me sprawled across him.

"Oh, so that wasn't a nightmare," he grumbles, and I smirk at him.

"Nah. That's all me, baby. A dream come true."

"Oh, Jesus. Get off of me," he groans but there's no conviction in his voice.

I nuzzle a little further into him, rubbing my cheek against his firm chest. This dude works out.

"Nah."

Elliot sighs and runs a hand through my hair, and then tugs on it roughly. It sends a jolt right to my balls, and my dick twitches in my pants.

Damn. That's new.

"I have things to do today. So, get off of me."

Reluctantly, I push myself up and stretch out, running a hand across my stomach.

"What are we going to do today?" I ask, eyeing my new friend, who just so happens to make my dick a little hard. Never happened before, but I'm good with trying new things.

"I'm doing things. But not with you."

I spread my legs and scratch at my neck. "That's not very nice."

He glances at the clock on the wall and mutters a string of curses.

"You need to go. *Now.*"

I refuse to move quickly because, damn, I'm curious. Where is he off to in such a hurry?

"Why do you want me out of here? Got a date?"

"No. It's much worse..." his voice trails off when the doorbell rings, and he hangs his head with a loud sigh. "Goddammit. Is there any way I can convince you to slink out the back door or a window, perhaps? You have that criminal mentality. I think you could manage it."

"Nah, I don't feel like being a criminal today," I say, pushing myself up and moving toward the front door. "How about I get this, instead?" I ask, but I don't wait for his response.

I pull the door open and see three women standing there. Their heads all swivel toward me, and then their eyes move from the top of my head to my toes, and right back up again. They're totally in sync, and I wonder if they practice this shit at home.

The heavily pregnant one pokes at my chest.

"Oh my god. He's real," she whispers, and all of their eyes widen.

"Elliot!" the brown-haired one squeals and pushes her way past the pregnant one. "Who is this fine specimen? And why did we not know about him? You've been keeping secrets, brother. We made a pact, and you broke it. We always keep one another in the loop, no matter what. Does our group chat mean nothing to you?"

I turn my head and see Elliot pouring himself a large glass of wine. It's not even nine o'clock in the morning.

"Let us in, you goddamn miracle," the third woman with short hair says and pushes her way past me, brushing against me. I flex to make it more enjoyable for her.

"Oh, a morning drink," the pregnant woman says. "Pity I can't have one." She opens the fridge and peers inside as the other two come to stand near Elliot.

"You're early," Elliot mutters, taking a large sip of wine. "Why can't you be late like normal people?"

"You are such a boob, El. We're on time. It was in our *group chat*," the pregnant one says.

Elliot frowns when the brown-haired woman grabs the glass from Elliot's hand and downs it.

She sputters and coughs. "Jesus. That's cheap-ass wine. You've got money, El. At least buy something that doesn't come in a box."

Elliot glowers, and then all of the women turn to look at me once more.

"And what is your name, handsome?" the pregnant one asks.

"Luke," I say with a grin and give a half bow.

The women smile widely, and then the pregnant woman walks up to me, holding out a hand. "I'm Eliza. This is Jane," she gestures to the brown-haired woman who just waves, pouring herself another glass of wine. "And that's Kate," she says, pointing to the short-haired woman gaping at me.

"We're Elliot's sisters," Eliza explains.

"Is that so," I say, looking over at Elliot, who is looking everywhere but at me.

"And you are?" Eliza says.

"I'm Eli's best friend."

"He's *not* my friend. I barely know the man," Elliot interjects.

I roll my eyes. "Nah, we spent the night together. So, we're probably more like lovers."

Eliza squeals, and Jane chokes on her drink, some of it dribbling down her chin.

"We are not lovers," Elliot bites out, and Kate squeaks. "I repeat. *Not. Lovers.*"

"El, you haven't had a lover in years. Ever since—"

"He's not my lover. Jesus. Who even calls it that anymore?" Elliot sends me a glare, and he points to the bedroom.

"I need to speak to you."

I waggle my eyebrows at Elliot's sisters, and they all squeal in unison as I follow Elliot down the hallway and into his bedroom.

He fists my shirt and roughly tugs me inside and shuts the door, locking it. Fuck, he's strong. Fixing my rumpled shirt, I glance around the space and whistle. Looks like a prince sleeps here. A fancy interior designer probably came in and picked out pillows and shit.

"You make your bed?" I ask.

"Of course, I do. I'm not a barbarian. And I assume, by just looking at you, that you do not."

"Nope, lover, I do not. What's the point when you get right back in a few hours later?" I smirk, and Elliot shakes his head.

"Do not call me your lover when they're around. They're never going to let it go," he hisses.

I shrug. "So?"

"So..." he pulls me farther away from the door, and then we're in the bathroom. He shuts the door, locks it, and then turns on the sink faucet.

"Whoa, what's with the weird CIA shit? You got cameras in here? Kind of kinky if you do. You like watching people take shits?"

"Wha—of course I don't have cameras in here. What is the matter with you? It's just that they listen. They're *always* listening and they hear all."

"Ah, kind of like my Superman hearing. I have to admit, it's a blessing and a curse."

"That's not a thing," Elliot says as he rubs his temple, and his eyes meet mine. "You need to leave. I cannot have you here with them. You and my sisters will not mix well."

"Nah. They seem like fun. They already like me."

"They're not fun and they only like you for your muscles. It's sexual harassment."

"So? At least someone appreciates them."

Elliot eyes my arms, and I flex them one at a time for his enjoyment, but he just pinches the bridge of his nose.

"You aren't leaving, are you?" he says, defeatedly.

"Nah," I chuckle. "I'd like to stay. If you'll let me."

Elliot huffs and then points at me, his eyebrows meeting. "If you stay, you behave. Seriously. Got it?"

I press a hand over my heart. "Cross my heart, hope to die."

"You're a child."

"At heart. Lighten up. I'll live to be a hundred, and you'll be dead by forty if you keep this up."

"Oh, goodie. Five more years, and then I'll finally escape you."

I roll my eyes, and Elliot pulls the bathroom door open and walks out.

"Leave while I change," he commands, and his deep, stern voice makes my dick perk up. I still don't really know what's going on there, but I think I've decided it needs to be examined closely, very closely. Maybe later I'll jack off to thoughts of him bossing me around and see where that goes.

"I can't watch?" I tease.

"Absolutely not."

"Cool. I can respect that," I say. "I am respectable. You'll see."

"You are the furthest person from respectable that I have ever met."

I smirk at him, move toward the bedroom door, and shoot him an air gun.

"See ya out there, lover."

"Dear lord. Go away."

I chuckle, opening the door, and his three sisters fall through. It's fucking comical, and Elliot looks like he's about to blow a gasket. I want to stay and watch his head explode.

"How is this my life?" Elliot grumbles, moving to the dresser and grabbing a pair of pants and a shirt. "You can all leave now and go gossip in the other room."

"We would *never*," Jane says, and Kate waggles a finger at Elliot, who is disappearing into the bathroom.

"He's very sensitive," Kate tells me as we move into the kitchen, and Jane pours us all large mimosas. Actually, it's just Prosecco with a drop of orange juice for color. So basically, just straight alcohol. These are my type of ladies.

Elliot thinks we won't mix well. Nah, we will mix just fine.

I swallow my drink in two gulps and hold my cup out for more. They examine me, and then Jane pours me four more glasses while we wait for Elliot to appear. He takes a long-ass time too. Probably combing his hair into submission.

Fuck, I'm thirsty. Gotta hydrate.

That's when I start to feel it, the slight buzz. Nothing I haven't had before. Could probably have a few more glasses before I pass out.

"Shouldn't have drunk those so fast," I say with a burp.

Elliot meanders in and sighs. "Don't tell me he's drunk already. It's only nine-thirty."

"I'm not drunk," I grunt, leaning back in my bar chair, and I smirk at Elliot, who is freshly dressed and shaven. Well, his time in the bathroom was well spent because he looks *good*. Really fucking good. It may be the alcohol talking, but I don't think so.

"I can get drunk though if you want to take advantage of this." I flex my bicep, and his sisters all stare at it for a moment and then start talking all at once until Elliot shouts at them to be quiet.

"Please do not egg him on. He won't stop if you do," Elliot says, glaring at me. "Eliza, Jane, and Kate, let's just get on with the morning, so I can finish off my day in peace."

I hold out my cup for another drink, and Jane refills it. I slurp at it, and Elliot sighs loudly again.

"So, what's the plan?" I ask, eyeing his sisters. "What do you all normally do on a Sunday? Church?"

"Hell no. We'd burn. No, we usually go out to brunch. Well, actually, we drag Elliot kicking and screaming," Eliza says.

"Because if we don't do this, we'd never see him. He'd just disappear into the ether, never to be seen again," Kate adds. "Plus, we're nosy and we like to know what this naughty boy has been up to."

"And he needs socialization, or he reverts back to being an unlikable caveman," Jane adds.

"That's because he doesn't like people," Eliza explains, taking a large gulp of orange juice.

"Yes, he hates them all," Jane says.

"Except you," Kate exclaims, and when I glance over at Elliot, he has his eyes closed. He's so still that he looks like a vampire. Or a corpse. Like he just died on the spot. He probably expired from the stress of it all.

"Think he's asleep?" Jane asks, and I reach over and poke his side.

His eyes open slowly, and he glowers at me.

"What. Do you. Want?" he drawls, and I smile at him.

"I'm starving. I need to eat like ten meals a day to remain alive. Can we go?"

"I'd rather if you didn't join us," Elliot says, and I clutch a hand over my heart.

"Don't be an asshole. Your sisters love me."

"We do," they all say simultaneously, and Elliot's chin hits his chest.

"Fine. Fine. Let's go, but all of you need to behave. I'm serious."

I throw my arm over his shoulders as we exit. "Ah, lover. You know us. We'll be on our best behavior."

———

ELLIOT

He is not on his best behavior. And neither are my sisters. The entire restaurant is staring because they're so fucking obnoxious. We won't be allowed back in next week. Even Bradley, our regular waiter, is eyeing us with mortification. I don't know how they talk me into this every week when I know how it goes. I'm usually leaving outrageous tips to make up for the fact that I have a family of wild animals.

My sisters have always been nosy and mostly overbearing, but it seems to have amped up ever since I had my heart ripped out a few years ago. I know they're just concerned about me, and that they love me deeply, but this, right now, is not my older sisters being concerned. No, this is them embarrassing the shit out of me. Yet, here I am, sitting in the front row watching this circus show. There's no escaping it.

Eliza is groaning about having to pee constantly, Jane is drinking herself under the table, and Kate is snorting like a pig in a pen at everything Luke says.

And Luke...he's charming and his laugh is infectious, and

all the women in the restaurant can't stop staring at him. It's making my eye twitch.

I mean, sure he's young and attractive…in a muscly, primal, He-Man sort of way. If you're actually into that sort of thing. But do they have no shame? Can't they keep their eyes to themselves?

I spend the entire time shooting withering looks across the restaurant at strangers who just happen to look our way.

When it's finally over, I have a raging headache.

"That was awful," I tell Luke as we move to my Tesla, and I pull the driver's side door open.

He slides inside the passenger seat and buckles up.

Yes, I drove him to the restaurant. He didn't even ask. He just followed me into my car like a stray dog.

"Nah, that was fun," he chuckles. "I like your sisters. They remind me of my brothers."

I eyeball him. "Oh, dear god. There are more of you?"

"Yep, and a cousin. We are fucking awesome. Just like your sisters. You'll meet them one day and fall in love."

"Well, all I can say is that A, I will not be meeting your family, and B, you will not be seeing my sisters again."

"Nah, Eli. We exchanged phone numbers when you went to the bathroom. Had to be all covert about it since you looked like you were about to have an aneurism. I think you had too much fun."

Shaking my head, I pull out of the parking lot, and begin the short drive back to my house.

His phone pings when I'm stopped at a light, and he glances down at it and snorts.

"Your sisters," he beams and waggles the phone in his large hand. "Fuck. They're fun. I hope someday they'll add me to your group chat." When I scoff, he looks at me. "How are you all related? You're the definition of un-fun."

"I've been asking myself that question for as long as I can remember."

When I pull into the garage, Luke hops out and follows me inside. I didn't invite him in, but he waltzes right in like he lives here. This is a pattern, one that I'll need to break very soon. Before something terrible happens...like I start to like him.

"Do you mind?" I ask when he flops down on the couch and spreads his thick thighs out in front of him. They're very nice thighs. Very muscular. I should not be noticing them or how nicely his bulky body fills out his jeans and tight T-shirt.

"What?" he asks, closing his eyes.

"You're not hanging out here today. You need to go back to wherever you came from."

He peels an eye open and then holds a finger up to his lips.

"Shhh, Doc. I drank too much. Your sister Jane is like a fucking fish. Never seen a woman down so much alcohol in such a short amount of time. I just need to sleep this buzz off. Then I'll go. Cross my heart."

I run a hand through my hair and watch in amazement as he just slips off into sleep. Seriously, he just closes his eyes, and he's out like a light. It's been less than a minute and he's actually snoring.

How did I manage to acquire this large man? Will I ever get rid of him?

With my luck, probably not.

I sigh, resigned to my fate, which doesn't seem so terrible at the moment and lower myself down next to him, pulling out my laptop. Better do some research while I have the time. There's a conference I'm attending soon, and I need to pick out which workshops I plan to join before I get stuck in some that are utterly useless and a waste of my life.

I'm already regretting my decision to attend. My sisters are right. I hate interacting with people. Networking? Who needs it? I could live in a cabin in the woods for the rest of my days and be utterly happy. I'd make friends with the bears and have food air-dropped nearby.

An hour later, I'm in the middle of reading through a seminar description, my glasses perched on the end of my nose, when Luke wakes up.

"Hey," he says, his voice rumbling with sleep. Then a smile pulls the corner of his mouth up, making him look adorable and edible. Apparently, I have turned into a cannibal.

"Have I told you I like those glasses on you? Very distinguished."

I push them higher on my face and blink at him.

"What are you doing?" he asks, sitting up and leaning into my space. Why is he always so close? Does he not know the meaning of personal space?

He was most definitely raised by wolves.

"Research."

He rests his head against my shoulder and yawns. "Tell me about it."

I don't know why I am even engaging him in this, but I go on to describe the different workshops I'm still debating on attending. He asks me questions that surprise me, and I wonder if he's not more intelligent than he looks. I've always been told not to judge a book by its cover, but that's exactly what I did, didn't I? I should know better. I hate it when people do that to me.

"And these workshops are for...?"

"A conference I'll be going to soon."

"Nice," Luke replies and then says. "Where is this thing taking place? Maybe I'll come with."

Don't do it. Don't say it....

"Colorado. Colorado Springs, to be exact," I say much too clearly. I even enunciate each syllable.

"Oh, I fucking love Colorado. There are a shit ton of things to do there. I could make an itinerary of all the things the two of us can do."

I just blink at him because he's invited himself. *On my trip.* When I planned on going solo. Who is this guy? I never knew people like him existed in real life.

"...Plus, I want to climb the Manitou Incline, and that's near the Springs. It's on my bucket list."

And I can't do anything but ask, "What's that?"

He shifts and meets my gaze, excitement in those hazel depths. "It's like three thousand stairs up a mile-long incline."

"Sounds like purgatory. People do this for fun?"

"Fuck yeah."

"Well," I say, pulling my glasses off and rubbing my fingers into my tired eyes. "I don't even know if we'll be associating with one another at that time, so let's not make any hasty plans."

Luke snorts. "Hasty plans? Dude, I like you. We'll be friends for a long-ass time. You can't get rid of me that easily."

I don't doubt that, but Luke will learn his lesson shortly. I don't have friends. People and I don't mesh well. But I don't say any of that because Luke is standing up and stretching, his shirt riding up and revealing a flat, defined stomach. I can't tear my eyes away. Something long-dormant inside of me sits up and takes notice. And it notices in graphic detail.

"Alright. I said I'd go when I woke up. Probably for the

best. I have work tomorrow. Unless you want to watch the second *Lethal Weapon*."

"I already watched it," I reply. "While you were asleep, and snoring so loudly I had to turn the captions on to know what they were saying."

Luke smiles widely at me. "Ah, see, told you you'd love it. Couldn't tear your eyes away, huh? We could watch the third one instead. I've seen them like ten times, so I could totally do that."

I glance down at my computer and seriously debate telling him to stay because he's infected me like some kind of virus, but then common sense wins over, and I just shake my head. I cannot be entertaining this massive, odd man. I'm not delusional or naive. I'm not quite sure what he wants from me, but whatever it is, he can't have it.

"No. Not today. I'm much too busy."

Luke's smile slips just a little, but then he shrugs like it's no big deal. "Cool. No problem. I'll see you later."

He stands in my living room staring at me, and then he runs a hand through his hair.

"Alright, Doc, see ya."

And then he's out of my house, and I can breathe again.

But fuck, if it isn't lonely.

When such a big presence is suddenly absent, you can't help but feel the void.

I mess around on my computer for a bit longer, make myself something to eat, go for a run and do some push-ups, shower, play the piano, and then when the sun starts to set, I change into my pajamas. I switch on a documentary, trying to focus on what is being said about black holes in the galaxy, but then my phone pings, and my concentration is obliterated.

Luke: I'm outside.

My stupid heart flutters in my chest.

Me: I thought you went home hours ago.
Luke: Nah.
Luke: Changed my mind.

I push myself off the couch and walk to the window, moving the curtains aside and peering out. The silhouette of Luke on my porch has my lips twitching slightly.

Me: Well, have fun sleeping outside. I'll toss you out a sleeping bag.

I see him glance down at his phone and run a hand along his jaw before his fingers fly across the screen.

Luke: How about I sleep inside instead?
Luke: We can share your giant bed.
Luke: I won't even hog the covers.

I stare at my phone. He is insane. I need to buy new locks for my doors, extra strength ones, to keep this guy out.

Even as I think this, I walk to the front door and open it. In the distance, I can see a large truck with some kind of equipment in its bed. I wonder what he does for work. Does he even have a place to live, or is this guy homeless?

But I can't analyze it all too much because Luke is standing right in front of me with a duffle bag in his hand. His bicep bulges from its weight. When he sees me, he smiles, squeezes past me, and makes his way through the living room.

"Knew you'd change your mind, lover."

"I didn't change my mind," I reply. "You hovered on my porch like the boogeyman until I caved. Did you just lurk out there for hours?" I wouldn't put anything past this guy.

"Nah, I drove around, got some food, took another nap in my truck." Luke shrugs and then moves toward the bedrooms.

"I have a guest room," I shout after him, and Luke turns to look at me.

"Yeah, but I've peeked in there. The bed is too small. I'll hang off it and I'll sleep terribly. I should probably just share yours."

I need to protest, to tell him absolutely not. But instead, I watch him disappear into my bedroom and return a moment later without his duffle bag.

Apparently, I am sharing a bed with this ruffian tonight.

"What are you watching?" he asks, taking in my pajamas with a small smile.

I push my glasses up my nose. "A documentary about space and black holes."

"Cool," he says and then grabs the remote from the table and flops down on the couch. "I love space shit."

"No, you do not."

"I do too. What do I have to say to convince you?" He taps his chin and then says, "How about, scientists have found evidence that in the center of the Milky Way there is a large black hole, or, oh, here's a cool one. Did you know a star can weigh so much that it can bend the nature of time and space? That's like some *Doctor Strange* shit right there...."

I blink at him, my mind not even comprehending that *this* just came out of *that*.

Books and covers. I need to keep reminding myself not to judge.

"Come on, Doc. I want to watch this with you. I'm like Spock, you'll see."

"You're the furthest man from Spock I've ever met."

"Yeah, you're right. I'm a rollercoaster of emotion." He looks at me with a wry smile.

"I'm... You're..." I've lost the ability to speak. "The fact is, you won't stay awake through the show. I'm willing to bet you'll be asleep in a matter of minutes."

"Pfft. I have amazing stamina. Never had a single complaint."

"How did you take what I just said and make it about sex? We were talking about you making it through a movie."

"Everything leads back to sex."

I stare at him and shift on my feet.

"It absolutely does not. A lot of things don't lead back to sex. Like...blood panels and prostate exams. Neither of those is sexual."

Luke eyes me like I'm insane. "Nah, I heard prostate massages are hot. My cousin says so."

"Okay, to clarify, I said *exam*, not massage."

"Both could finish with a happy ending."

"Oh my god, okay, enough of this. Let's just watch the show."

I reluctantly lower myself onto the couch, and Luke wastes no time. He scoots toward me until our thighs are touching. I can feel the warmth of his leg seeping through my pajama pants and I can't help but notice he smells like sunshine and grass, with just a hint of gasoline. I don't totally hate it. I should tell him to move away, but I don't. It's been such a long time since I've been close to another person like this. My sisters barrel their way into my life every week, but I don't really have friends.

Not since Andrew. All of our friends sided with him when things ended. That's when I realized that perhaps I'm not likeable enough to keep around. Perhaps there's something deep within me that's just not wired right, that repels people away from me.

I push the thought aside and focus on the screen as Luke's large arm bumps into mine. He presses play on the controller and then leans even more toward me.

"Do you always sit this close to people?" I ask.

"Nah, only you, Doc. You're special."

CHAPTER THREE

ELLIOT

L uke slept through the documentary like I knew he would, and I had to shake him awake when it was finished. But not before I ran my hand through his hair while he snored softly against me. I have no explanation for doing this, other than I am a masochist, and my hands seem to be attracted to him. He's probably only about ten years younger than me, so still a full-grown man, but he looks so youthful and sweet when he sleeps

Last night when he'd shown up at my house unexpectedly, he didn't even make it through the second movie before conking out. He'd just leaned over, pressed his face against my thighs, and closed his eyes. He didn't even ask permission. I should have felt livid; I don't normally like strangers touching me. But livid was far from what I felt.

I'd just gazed down at his face and stroked my fingers through his dark blond hair, my mind spinning in ridiculous, unseemly directions. I thought about how soft his hair felt, how he was quite possibly the most handsome man I'd ever met, how goddamn weird he was, and yet, despite all his quirks, how a little less lonely I'd felt with him in my space.

I probably shouldn't have called the cops on him. It was a dick move, but I'd wanted to see what he would do.

And he certainly didn't disappoint. He hid in a fucking bush right outside my window, so yes, as I assumed, he's slightly insane.

"Luke, wake up," I say and tug firmly on his blond strands until he groans awake.

"Damn, Doc. Don't do that when I'm asleep. Gives me all sorts of ideas," he mutters and pushes himself up straighter. He adjusts his pants, and I note the bulge in his jeans. It's ridiculously large, a mammoth, and I've suddenly envisioned myself as a caveman hunting it down. I've lost my mind.

Luke yawns and runs a hand under his shirt, utterly oblivious to my straying eyes. And they are straying. I'm so far off the beaten path. The mist is rolling in and I'm completely lost.

"Fuck, I missed the movie, huh?" he asks.

I swallow and try to focus on his face. "Are you really surprised?"

"Nah," he says and then nods to the room. "I'm gonna go lie down before I fall asleep standing up. It's happened before."

I just watch as he strides down the hallway and disappears into my room.

I don't move. I sit, frozen, and watch the credits scroll across the screen while debating the merits of just sleeping here on the couch. It would be safer than going in there with him. But I don't do it. Of course, I don't. This is my house. I will not give up my bed because this man has inexplicably moved in and taken over my space.

I cautiously walk into my room and see Luke sprawled out on his back on my bed, the sheets dangerously low on his narrow hips. His chest muscles ripple as he leans up and watches me approach.

"Don't worry. I'm not naked," he pulls down the sheets a bit and reveals a pair of black boxers with...are those pink squids?

"I mean, I'd like to be, because wearing clothes to bed feels a little like prison, but I didn't want to scare you off. Now if *you* want to undress...." His eyes slide down my pajama-clad body, and I resist the urge to button up the top button. I don't know why because Luke seems to have no qualms about me.

He seems more interested than anything.

But interested in what? What parts I have? Or does he just like...me?

I'm comfortable with who I am. I worked through all of that years ago, but it makes me nervous that I don't know exactly what he's getting at.

I barely know the guy, but he seems to have no issue spending the night in my bed with another man.

"Are you gay?" I blurt.

He rolls his lips between his teeth, eyeing me. "Nah, don't think so. Are you?"

"Yes."

He cocks his head and then pulls the sheets back. "Yeah. No big deal. Come on, Doc. In you go."

I eyeball the bed like its rabid. "I cannot believe I'm doing this."

"Believe it, baby," he says with a smile as I move to the other side of the bed and slide beneath the covers.

Luke scoots over until he's ridiculously close. It's a habit with this man. A dangerous one.

"I didn't take you for a cuddler," I mutter.

"I am discovering new things about myself each day."

I arch an eyebrow at him. "Is that so?"

"Yeah."

That word hangs in the air between us, and I find myself shifting a little closer to him. Only because it's cold and he's so very warm.

"Just for this one night, and then you need to go back home and stay there. You can't just move in."

"Whatever you want," he says, and then that thick arm of his is wrapping around me. He grunts a little, pulling my back into his chest, and then nuzzles his face against my head. His hand splays across my stomach, and I feel something similar to desire move across my abdomen.

But that's just silly, because there is no way I am interested in this man.

Man-child is a more accurate description.

I sigh and mutter, "This really cannot happen again."

But a soft snore is his only reply. He's already asleep. I'll just reaffirm this decision in the morning. Luke will respect it. He has to.

———

I wake up with Luke nearly sprawled across me. Again. His arm is across my chest, his leg thrown over my thighs, his face tucked into my armpit, and, yeah, that's his dick—hard, and pressed against my hip.

Gah!

"Luke," I hiss, and he grumbles and seems to grow heavier against me.

I poke him, and he jolts slightly. He pushes himself up, and his eyes blink open as he looks down at me.

"Morning, Doc."

His raspy voice in the morning is sinful, but I push the thought away. I will not be sinning with this man.

Plus, there is no time, even if I wanted to. Which I don't. I absolutely *do not*. I have to get to work, and his body is still plastered to mine.

"Do you mind?" I ask, but Luke just tilts his head, not moving an inch from me.

"Spell it out for me. It's too early to think."

"You need to move. I have to get to work."

Luke presses his forehead to my chest and sighs before rolling off of me. The sheet tents around his crotch, and I force myself to look away. That's not what this is. There is no way I am going there with this man. He's not even gay anyway. And even if he was bi or pan, a man like that wouldn't ever be into the things...never mind.

I am *not* going to think about this.

"Got to get to work too," Luke says. "We're finishing up a welding contract this week down at the shipyard. Got so much shit to do," he says, placing his hands behind his head, his eyes still closed. He's making no move to leave my bed or my house. Or my life.

"Then why are you still in bed?" I ask, grabbing a pair of underwear from my drawer and holding it to my chest.

He peeks an eye open. "Always rushing, Eli. It's not good for your health. And yeah, I'll get up soon. Just need a moment of meditation before I move. This is going to be a long-ass day."

I move toward the bathroom and then glance over my shoulder at him. "Please be gone when I'm done. I don't have time to wait around for you to get ready."

He salutes me and then closes his eyes again.

When I'm done with my shower, I peek out of the bathroom, thinking I'll still find Luke in my bed, but he's not. He's gone.

Disappointment surges through me, and I pinch the bridge of my nose.

No.

I am stronger than this.

He's a stalker and a menace. I do not like him.

I walk to my closet, pull on my freshly pressed clothes, and then I'm driving to work, sipping my coffee.

When my phone pings, my straying eyes can't help but look down at it.

Luke: What are your plans for after work?
Luke: We could hang out. I'm off at six.

I fumble with my phone, driving with my knee, and placing my mug in the cup holder. I've never driven so recklessly in my entire life, yet the minute Luke texts me, here I am, riding up on the shoulder of the road like a drunk. I chastise myself as I reply.

Me: Depends on what you have planned.
Luke: I'm easy.

I pull my eyes back to the road and tap my fingers on the

steering wheel. Because that phrase means more than he thinks, but I am not going there with him. I've made that mistake before and I'm never doing that again.

Luke: How about I bring drinks and dinner to your place. Then we can watch the next movie in the *Lethal Weapon* series. Black holes are cool, but guns are cooler.
Me: Your taste in movies is ridiculous. And guns are criminal.

I will never admit I kind of like the damn movies. I'll take that confession to the grave. Luke will never know the truth. He keeps snoozing through them anyway. And yet, both times, I found myself intrigued by the characters and the silly banter. One time, I even chuckled. I'd bitten my cheek afterward, peering down at Luke, who was snuggled against my thighs, worried I'd been caught. But he'd slept through my little slip up.

Luke: Come on, Doc. Don't make me beg.
Me: Fine.
Luke: Fuck yeah! It'll be fun. Trust me. I'm the most fun you'll ever have.

I quickly put my phone down and grab my coffee mug again. Fun is one word for it. More like torture.

Because what if I actually do have fun and then I start to really like him?

The horror.

When I'm finally at work, my phone pings again, and I quickly grasp for it before forcing myself to move more purposefully. I am thirty-five years old. There is no reason to

get excited over an excessively attached man. I do not trust
him. And more importantly, I do not trust myself.

I glance down at my phone and sigh heavily. I'd rather it
was Luke. But no, this is the insufferable group chat my
sisters insist I stay a part of.

Jane: What are you guys doing this weekend?
Me: I would like to request to be removed from this chat.

I, of course, go ignored.

Kate: Stalking Elliot and his hottie lover, duh.
Eliza: A stakeout! I'll bring the chips and dip. And the
chocolate.
Me: Go away.
Jane: Ooh. I'll bring the drinks.
Kate: I have the binoculars.
Me: Don't you dare. There is nothing to see here.
Eliza: Don't be such a grump.

I click my phone off and set it on my desk. If I was to find
a minivan full of my sisters outside of my house, I would not
be surprised. They've done this before. Once, I hate to admit,
I had been in there with them, sneaking around and spying.

They were terrible at it.

Cops were called and we were issued a citation.

I'll never live down the embarrassment.

They bring it up on every holiday and cackle relentlessly.

The next hour passes, and I see a few patients. I absolutely refuse to look at my phone to see if he's texted. I will
not check it until tonight when I am done with work. Then,

and only if he's texted, will I respond. I am not an overeager teen with a crush.

I make it until lunch before my magnet hands pull that phone right into my fingers. I glance at the screen and see a message from Luke. It's a selfie of him at a shipyard, a welding helmet pushed back over his hair, a ridiculously cheesy smile pulling those full lips up.

Dammit.

I click my phone off and then click it back on. I stare at that picture for a long minute and then do something so unlike me that I'll cringe for years to come.

I hold my camera up and snap a picture of myself, wearing my white lab coat, arching an eyebrow behind my glasses.

My finger hits *send* before I can overthink it.

And then I overthink it. My mind is reeling and panicking. *What have you done?* But a moment later, a text comes in, and I blush.

Luke: Damn.

My cheeks burn hotter, and I slam my phone face down on my desk, before picking it up again and staring at the screen.

Luke: Show me more, Doc.

Is he flirting? Is this sexting? Andrew refused to do this with me; he said it was juvenile.

Before I can analyze it, my phone pings again, and I see a picture of Luke pulling the hem of his dark blue shirt up, revealing a defined six-pack. His skin is a little dirty, and when

I zoom in, for scientific purposes only, I can see sweat glistening off his muscles.

Oh, for fuck's sake.

Amanda pokes her head into my office, and my phone clatters to the ground. She eyes it and then me, popping gum between her purple lips.

"Next patient is here."

"Fine," I say, clearing my throat. My face is positively on fire. "Send them to room two."

"Already did. Was just reminding you that you have to work and to stop looking at porn."

"I'm not...." My words trail off.

Amanda keeps looking at me, and I glower at her. I do not need her all up in my business. My sisters are enough.

As soon as the door is closed, I swipe my phone up from the ground and tuck it in my pocket.

I will not engage with him anymore.

It's bad enough that I have to see this man when I get home.

And yet, I can't help the excitement that zips through me at the thought.

————

Luke arrives an hour after me, and I walk as slowly as possible toward the front door. I will not scamper about and seem eager for this.

I will *not*.

As soon as I pull the door open, Luke smiles widely at me and holds up a six-pack of beer and a large brown paper bag with grease stains lining the sides.

"Hey," he says as he strolls past me. He smells like engine

smoke and gasoline. It's not intoxicating in the least. No, it's dirty and filthy and is making my mouth water.

I stare at him as he sets the beer on the counter and pries the brown paper bag open.

"I got burgers and fries."

"How healthy," I reply, and he smirks at me.

"Gotta live a little, Doc. It's not good to be so uptight. You're puckered tighter than my virgin asshole."

I flush and somehow manage to choke on my own saliva. He twists the cap off a beer and holds it out to me.

I clear my throat. "I prefer wine, so, no, thank you."

He shrugs and gulps it down. I watch in morbid fascination as he consumes the entire thing in four swallows. He sets the empty bottle down on the counter with a clink and swipes the back of his hand across his mouth. Then he opens another one and takes a long sip.

"Can I take a shower? I'm filthy," he asks, meeting my gaping stare.

He absolutely is. And now I'm thinking about those sweaty abs I'd ogled earlier.

"Yes," I manage to say, and he peels his shirt off and flings it over his shoulder, and then he grabs his beer and moves back to the bedroom.

I absolutely do not watch him go.

I would never do that.

I have the self-control of a monk.

Reaching up, I grab a wine glass, fill it to the brim, and take measured sips. There is no way in hell I can get drunk around Luke. There's no telling what I'd do; what hidden, carefully guarded part of me I'd show him.

Luke saunters out ten minutes later with wet hair, wearing a pair of my sweatpants. And holy hell, they're tight. Too damn tight, and about three inches too short. His ankles are showing and flexing as he walks, and I've never once had the thought that ankles were sexy, but fuck, his are. My eyes travel up and he's not wearing a shirt. I'm slightly horrified with myself as I stare wide-eyed at the water droplets dribbling from his hair, down his muscled chest.

"Oh, please. Just help yourself to my clothes," I say, gulping down my second glass of wine.

So much for measured sips.

"Thanks, Doc. You're so generous. Did you eat yet?" he asks, eyeing the unopened bag of food, and I shake my head, licking my lips. His eyes track the movement, and I feel myself grow warm.

I should turn the heat down in here.

"It's polite to wait," I say, feeling slightly buzzed. Perhaps I should have eaten to negate this drunken state I'm almost in. I'm a total lightweight.

He snorts. "No need for any kind of formality with me, Eli." He reaches into the bag and then hands me a burger and fries. "You can just be yourself."

No, I absolutely *cannot*. I will not let myself be vulnerable like that again.

Luke rips into a burger and leans a hip against the counter, grabbing a third beer and popping the cap open.

"Did you drink your other beer in the shower?" I ask.

"'Course. Best way to do it. Hot shower, cold beer. Life can't get any better than that."

I sigh, pour myself a third glass of wine, and take a tentative bite of the hamburger. It's greasy and cheesy and fucking delicious. I will not moan or show him how much I am enjoying this. It's a slippery slope from here. Next thing I know, his dick will be in my hole.

And then I'll be so overcome with emotion, I'll end up on one knee, proposing.

Fuck, I am never doing that again.

"It's good, huh? All that grease. You can feel it clogging your arteries with each swallow," Luke says with a smirk, not realizing where my thoughts have gone. "I can see you orgasming from over here."

I take another bite. "I am not."

He stuffs his mouth full of more burger and even fits a few fries in. It's impressive how much he can shove in there. That only comes with practice.

Luke gulps it all down, then pulls out a second hamburger, ripping into it.

"You eat like an animal," I say, resisting the urge to lick my fingers.

"You eat like a pigeon. You gonna finish that?" he asks, eyeing my half-eaten burger.

"Do not move in on my food," I grumble. "I will finish it."

He chuckles at that and then proceeds to finish off all his fries and the rest of his second burger by the time I'm done with mine.

And I may be slightly drunk now because everything seems less daunting.

I should not have had that third glass of wine. I've got to keep my defenses up.

"Ready for the movie?" he asks, reaching over and swiping a bit of ketchup from the corner of my mouth with his thumb and then slipping it in between his lips. He sucks it clean as I gape at him. But he doesn't notice. He just saunters over to the couch and plops down onto it.

I walk as steadily as I can to where he's sprawled out.

Instead of sitting far, far away like I should, I sit much too close. Our thighs brush, and our arms are pressed against each other. Luke doesn't comment on my proximity. He just grabs the remote, leans his head against my shoulder, and presses play.

"Are you going to stay awake for the entire thing this time?" I ask, rubbing my cheek against the top of his head like some kind of animal.

"Fuck yeah, I am."

He's asleep thirty minutes in.

I, of course, suffer through the entire movie before shutting my eyes.

I wake a few hours later with him wrapped around me, one of my hands in his hair, the other down the back of his shirt.

Tomorrow. I will end this madness tomorrow.

CHAPTER FOUR

LUKE

I've spent all week with Elliot. I mean, we both go to work during the day, but I'm with him every night.

He hasn't kicked me out yet, although he grumbles that he will. Nah, I think he's keeping me. I told you—motherfucking glue.

Hell, if Elliot isn't intriguing. I cannot peel my eyes away.

And the texting.

Those dirty little pictures he sends me—that aren't actually dirty at all because he's always fully clothed—still somehow manage to be *so damn hot*. I'm a little addicted to them.

I keep sending him ones of myself in various stages of undress because I like pushing his buttons, and every once in a while, he'll cave and do something naughty. It excites me that, despite all his grumbling, he still flirts with me. He doesn't want me to know how much he likes it.

Yesterday he sent me a picture of him sitting at his office desk, his legs spread, his fingers lingering on the buttons of his shirt, like he was ready to undress for me.

Or, the one that I shamelessly ogled for far too long, of him with those glasses on, a finger between his teeth as he bites down on it.

I haven't brought up this little game we play because I'm afraid he'll stop doing it. So, I just act cool when we're together and pretend like we don't do this shit.

But every day, I wait eagerly for those pictures. They're so rare that I save *and* favorite the ones he sends so I can look at them later.

And I do look at them later. I look real hard.

I'm fucking confused.

I've only ever dated women and I never thought I'd be into a guy. But damn, if I'm not into Elliot. I thought we could just hang out as friends until I figured out what was going on with me, but my dick already knows.

My dick wants him.

I need answers to these burning questions cluttering my mind, so I do the only sensible thing. I head over to Caleb and Whit's place after work. I don't even text them to let them know I'm on my way because they never respond anyway. Whit's so far up Caleb's ass, literally and figuratively, they don't have time for anything else...like socializing with their family.

Well, it's family time now, fuckers.

I park my truck on the street and jog across to their large apartment complex. They rent a small studio in a sort of shitty neighborhood, but it's all they can afford. Not that they complain. They're so damn happy, just the two of them, in their little love bubble.

I want that.

I want it bad.

No one ever seems to pick me though. Seems like I'm the disposable one.

I jog up the four flights of stairs and knock loudly on their door. They better not be fucking right now. I've heard that shit one too many times; Caleb moans like a whore and I can't Ctrl+Alt+Delete those sounds from my brain.

"Open up, fuckers!" I shout, and a minute later, the door swings open, and Whit stands there, eyeing me. He's wearing all black, like usual. Black pants and a long-sleeved black shirt. He even has on black socks. I've never seen him wear any other color. For Halloween he should dress in all white just to freak everyone the fuck out.

Whit clears his throat and tucks a wayward strand of dark hair behind his ear as he meets my stare.

"Luke, what a surprise," he says, deadpan, as he arches an eyebrow, and I can't help but ask.

"Whit, man, you got a relative named Elliot? Because you two are eerily similar."

Whit shakes his head. "No, not that I know of. All my relatives are in Romania."

"Cool, cool," I say and hold out my fist, and he bumps it as Caleb rounds the corner and pulls me into a hug, slapping me roughly on the back.

"Hey, man. Where have you been? What are you up to?" he asks with a wide smile. He's wearing torn jeans, a stained white T-shirt, and a backward baseball cap. I glance over at Whit and smirk. The two of them couldn't be more different if they tried.

When we pull away, Whit places a hand around Caleb's waist, and Caleb just sinks back into him.

These two are very handsy; makes me kinda jealous.

I want someone to be all handsy with me, touching me all the time.

"Not much, dude. Just came by to hang."

Caleb socks me in the arm. "Cool. Want a beer?"

"Hell yeah. I want all the beers."

Caleb pulls away from Whit, walks to the fridge, and uncaps a bottle, handing it to me.

"I was just about to start dinner. Are you staying?" Whit asks, moving toward Caleb and pressing a hand to his neck.

See, what did I tell you? Handsy. All the damn time.

"Yeah, man. I could always eat," I say.

"Better double the recipe then, babe," Caleb says, grabbing a beer for himself and gesturing to the small, worn couch.

We sink down onto it as Whit moves around in the small kitchen.

Caleb takes a swig of beer and then tilts the bottle toward me. "So, what's up, man? Why you hanging with us on a Friday night?"

"Can't I chill with my favorite cousin?"

"Just figured you'd have plans. You know, out there causing chaos. Didn't expect you here with us."

"Well, Ma wanted me to go home and visit, but I have other plans this weekend."

"Oh yeah? With who?"

I take a long swig of my beer. "Elliot."

Caleb's eyebrows rise. "Who's that?"

"A friend."

Caleb cocks his head and runs a hand across his chest. "A new friend?"

"Yep."

Damn, the way he's inspecting me makes me fidget like I'm six years old again and Dad's just asked me where all the matches went.

"Why you moving around like that? You not wipe good enough?"

I narrow my eyes at him. "Nah, man. I wipe just fine. My ass is squeaky clean. Just getting nervous with you looking at me and shit."

He arches an eyebrow, and I glance over at the kitchen and see Whit meticulously measuring out ingredients. It's like he's in a chemistry lab or some shit. Pretty soon, he'll pull out some goggles.

I lean forward a little and say, "Fine. Pry it out of me, why don't you? I think my dick likes a dude."

Caleb's eyebrows both raise, and he freezes. "Is that so?"

"Yeah, man. And I don't know what to do."

"What do you mean?"

"I mean, I've never been into a guy before. Well, Elliot's trans. I mean, I'm not even sure what he's got...down there. But does that even matter? He's definitely a dude and my dick wants him. What do I do?"

I take another long swig of my beer, my mind rightly fucked at this moment.

"I have no clue. I would ask him about all this. Just be upfront with him."

I lean forward and say quietly, "But cuz, listen to me. I get hard thinking of him. He sends me these pictures, and I could totally jack off to them."

"Whoa," Caleb says and then chuckles slightly. "TMI, man."

"Shit," I grumble and then lean my head against the back of the couch. A frustrated groan exits my mouth, and Whit moves over toward us. He's wearing an apron and plastic gloves.

This guy has issues.

"Everything okay?"

"Yeah, babe. Luke is just into a guy, and he's all confused."

"Ah," Whit says, and I eyeball my cousin's fiancé.

"What's that 'ah' mean, Whit? Care to enlighten me with that big brain of yours?"

"I just mean 'ah' as in, that's interesting. Nothing else."

I snort. "Yeah, sure. Whatever. So, what should I do? Tell me what to do. I need a little guidance."

"I think you should do what feels right, Luke," Caleb says. "Your dick is never wrong."

"So very true. So, I should let him fuck me if he's into me? Or do I fuck him? How does that work?"

I glance at Whit and lift my chin up at him. "You know anything about gay trans dudes?"

Whit shakes his head. "Everyone is different. You'll have to ask him."

"Nah, man. We're not there yet. I don't know what he wants. Mostly I think he doesn't like me. But he still lets me snuggle with him, so I dunno."

"Who couldn't love you?" Caleb replies, then grabs onto the back of my neck and pulls me toward him. We wrestle on the couch for a few minutes and when we look up, Whit is gone, back in the kitchen, wiping the counters down with Clorox wipes.

"I'll just ask him," I say.

"Do it," Caleb says. "Just put it all out there. Be like, do you like me? Check yes or no."

I pull out my phone, roll my lips between my teeth and then type.

Me: Could you ever like a guy like me?

I tap my foot and seconds later his response pops up on my screen.

Doc: What kind of question is that?

Caleb peers over my shoulder and nudges me. "Just tell him that you're curious."

Me: Just curious.
Doc: It's none of your business.

I glance over at Caleb, and he runs a hand over his mouth. "Just tell him you're interested."

"Nah, I can't do that. It'll scare him off. He's already trying to get rid of me. I don't want to give him a reason to kick me to the curb."

Me: Do you have a type?
Doc: I do.

My phone pings again, and I frown.

Doc: Where are you?
Me: I'll tell you when you tell me what I want to know.

I can almost hear him sighing, and my fingers fly across the screen.

Me: Come on. Tell me. What is this type of yours?
Doc: Where are you?

I stare at my phone and then shove it between my thighs.

"He's not going to answer me. He's elusive. Like a slippery little eel."

Caleb scratches his stomach, deep in thought.

I lean my head back. "He probably doesn't want to hurt my feelings. That's gotta be it."

"You think he's not into you?" Caleb says. "Because you're fucking awesome. So, if he isn't, he must have terrible taste."

"Meh, I dunno, but Eli is..." I bite the inside of my cheek and stare at the ceiling. "He's different. He's hard to get to know. He's all closed off and quiet."

"So? When has that ever stopped you? Just keep sticking around, and he'll fall for you one day."

"Yeah?"

"Fuck yeah," Caleb says. "It worked with Whit, and now look at me." He holds up his hand and shows off the ring on his finger, and I sock him in the shoulder, and then we're wrestling again, knocking into the coffee table and toppling over a stack of books.

"Caleb," Whit says from the kitchen, his fingers tapping on the counter.

"Sorry, babe," Caleb says and pushes himself up, and I help right the mess we've made. Caleb lopes over to Whit and pulls him into his arms, and presses a long-drawn-out kiss to his mouth.

"Keep it in your pants, guys," I grunt, feeling my chest ache. "You're making me jealous."

Caleb pulls away from Whit reluctantly and then grabs another beer.

"Sorry, I just can't help it," Caleb says. "Hey, how about we play a game before we eat. Bet I can kick your ass."

"You're on," I reply.

Many hours later, I wake up to the sound of moaning. I glance at my phone. Damn, I slept in. But shit, can't these two keep it together while they have guests? Rude.

I push myself up off the couch and swipe my keys from the counter. I'm not going to stick around and listen to the crescendo.

Nope. Don't need to hear that.

―――――

"You didn't show up last night, nor did you respond to my text messages," Elliot mutters, frowning, as I push past him into his house. "Not that I cared where you were or what you were doing. I had a lovely night. Alone," he says to my back.

"Aw. You fucking missed me. I knew you would. And just so you know, I fell asleep at Caleb's."

"And who is Caleb?" he asks, his mouth frowning even further. I didn't know that was possible, but apparently, he can bend the laws of physics with his grump face.

"My cousin. Don't worry, Eli. You're still my bestie."

He purses his lips. "Do you have a home, Luke? Or are you homeless?"

"Nah, Eli. I have a home. I just couch surf during the work week. Saves me a shit ton of money on gas and I don't have to commute for hours."

He doesn't look like he believes me, but whatever. I got more important things on my mind, like our plans for later today.

"Hey, I thought we could hang with my brother today."

"I'd rather not."

I nudge him lightly, and he huffs. "Fine. But only because you're insisting. You're really twisting my arm."

I snort a laugh. "Awesome, man. Let me just shower and change."

Elliot is pouring himself a cup of coffee when I come back out. His eyes slip across me, and I roll my lips. Yeah, maybe I'm not his type, but he can't stop looking at me.

I see you, Eli. I *so* see you.

"Can we grab a coffee on the way over?" I ask because this guy doesn't even have creamer. Or sprinkles. Or anything fun in this entire damn house.

Although I did hear him playing the piano two nights ago. He thought I was asleep, but I heard it, and it made me unreasonably horny.

I want him to play for me one day.

I also want him to spread me out on those keys and eat my dick.

Yes, my imagination has evolved over the last week and has become completely bent since last night. I have accepted my attraction and refuse to go back.

I am into Elliot.

"Fine," he says, caps his portable coffee mug, and gestures to the garage. "Let's go."

After stopping at the coffee shop, we make our way to my brother Sem's place across town. Elliot has soft classical music playing over the speakers in his car, and his fingers tap a rhythm on the steering wheel. Outside it's cold and grey, and I wonder for a moment if it's going to rain.

"Do they know we're coming?" Elliot asks as I moan around a mouthful of whipped cream and white mocha.

"Nah, it's best to surprise them."

He eyes me. "It's eerie how similar you are to my sisters. They show up randomly, as well."

"You know, I think we were fated, Eli. You and I. God

made us just for one another." I gesture to a side street. "Turn right here where that red car is."

Elliot follows my instructions, and a minute later, we are pulling up in front of Sem's motorhome in the RV park he currently resides. My little bro said he'd moved here a while back to be closer to work. Fucker was tryin' to trick us. We all knew it was so he could be closer to Magnus. He was a little obsessed. Hell, he's still obsessed.

"They should be home," I say as I push the door to the Tesla open and hop out. My feet crunch under the gravel as I walk around the car.

"Your brother lives *here?*" Elliot asks, glancing around, and I eye him.

"Don't be a judgmental asshole, Eli. Not everyone lives in fancy houses."

His cheeks turn pink, and he stutters for the first time since meeting him. "I was...was not...I didn't mean...."

I can't stand it, him looking so flustered and embarrassed, so I just move toward him and pull him into my side.

"No worries, Doc."

He glances up at me. "I didn't mean to sound judgmental."

"I know. You can't help it. Let's go knock."

A second later, I'm pounding on the door, shouting for someone to answer. I hear footsteps moving through the RV, and a moment later, the door swings open. Magnus stands in front of me, rolling his eyes. He's wearing tight skinny jeans and a pale pink shirt. His fingernails are painted a bright red and is that eyeliner?

"Oh, Luke. How ever did I guess it was you?"

I snort and flick his hip. "Where's my brother, tiny?"

Magnus ignores me, peers over my shoulder, and then

raises his eyebrows. "Oh, who is this, Luke? You have been mysteriously absent lately. Is this the reason why?"

"Yep. He's my BFF," I say.

"Is he now? Because Caleb called me last night...." Magnus begins, but I cut him off.

"Damn, Caleb. Such a fucking gossip. He can't keep a secret to save his life."

Magnus hops down the stairs and pushes past me, holding out his hand to Elliot. "Hello there, handsome. I've heard *all* about you. I'm Magnus, Luke's brother-in-law."

Elliot looks at me before glancing down at Magnus. He nods once and extends his hand. "Elliot."

Sem suddenly appears, watching Magnus vigorously pumping Elliot's hand, then my brother's blue eyes swivel to meet mine.

"Hey, bro. What are you doing here?" Sem asks me as we both move to stand where Elliot and Magnus are chatting.

Before I can answer, Magnus chimes in. "Look, Sem. Luke brought a *friend*." The way Magnus says that word makes me snort and causes Elliot to arch an eyebrow.

Sem eyes Elliot and Elliot eyes Sem and then my brother turns to me and smirks, "He does that thing with his eyebrows, like Whit."

"Fuck, I know."

"Who's Whit?" Elliot asks. "You've mentioned him before."

"My cousin's fiancé. You'll meet him one day," I tell Elliot and then turn to Sem and Magnus. "So, what are you guys up to? We hangin' or what?"

Magnus moves over to Sem and tucks himself into his side. "We were just leaving, actually. We're meeting August and Emery for food and some laser tag."

"Fuck," I say and then smile widely. "Why didn't I know about this? Elliot and I love laser tag."

"You may, but I do not," Elliot mumbles.

I don't listen to his protests, I just nudge Elliot gently until he sighs and agrees to go with me. He pretends like I'm forcing him, but I see that gleam of excitement in his eyes. He's probably never played laser tag in his entire life. He probably scoffs at it and mocks it, but secretly, deep down, he wants to smear paint on his face and howl at the moon.

"Never played a game in your life, huh? Is this going to be your first?" I ask Elliot as we move into his car.

He just eyes me. "I play games."

I scoff, buckle up, and then reach out and tug on his earlobe. And that fucker presses into me, just enough that I take notice, so I move my hand around and cup the back of his neck.

"You're going to love it, Eli. Laser tag is fun."

"I think love is a strong word."

I lean into him and say softly in his ear, "Just give it a chance, yeah? For me?"

Elliot shivers, it's slight but I catch it. Biting at his lower lip, he gives a clipped nod. "Fine. For you."

And damn, if that doesn't make me light up inside, because Elliot doesn't seem like the type to give in easily. Not to just anyone.

No, he seems stern and obstinate. God, I want to see him loosen up for me, to bend just a little.

My mind is straying down a very sexy path when my stomach rumbles loudly, and I rub at it. "Fuck, I'm hungry."

"Well, it's a good thing we're eating first then; don't want you to pass out from hunger," Elliot replies, and I chuckle softly.

I squeeze his neck again, and he presses back into my palm. So, I just keep it there, massaging his tense muscles until we arrive at the small diner outside of town. What really makes me grin is that he doesn't even huff and puff about how close I am. He's usually such a prickly pear but I'm growing on him.

"Ready?" I ask when he parks the car.

He eyes the restaurant, and I squeeze his shoulder. "I eat here all the time. It's totally sanitary."

"It has nothing to do with that. I just..." he huffs. "I'm nervous."

My eyes widen at that because...did Elliot just open up? To me?

I shift in my seat, so I can face him. "You're nervous?"

"Forget I said anything," Elliot says, and I clutch onto him tighter, forcing him to stay right where he is.

"Why you nervous, Eli?"

"I don't do well with...people."

"You're a doctor. You're with people all day long. They all seem to love you."

"Yes, but that's different. There's a power imbalance in those types of interactions. I know what's expected of me and I know I'm good at it. Here, I'm just Elliot."

"Eli..."

"There is a good chance they won't like me. I will say the wrong thing or come off as rude. I don't have friends for a reason."

"Nah," I say and tilt his chin toward me. "They'll like you. Hell, I like you, and you're a grumpy bitch who ran me over with his car."

He snorts but then his face falls again. He looks so uncertain, gnawing on his lip, that part of me wants to lean forward and suck on those lips, just pull that insecurity right out of him with my mouth. If I knew it would help, I'd do it. But I don't, because that's not our thing. Not yet, at least.

"I promise those dudes out there will like you."

"I just...never mind. I shouldn't have said anything. Can you please just forget it?"

He pushes his way out of the car, and I rush out after him.

"Not sure I can forget that, Eli. You actually opened up to me. I'll remember it forever."

"It was a moment of insanity. I'm fine now. Won't happen again," he mutters and then eyeballs a black SUV in the distance where Sem and Magnus are hovering.

My brother and Magnus both watch as we approach, and then Magnus turns to talk to his best friend, August, who is sitting in the driver's seat of the SUV with a tattooed guy straddling his lap.

Huh. I've hung out with August a few times before when I've crashed at Sem and Magnus' place. I thought he was a straight dude. Guess I was wrong. Apparently, I've been wrong about a lot of people being straight. My dick is totally smirking at me right now.

"So, guys," Magnus begins with a wide smile. "Luke just showed up while we were leaving. Therefore, this is no longer a double date. It is hereby dubbed a triple date."

"This is not a date," Elliot grumbles to no one in particular. I just throw my arm around him and squeeze his hard body right into mine.

"Fuck you going on about, Eli? Don't make this weird."

"I am most likely the least weird person here," Eli says, and I pull him closer to me. Damn, I like him close. Plus, he smells good. I lean in and sniff a little.

Fuck, yeah. He really does.

When I turn back around, Magnus is rolling his eyes.

"I take issue with that," Magnus says loudly. "I happen to think that I am *very* normal."

That just makes me laugh because I know all about the weird shit Sem and him did a while back. I know too much, actually. The van Beek family is tight, a little too tight at times. Sem blathered on and on one night about their kinky sex, in great, exaggerated detail. Yet another reason why my brain needs a bleach bath.

"Oh, fuck off, tiny. You're crazier than a soup sandwich," I say, reaching out and scooping Magnus right into my arms.

My brother growls loudly and grabs his husband away, cradling him to his chest.

"Don't touch him, Luke," Sem mutters. "You trying to die?"

I grin, and Elliot pinches the bridge of his nose. Nah, he pretends he's annoyed, but I see how his lips twitch. He's trying not to smile.

Suddenly the SUV door is thrown open, and the tattooed guy comes tumbling out. He stumbles into the dirt and then brushes his pants off and straightens his shirt. A smile lines his face, and he meets my eyes.

"Hey, I'm Emery. I haven't met you two." He flicks his hand between Elliot and me, and while I smile, Elliot just stares at him. He's probably never seen so many tattoos before.

"I'm Luke, Sem's older brother. And this is Elliot, my best friend," I say.

"He uses that word too loosely," Elliot interrupts. "This man just invaded my space one day, and I can't get rid of him."

Fucker. He jokes. No one gets them but me.

I reach out and pat Elliot's head to irritate him even further. "Nah, he secretly loves me. Keeps me around to show off. He likes my muscles. Told me so himself."

Elliot sighs and looks to the sky mumbling something under his breath but makes no move to extricate himself from my side. Instead, he subtly leans into me.

Asshole thinks I don't notice, but I do. I notice all the things when it comes to him.

"Alright, this is fucking awkward, but then again, with this family, why am I surprised?" Magnus mutters and then announces, "Alright, everyone, listen up. For expediency, this is August, my best friend," he points to the guy with golden blond hair and a muscular body. "And today, August and Emery have officially become boyfriends."

Emery links his arm with August and bounces a little. "Why, yes, we have. And we are also stepbrothers. It's all very scandalous. But yeah, he's all fucking mine. And he is fabulous at sex. I mean, look at him. Mr. Rogers. Who knew? Mind blown."

August blushes bright red as Emery bumps Sem's fist and then mine. Because congratulations are in order, especially when it comes to getting some.

Which I have not been getting.

I am on a sexual fast, and my dick notices. It's aching in a not-fun way. The other day, I came in my pants when I took a nap in my truck. I woke up feeling like I was twelve years old all over again.

I've taken to bringing a change of underwear with me when I leave the house because I'm dreaming of Eli all the time. I should probably stop looking at all those damn sexy pictures he's been sending me.

They aren't even explicit, but I imagine they are. The one

where he's biting his finger, I imagine it's my dick. But instead of biting, maybe just a little nibble. Really, anywhere in the vicinity of his lips and tongue would be good. I'm not picky.

There was one picture where he had his hand on the button of his pants, serious eyes and a firm jaw, and he looked so goddamn authoritative. I imagined him bending me over and giving me a stern talking to.

If he ever sent me an actual nude pic, I'd probably come right on the spot, just jizz right across my phone screen.

I shift on my feet and tuck Elliot further into me. He has no idea what he does to me.

"It's always the quiet ones, huh?" I murmur and smirk.

"Oh yeah, totally. Like, it's the best kind of surprise," Emery says with a cheery smile, obviously referring to his new boyfriend.

Magnus interrupts our side conversation by clearing his throat. "Okay, enough of this. Let's go inside and get food because we have a reservation for laser tag at two, and Luke eats *for fucking ever*. The kitchen needs time to accommodate his order."

"That's right. I'm a growing boy," I say and pull Elliot up the stairs. He pretends to resist, but he still walks right up into the diner with me without a fuss.

"You're trying to hide it, but I know you're having a fucking blast," I say in his ear.

"I am not," he grumbles as he slides into a booth, and I move in next to him, handing him a menu. He stares down at it as the others pile in around us.

When we're all ordering, Emery asks me if I have any tattoos. I tell him that I do, right on the back of my thigh.

"It's a mermaid," I say. "A fucking big one too. All colorful and intricate."

Emery wiggles in his seat, looking like an excitable puppy, and I quickly decide I like him. Kinda want to boop him on the nose.

I can feel Elliot eyeing me. He didn't know about my tattoo because he hasn't seen the back of my thigh.

Yet.

But I can tell he's intrigued.

I lean toward him and whisper in his ear, "I'll show it to you if you want. I'll pull my pants down and bend over so you can get on your knees and examine it, Doc."

He clears his throat and I don't miss how his face pinkens. "No, thank you," he mutters as our food is brought out.

"Let me know if you change your mind," I say and waggle my eyebrows at him. Because I would very much like him behind me in any way, shape, or form. Preferably naked.

Doing things with his tongue and his hands.

I've fully accepted it now.

There's no going back.

Like Caleb said, my dick is never wrong.

Elliot ignores my stare and just nibbles his food like a little bird. I eye August and Emery and watch how August feeds his guy. He slips a french fry right into Emery's mouth, and for a moment, I'm envious.

I turn toward Elliot, and open my mouth wide.

Elliot scoffs, "I'm not feeding you. You're not my boyfriend."

I smirk and then rip into the back end of his sandwich. Because he doesn't need to remind me that he's not into me. I already know.

He eyes the large bite mark in his food, and sighs softly, "I've made mistakes in my life that have led to this."

I laugh. "Nah, man. I'm the best thing that's ever

happened to you. You told me that one night while you were asleep."

Elliot looks like he could die. He makes a slightly strangled sound in his throat as Magnus shifts suddenly toward us in his seat.

"I'm sorry, are you two sleeping together?" Magnus asks.

"Absolutely not," Elliot remarks in a clipped tone, finally finding his voice.

I laugh and throw my arm across the back of the booth.

"He's just being shy. I sleep in his bed most nights. It's fucking comfy. He has this fancy mattress that feels like sleeping on a cloud. He said it was ten grand. This dude is Mr. Moneybags. He's a doctor too."

Elliot stares at me, completely perplexed, and I fiddle with his earlobe a little. Despite the dismay on his face, Elliot leans into my touch and I smile.

But then my attention is drawn to Emery, who is suddenly holding out a handful of lollipops.

"I brought something for you," he announces with a grin.

Elliot shakes his head when they're offered to him—because, of course he does—so I grab two. Don't want to be rude. Plus, I love candy. I unwrap and pop both suckers in my mouth simultaneously because I'm an adult, and the only good part about being adult is getting to do what you want, am I right?

"Fuck yeah. These are good," I grumble, my words coming out muffled.

Magnus rolls his eyes and pockets a sucker. "I'll save this for later then. Apparently, Luke may need it. He's having a mini orgasm over there."

I just continue to suck on them, and from the corner of my eye, I can see Elliot watching me in...something. I'm just hoping it's not disgust. But I'm not changing for him. He can take me or leave me.

I mean, I hope he takes me. I really, really want him to take me. To pick me.

Magnus scoots out of the booth and claps his hands to get our attention.

"Alright, listen up. So, we need to go like *now*. It will take about fifteen minutes to get to the laser tag place, and we need to check in...Luke, do not do that with your sucker. That is not sanitary."

I eyeball my brother's husband as Elliot continues to watch me.

"I guess I can't get out of this," Elliot asks me softly.

"Fuck no. You're stuck with me all damn day."

"Fine, but my sisters do not find out about this," Elliot replies, and I smirk at him.

"Too late," I say, and Elliot groans.

———

Fuck, laser tag is fun.

I can't stop howling. I feel like a badass motherfucker right now because we are annihilating the other team. We are in a battle to the death, and I am winning.

It's Sem, Emery, and I versus Elliot, Magnus, and August. And damn, I'm glad we did it this way. My teammates are crushing them to dust. We don't mess around.

Well, more like I don't mess around. I'm taking no prisoners. Sem keeps eyeing Magnus with what looks like equal parts worry and lust. Emery is shirtless and bouncing around like a pogo stick.

But still, there is no way those weak fuckers are going to

win. No. Way. We have just a few more minutes before our time is up, and we are so far ahead that I know we will come out on top.

I'm behind a hay bale, and another howl erupts from me. I can't contain it. I'm part werewolf now.

I glance over and see Sem's painted face peeking behind a tree, while Emery hides behind a giant tire. They're going to do some kind of sneak attack. I just know it.

I'm so distracted plotting my next move that I don't feel a presence moving up behind me.

"What the hell are you doing?" Elliot asks harshly, and I clamp my mouth shut mid-howl and try to turn, but his hands are suddenly on my hips and his body is pressed up against my back. He's firmly holding me still.

Oh, shit. I like this far too much. My hungry dick likes it too.

It's getting hard and weepy.

"Why are you howling like an animal?" he asks, and that low voice in my ear makes my skin prickle and my imagination soar. It's off into outer space now.

"Answer. Me," Elliot growls and presses himself harder into my back, his fingers digging into my sides.

"Uh," I say, and I can't even form words. My brain has lost all ability to function. Goddamn, is it weird to hope he anally probes me right now?

"You were saying?" Elliot drawls. Then his breath hits my earlobe, and I'm flushed and sweating, my gun hanging limply by my side.

"You're scrambling my brain," I manage to mutter. Elliot chuckles darkly, and my dick twitches painfully behind my zipper.

Damn. Who knew I'd be so into this domination shit?

He could probably tell me to do anything at this point, and I'd do it.

One of his hands slowly moves down to the bulge in my pants, and then he squeezes.

He squeezes my dick, and I slump right into the haybale. I'm surprised it doesn't just topple over with my weight pressed against it.

"Elliot," I groan, my gun dropping into the dirt with a loud clatter.

"Acting like an animal," Elliot grumbles. "Perhaps I should make you get on your knees and beg."

I'm panting now, like a dog.

He wouldn't be too far off; I'd beg for him.

He flexes his fingers once more, and I'm in literal pain. My dick is ready to explode. It's been so long. Too long. So, I do the only sensible thing.

I thrust up into his hand once and come in my fucking pants.

Self-control, who needs it? Not me.

I shudder through the release and then breathe deeply through my nose. And as the haze wears away, I kind of feel like shit. My boxers are uncomfortably damp, and Elliot has backed away from me and is rubbing his temple in my peripheral. He looks smug and slightly annoyed.

"We won!" I hear through the roar in my ears.

Did he fucking do this shit to win? Was this a trick?

"Let's go," he mutters.

I eyeball him, but still follow him out from behind the hay bale like a disobedient child. But I'm kind of pissed too. Asshole is playing with me.

"Hey, man, you okay?" Emery blurts, and I open my mouth and then close it. Then open it again and gesture to my right where Elliot is standing, pinching the bridge of his nose.

"He just...he jacked me off behind a hay bale."

Everyone swivels to look at Elliot.

"No. I accidentally touched your dick. There were no wrist movements."

I just open my mouth and stare. "You reached on down and grabbed it, Eli. Admit it."

"Like I said, it was an accident, Luke."

"Nah, you did that on purpose. So, you could win. You sneaky fucker."

Now I'm sort of proud and pissed. And embarrassed. I hate being embarrassed. Rarely happens to me, but when it does, it throws me off-kilter.

"Just so you know, I enjoyed that about as much as receiving an enema. So no, it was not on purpose. You shifted, and my hand slipped."

Damn, that hurts a little, even though it's obvious to me he's lying. But there's nothing I can do about it now. I glance down at my crotch and sigh. It's growing wet. My come is seeping through my jeans.

"You have got to be kidding me? I barely touched you," Elliot grumbles and then snaps, "Luke van Beek, go clean yourself up. Now."

My eyes shoot up to meet Elliot's.

"You ordering me, Eli?"

"I am. Go."

Fuck. Part of me wants to rebel, but I can't make myself do it. He has some strange pull over me that I can't explain, and it turns me on. I stomp off toward the bathrooms, rubbing the back of my neck as I replay what just happened. As I relive it, I'm confused, irritated, and horny all over again.

Inside the bathroom, I do my best to clean myself up but just end up stuffing my boxers in the trashcan. I don't need them anyway. I have a six-pack of new ones waiting for me in my truck because I'm a horny fucker who can't stop coming in my pants.

Elliot is waiting for me outside the bathrooms, his legs crossed at the ankles as he leans against the building casually tapping on his phone. I stare at him, but he won't look at me.

Well, fuck him too. I have nothing to say to this duplicitous ass. Using my dick against me to win. Even I'm not that shady.

So, in protest, I glue my mouth shut the entire way home, and Elliot is equally as quiet.

When we arrive back at his place, I stomp my way inside the house and just stand in the kitchen, unsure of where to go from here. Should I leave? Stay? Say something? Not say anything at all?

I fidget anxiously as Elliot locks the front door, and then he leans against it. Our eyes meet across the space. Something electric snaps in the air around us, and I swallow roughly.

Fuck.

Suddenly, he's pushing off the door and stalking toward me, and I step back until I hit the wall with a thump.

When he's directly in front of me, he narrows his eyes slightly.

"I think we had a misunderstanding," he says, and I gulp.

"What about, Doc?"

"The definition of a hand job."

"Nah," I choke out. "I know what that shit is. Do it all the time. I'm a gold medalist."

He glances at my crotch, then reaches out and grabs onto my neck, squeezing it tightly.

"Would you like me to show you what me jacking you off looks like?" he asks.

Oh shit, my dick is hardening so quickly I'm lightheaded. All my blood flows south in record time.

I swallow roughly and try to breathe.

"Because what happened earlier was *not* me jacking you off. That was me playing with you."

He reaches down, roughly grabs onto my hardened dick, and pushes his palm against it.

My breath comes out in a whoosh. "Oh, fuck."

He smirks, and squeezes my neck tighter.

"Turn around."

He loosens his grip on me, and I can't think of doing anything else but what he says. Okay, so this clarifies that there's a good chance that I'll be the one getting fucked in this relationship...or whatever this is.

And I am so here for it.

"Hands flat on the wall," he commands.

I slap my hands onto the wall as he grabs my hips and kicks my legs apart.

His fingers hook into the waistband of my pants, and he tugs them down until they're stretched across my thighs. His hand rubs against my left thigh, right where the mermaid tattoo is, before traveling higher, over my ass cheek, and reaching around to my front.

My dick is almost painfully hard now, and I lower my head to watch as his hands slip across my abdomen, one grabbing onto my dick, the other my balls. A guttural groan escapes my mouth.

"Uh, uh, uh," he reprimands, squeezing my dick almost painfully. "Not a fucking sound from you."

Holy fuck.

I bite down on my bottom lip and let out a broken breath. I have never, ever been submissive, but damn, if this isn't something I like.

"Good boy," Elliot says in my ear, and then his dominant hand slowly pumps me. Pleasure shoots through my entire body as I watch his fingers move up and down my thick, straining cock.

I'm sweating. It's rolling down my fucking temples and onto my cheeks. Elliot is pressed against my back, his breath tickling my ear as he breathes.

He's not even out of breath. He's always so in control. What would it take for him to come undone like I am right now? I want to see that so fucking bad.

"See," he says, his lips moving against my earlobe. "This is me jacking you off. Do you feel the difference?"

I gulp and nod, but he can't see it because my head hangs like an anvil between my shoulders as I watch his soft, long fingers work me over the edge.

I'm huffing, my fingernails digging into the wall as he rolls my balls in his other hand. I'm so fucking close.

"No, you don't," Elliot mutters, and he stops, his thumb and forefinger pinching the tip of my dick. "You come when I say you can."

A whimper escapes me, and I slam my eyes shut because who does he think I am? I have like zero self-control. Didn't he see me behind that hay bale? That's my life in a nutshell.

I. Cannot. Wait.

As if he can read my thoughts, he says, "Oh yes, you can."

Then he starts pumping me again, faster this time. I'm swallowing my moans because I worry he'll punish me more if I let one escape.

Why does that make this even hotter?

Maybe he'll spank me. Tie me up and fuck my ass.

Yeah, I am totally a bottom.

I'm rutting into his hands now. Desperate. Aching. Needy.

"Come," he rasps, and my dick hears his command and can't help but obey. It erupts almost painfully as come shoots everywhere. It hits my stomach, his hands, the wall.

He strokes me through my orgasm until I sag heavily, my forehead pressed against the wall, and then his fingers release me as he steps back.

"I expect you to clean up your mess."

I am parched. I can't even respond. I just grunt and give a minuscule nod.

Yeah, Eli. I'll get right to it after I can fucking move. You turned me to jelly. I've lost all coordination.

What would sex be like with this guy?

I'd be reduced to ash.

CHAPTER FIVE

ELLIOT

It is official. I've had some kind of stroke. I told myself I wasn't going to get involved with him. But not only did I grab Luke's dick at laser tag, I also jerked him off...in my kitchen...against the wall.

And the worst part? I enjoyed it.

Luke is napping in my bed after cleaning up his mess, and I just shift on my feet, not wanting to get into bed with him because then I might hump him. I should have just kicked him out of my house right after he came, but he looked so dazed and tired.

So, I let him lie down for a bit, and now he's asleep. Just like I knew he would be. This man cannot stay awake to save his life.

I huff in frustration.

Damn him for being so wonderfully submissive. You would never guess just by looking at this hulking man that he'd be into giving up control, but he enjoyed it. He loved me telling him what to do.

I pace and press my hand against my groin. There is no way I am falling asleep now. I will be awake for hours if I don't get off. And I'm not about to do it next to Luke. I'm not that desperate.

Lies. I'm exactly that desperate.

But the rational part of my brain is still functioning. So instead, I move into the guest bedroom and lock the door.

This is what I've been reduced to—secretly masturbating alone in the dark, like a delinquent.

I sit down on the edge of the bed and press my fingers to my temples, breathing deeply through my nose. I will the ache away, but it only builds. It's been way too long since I've opened up to anyone. Since I've fucked anyone.

It's showing.

I'm wanton and needy, and it's making me reckless.

There's nothing to be done but to give in to it.

I flip onto my stomach and slide a pillow between my legs.

That insatiable ache is right between my thighs, and I thrust my hips forward, biting down on my lip to muffle any grunts I make. It would be just my luck for Luke to wake up from his slumber and hear this. I stuff another pillow against my face and arch my hips repeatedly until I feel myself cresting.

And I will never, ever admit it, but I imagine Luke the entire time—Luke underneath me, Luke writhing as I fuck into him, Luke submitting to me and giving in to all my desires.

With one final thrust, I push myself over the edge and then roll onto my back, panting. My chest heaves as I brush a hand over my damp forehead.

"Fuck," I mutter because it didn't help. No, it only made it worse.

I need to do it again.

So, I do.

Goddamn, I am so screwed.

———

My shirt is unbuttoned when Luke strides into my closet half-naked the next morning. His chest is still wet from the shower, his boxers practically glued to his thighs. And I see his cock straining toward me. It's almost like it's reaching out to shake my hand.

Ignore it.

I will ignore it.

He glances down at the thick length pressing out from his body and then meets my gaze.

"You gonna be impolite, Eli?" he teases, and I manage to roll my eyes even though my whole body is lit up like a Christmas tree.

Fuck.

There's nothing I can do about it now. I'll have to wait until tonight when Luke is asleep. I'll sneak into the guest room again and hump my pillow like the winner I am.

"You want a repeat of last night?" I ask, buttoning up my shirt and tucking it into my pants.

"I could do that," Luke replies, his hands on his hips, his head tilted slightly.

"Well, I have to get to work. You'll have to wait."

What the hell am I doing? I'm promising a repeat of something I shouldn't even be engaging in.

"Yeah, we'll see, Eli," he says with a smirk and then grabs onto his dick over his boxers and arches his hips.

My cheeks are flushed as I throw my tie around my neck. I need to get out of here before I do something stupid, like press my mouth to his or sink to my knees and take that big cock right down my throat.

"Yes, we will, won't we," I manage to say, moving past Luke. But not before rubbing against him as I do, making sure to let my fingers trail across his straining cock.

And when he mutters *that's just cruel,* I huff a small laugh.

Because this is payback for the misery I've been in.

But apparently, Luke is fluent in the ways of battle because when my phone pings on the way to work, I glance down at it and nearly crash into a tree.

Luke has snapped a picture of himself with his pants undone, showing off the muscular V where his abs meet his groin, his hand cupping himself. My phone pings again, and it's a picture of him grasping onto his bare length, legs spread, everything on display.

I pull over to the side of the road and quickly place my car in park.

Then, because I'm on a complete power trip, I send him a text.

Me: You will not come.
Me: You will wait for me.

I bite my lip and shift in my seat, waiting for his answer.

Luke: You gonna punish me if I don't listen?

Oh god, yes, I will. I will do so many filthy things to him.

Me: Yes.

My breathing is ragged as I wait for his response.

When it comes, all the air in my lungs dissipates.

It's a video of him fucking his fist, and I watch it all, *every last second*. I watch his thick, callused fingers squeeze his long length and move from base to tip in quick, steady movements. My mouth waters as a bit of precum beads at the tip of his cock, his thumb brushing it away. And seconds later, when his come shoots across his stomach, I know I am in for a fucking treat when I get home.

I am going to take a paddle to that ass.

Spank it red.

A sudden knock on my window has me jumping, and my phone slips between the seat and the center console.

My heart smashes against my sternum as I roll down the window, meeting the stare of a concerned police officer.

"You okay?" the officer asks, and I gulp loudly, feeling overheated and flushed.

"Yes, I apologize. I had an important call and had to pull over," I explain. The officer eyes me suspiciously because I probably look high, like I just snorted a brick of cocaine.

"I'm a doctor," I explain, my tone as even as it can be when I'm fucking breathless. "I'm on my way to see patients."

I swear to god, if I get a ticket for this shit, Luke will be in so much fucking trouble. I'll edge him so hard, he'll cry.

But luckily, the officer lets me go after checking my license and registration, and I'm on my way to work, my phone still wedged impossibly between the seats.

I should burn it. Just douse it in lighter fluid and light a match because it's caused me nothing but trouble. Ever since I gave Luke my number, he's been turning me inside out.

But, of course, when I arrive at work, I frantically pry my phone free with trembling fingers, and when I click on the screen, my heart restarts.

Luke: What's my punishment, Doc?

Oh, I'm not going to respond. I get a sick sense of glee, knowing he's going to squirm all day over this, and then I spend every minute between patients thinking up ways to make him beg. Which only makes me hotter and hornier.

By the time I get home to an empty house, I'm agitated and frustrated. I need to get off again.

I'll have to wait for Luke though, because I have plans.

So. Many. Plans.

I spend an hour going through all of my toys, cataloging each one, and spending way too much time thinking about what I'll do with that ass of his.

But he doesn't come home.

He doesn't even text.

I wait for him, playing scales on the piano until my fingers ache, running around the block until my legs collapse.

Then I'm up until midnight, pacing.

I should text him and see where he is, see if he's okay. But I resist, because that's not what this is.

I don't even like the guy.

Shit. That's not true.

I like him too much.

Worry gnaws at me, and I sleep terribly, tossing and turning, my mind unable to shut off.

The next day, I'm a miserable cow. I'm exhausted and end up snapping at everyone. Amanda glares at me when I bite off her head for not moving fast enough. She just smacks her gum between her lips and clacks away on her computer. She's not even looking at the screen though. She's glowering at me. I have no idea how she does that. It's creepy.

I move away from her and stare at my phone screen, and my stomach drops.

He still hasn't contacted me.

Welding isn't that dangerous, right? Is he okay? Or maybe this isn't work-related at all. Maybe he grew tired of me. I'm not the easiest person to be around. I wouldn't be surprised if he dumped me.

I'm completely dumpable.

My phone pings, and I grasp it so hard, I swear I hear it crack.

Luke: Hey, Doc. Sorry I missed you last night, but I fell asleep in my truck and didn't wake up until morning.

My chest deflates, and I sag against my desk. Oh my god, my eyes sting. I blink frantically and then bite the inside of my cheek.

No. I will not cry over this man.

My phone pings again, and I stare at it through blurry eyes.

Luke: Good news tho. Got the itinerary for Colorado today.

Wait, what? Who the hell emailed that to him? It wasn't me. But then I remember the evil gleam in Amanda's eyes as she stared me down earlier. She's done this. I wouldn't be surprised if Luke exchanged numbers with her and they chatted regularly.

They probably plot and scheme against me.

Jesus.

There's no way I am escaping him now. He'll be on that plane with me to Colorado. I can't even bring myself to be mad about it.

Luke: I already have a shit ton of things planned. Be ready.

My fingers move across the screen before I can even think too hard about it.

Me: Next time, text me that you're safe.
Luke: Aw, worried about me, Doc?

I don't answer because enough has already been said. I've shown him too much. It's better to just hide away what little is left, for safety reasons.

When I finally arrive home, I am a mess of emotions. I hate emotions, they're so inconvenient.

But I'm human, and emotions come with the territory. I wish I had just been born an extraterrestrial being or maybe a shark. Whatever has an easy life and no emotions, I want to be that.

But I'm not. I'm just me. And I know there's only one thing that will help me feel in control.

One. Thing.

Luke's on the front porch, a beer in his hand. He's wearing oil-stained jeans, a grey shirt, and a grey beanie. He looks absolutely filthy, and I want nothing more than to smear that dirt right into his skin.

I stalk past him.

"Hey," he says, following me inside. "You look extra grumpy today."

If he only knew the absolute pain I've been in for the past twenty-four hours.

What I've suffered.

"On the bed. On your knees, facing the headboard. Hands behind your back."

He eyes me, and I arch an eyebrow at him. Why isn't he running to do as I ask? Why the hell does he have to push all the time?

"Is this my punishment, Doc?" Luke asks, tilting his head, looking intrigued.

I glance down at the bulge growing in his pants and meet his stare. "I think you already know what this is."

Luke opens a beer and takes a long sip before setting it down on the counter.

"Can't do that," he says, and I swear I'm hearing things, because Luke *did not* just turn me down.

"Your sisters are on their way here."

My mouth drops open, and I groan in frustration. "Do not joke! I'm not in the mood."

Luke adjusts himself and shakes his head. "Nah, Eli. This is no joking matter."

"Cancel," I mutter. "*Cancel. It.*"

"Nah, man. I can't. Eliza just texted. They're five minutes away." He glances down at his straining dick. "Guess we'll just have to suffer through."

"You invited my sisters...to my house?" I ask slowly.

"Well, no. Not really. I happened to mention I was coming over to hang because, you know, I need my punishment. But, you know, I didn't mention that part to them, and they said they'd be right over."

I sigh, removing my glasses, and press my fingers against the bridge of my nose. It will be another miserable few hours without any fucking relief. I'm going to bite my sisters' heads off, just snap them off like grapes being plucked from their stems.

As much as they live to annoy me, I do love them. They've had my back since the beginning, especially since I told them I was trans. They're the fiercest protectors I could ask for.

So, I'll suffer through this. For them. Even though I'm a mess, and I hate being messy like this. It makes me feel so out of control.

"Fine. We better order in then," I mutter.

I am never getting laid ever again.

I will die miserable and horny for *him*.

"Nah. No need. They're bringing food—something called a chartreuse board, whatever the fuck that is. Maybe it's all yellowish green foods? And Jane's bringing Prosecco and says I need to try it with pomegranate juice. Dunno, man. Sounds like I'm going to have the shits tomorrow."

I sigh and resist the urge to bang my head against the wall.

"That will not be enough food for you. They should know this. You consume more than any human I know. You're like a garbage disposal."

"Thanks for the compliment, but don't worry about me. I already ate. This will be my second dinner. Actually, more like an after-dinner treat."

I eye him and seriously wonder where he puts it. He's cut.

He lifts his shirt a little as if he knows where my thoughts went, and my eyes snap down to his exposed skin.

"Like it, huh? I look like a snack. Want to take a nibble?"

Before I can respond with the 'hell yes' forming on my lips, I hear my sisters coming up the walkway. They're so loud no one can miss them. It's like a Mardi Gras marching band. Welcome to my life.

Luke smirks at me, mouths *ready,* and opens the door. And they don't even pause; they just barrel right into him. Luke catches Jane first, her beloved Prosecco bottles clutched tightly in her hands. Then Kate, while balancing a large food container in her palms, still manages to reach up and press a kiss to his cheek. And lastly Eliza, who Luke just sweeps up and carries inside like a princess.

They swoon, positively melt, and my heart pounds so hard I can feel it behind my eyes. I have a headache. My jaw hurts from grinding my teeth. I ache everywhere. I'm going to disintegrate into a puddle of goo.

"Why, hello, brother," Eliza says as Luke gently sets her down in the kitchen. He rubs her stomach lightly, and she winks at me.

"Hi," I manage to say. It's all I'm capable of. Two-letter-word answers. Hi. No. Go.

"So, is this the food thingy?" Luke asks, eyeing the package Kate has set on the table. He pops the lid off and leans a little closer.

"Oh yeah. We got this one special just for you. You're going to love it."

"Fancy. Are those mini grapes."

"Of course they are. We are classy bitches," Eliza says.

"I brought the champagne," Jane chimes in. "They only let me bring two, though. I think five is a more appropriate number. One for each of us."

Luke holds out his hand, pops the top off of one, and helps pour the Prosecco into four glasses. A splash of pome-granate juice is added to each one and handed out to every-one, but Eliza just shakes her head, her lips wrapped around a straw shoved into an apple juice box. Jane swipes the extra cup off the counter and cradles both in her hands, taking sips from each.

"So, what's on the agenda, ladies?" Luke asks, gulping down his drink and getting a swift refill from Jane.

"Food, drinks, facials, and..." Kate holds up a small pouch and shakes it slightly. "Nails."

"Fuck, yes," Luke says and then helps carry everything over to the couch. They arrange the charcuterie board on the coffee table and set the glasses down, and I just watch in morbid fascination as they begin to chat, snack, and slather their faces with some green goop that emerges from a purse. I've been subjected to this on multiple occasions and yes, my face feels fantastic afterward, but no, I don't enjoy it. Much.

And there is no way I'm going to pretend to enjoy it right now. There is absolutely no way. I'm in too much pain.

Luke seems to have forgotten all about me though. He's having a grand old time. He lets all three of my sisters pamper him, and thirty minutes later, he's looking down at his nails and blowing on them.

"Black. Very goth. I like it," he says with a grin.

What the hell is my life right now? A year ago, if I had conjured this scenario up, I would have thought I'd gone insane. Am I hallucinating? Is this *The Matrix*? God, I hope I'm actually just asleep in some scary incubator pod.

When Jane offers me another glass of Prosecco, I suck it down and then glare at her when she tries to apply the green goop to my face.

"I will not," I say, and she rolls her eyes to the ceiling.

"Gosh, such a bore," Jane mutters, and Kate snickers.

But Luke looks over and blinks, his face slathered in green goop.

"Nah. He's fun. You just need to figure out what makes him smile. Got one out of him once. Felt like I won the lottery."

No one has ever called me fun in my entire life. Andrew was always harping on about how dull I was. It was an ongoing joke in our relationship. He laughed about it at parties.

But Luke isn't laughing. No, he's defending me, and it makes a tiny part of my ice-cold heart start to thaw.

This. Guy.

"Well, good luck with maintaining that record," Eliza says. "Elliot is the best, but he's always been a grouch. Even when he was little, he'd just scowl, remember that ya'll?" Jane and Kate nod and giggle. "It's not totally his fault, though. He gets that from *he who shall not be named*."

"Voldemort?" Luke asks.

The girls laugh, and Eliza says, "No, but close enough."

Luke eyes me but doesn't respond, just plucks a tiny grape from the board and pops it into his mouth.

"She means our dad. Both our parents are assholes. We have fully disowned them," Jane says, her words a little less crisp.

"Yeah. Goodbye fuckers!" Kate shouts.

"Fuck them all!" Eliza chimes in. "Bigoted assholes."

"The biggest asses!" Jane yells.

Luke pops some cheese into his mouth and cocks his head. "Eli hasn't shared any of his past with me. Care to fill me in?"

"Well damn, El. Why haven't you told him?" Eliza asks me.

I shift in my seat and gulp down some more Prosecco. "We have known each other for like two weeks. Do you share your life story with strangers?"

"Um, yeah. I do. My local Starbucks barista knows my due date and what I ate for dinner last night and I like them less than this guy. I feel like I've known Luke for years," Eliza replies.

"Yes, well, I don't just make friends as easily as you all do," I mutter.

"True, but that's just because you're shy," Kate blurts.

"I'm not shy."

"He is a total introvert," Jane adds.

"I just dislike people. It's different."

"Dislike is a nice word. No, he hates them," Eliza says. "But he likes you, Luke. He smiled once when he talked about you."

"I haven't seen you since the last time we were all together," I grumble, feeling entirely too exposed.

"Whatever. I heard the smile in your voice. Same thing," Eliza replies.

Luke eyes me and then grabs a handful of crackers and pops them into his mouth.

Eliza loud whispers, "Luke, El pushes everyone away. But if you cling on for dear life, maybe you can stick around. I'd love for you to be my brother-in-law. You're much better than Andrew."

Luke stops chewing. "Who's Andrew?"

"Oh gosh. His ex. He was trash. Pure garbage. I got into witchcraft just to rid ourselves of him."

I press my fingers into my eye sockets and then make my way into the kitchen to find the Advil. "That was not witchcraft. That was a scam. You ordered a box from a shady website and lit some herbs," I say over my shoulder.

"What the fuck ever. It worked, didn't it? Andrew is gone, and this man was conjured up," Eliza says.

"He's not a believer," Jane hisses to Luke.

"I believe in myself," I say.

"He doesn't even believe in love," Kate spews.

"No love, Eli?" Luke asks with an arched eyebrow. Some goop slides down his face and plops onto his shirt, and I snap.

"Will you please wash that shit off your face? It feels like I'm talking to a swamp monster."

"Nah, Eli. You have to keep this on for twenty minutes to ensure the antioxidants sink in."

I huff, "That's not a thing. I'm a doctor. I know."

"He's always such a showoff. Doctor this and doctor that," Eliza chimes in.

"I went to college for ten years. I can say whatever the fuck I want."

"See what we put up with?" she asks Luke.

"But we know he loves us, deep down," Jane says.

"Of course I do," I reply more softly. "I love you all very much. Even when I don't want to."

Jane leans toward Luke and adds, "But he thinks we're overbearing."

"Because you are."

"But he secretly loves it," she says. "He loves having us around. Once you get past the thorns and daggers, he's really just a big teddy bear."

"I can see that. He's sneaky that way. Did you know he's a bit of a cuddler?" Luke asks, and I stare holes into him. I'm definitely going to spank that ass when they leave—pull out my paddle and swat his ass red. There is no doubt about it now. He's been asking for it since that video.

I envision the entire scenario and feel myself grow warm with desire. I shift in my seat as I grow hotter for it. I'm almost on fire. I'm ready for them to leave.

But the night drags on. For. Fucking. Ever. They wash their faces, slowly. They finish off the food like sloths, and then finally, *fucking finally*, I manage to push them out the door. When the lock engages, I turn toward him.

He's standing so close. Much too close. And he smells like cucumbers and green tea.

I clutch my hands into fists. "On the bed. Hands behind your back. Now."

It's all I can say.

Luke runs a thumb across his bottom lip, tugging it down slightly, and then nods.

"If you say 'please'."

My eye tics.

"*Now*," I growl.

Luke's cheeks flush a little darker. "You got it, Doc."

And then he disappears down the hallway.

I feel my heart flutter at his compliance, and I second guess my decision for a swift moment, before I'm unbuttoning my shirt sleeves and rolling them up my forearms. When I get into the bedroom, I see Luke kneeling on the bed, his hands behind his back, his shirt off. He looks over at me, and our eyes meet.

I need this. I shouldn't, but I do.

"You were disobedient."

"Fuck yeah, I was," he says with a smirk, and I bristle slightly. The torture he put me through. I've been aching for days. He won't be smiling soon. No, he will be panting, and begging.

"Keep your hands behind you. If you move them...hm, just don't move them."

"Breaking the rules is very tempting," he says.

I grab onto his jaw firmly and force his eyes to meet mine. "Obey."

"When you say it like that," he mutters, and his cheeks flush. Oh, he likes being told what to do.

By me.

I move behind him, reach around, and unbutton his jeans, the sound of the zipper echoing throughout the quiet room. He's already hard, his cock pushing out against the denim. I lower his pants and boxers until the fabric is stretched across his thighs, then I slide my hands across his hips and grasp onto him. A low groan slips from his mouth.

"Not a sound," I say, and he huffs his frustration as I let go.

I press my hand against his spine and push him until he's face down on the bed, his ass up in the air. Then I work his pants off until he's completely naked.

"Spread those legs," I say, and he does, his cheek pressed against the sheets, his hands still clasped behind him, ass up.

And fuck, I could get off to this image for months.

"Have you ever bottomed before?" I ask, and he shakes his head slightly.

I reach down and grab onto his ass cheeks and spread them, glancing at his hole while kneading the hard flesh of his ass.

"Just because I'm trans doesn't mean I can't top. And Luke, I'm going to top you. You're going to come because I *let* you come."

He presses back against me, and I feel heat pooling in my abdomen. The ache is throbbing now.

I let go of him, walk to my closet, pull out what I need, and roll it out onto the bed.

Luke groans as he eyes it. "*Fuck. Me.* You're so hot. You even have a torture kit."

I slide my fingertip over each toy, and he follows the movement before I stop on a long slender plug.

"Fuck," he mutters, and I grab onto the paddle lying at the end and swat his ass. Hard.

"Shit!" he grunts, and I stare at the pink mark on his skin.

I run a hand over it and say, "I said, not a sound."

"Fuck you," he mutters, and then moans as I spank him again. And then once more just because I like how he looks, red ass propped up for me.

I grab onto his hair roughly and press my lips to his ear.

"You will do everything I say and if you're a good boy, you can come. But if you want me to stop, you say it. You say *stop*, and I will. You say *no*, and I keep going. Understand?"

He nods frantically.

"What do you say if you want me to stop?"

"Stop...but that ain't going to happen, Eli. I'm a fucking winner," he says, and I swat his ass again.

"You never learn, do you?" I ask, and he shakes his head.

"I was a terrible student," he replies, and I spank his ass again. And again, until he's writhing and whimpering on the mattress, his fingers nearly white from grasping them so tightly.

When I finally stop, and his delicious red apple ass is ready to be played with, I reach for the plug and some lube.

"Now. *Now*, you can make all the sounds. I want to hear you moaning," I say as I dribble some lube onto the silicone plug and press it against him. He's panting and grunting as I work it inside of him inch by inch, and when it's firmly planted against his prostate, I reach for the controller.

"This one's a vibrator," I explain and turn it on.

"Shit," he mutters and jerks slightly, sliding forward.

"Hm, not strong enough," I say, and then I turn it up, and Luke topples onto his side, humping the air.

"Eli," he moans. "What the fuck!"

Oh god. I'm giddy. My mouth is pulled up into a smile. I push him onto his back, reach over and grasp onto his dick. I dribble lube onto it, mixing it with his precum.

"Next time I say you'll be punished, think of this."

"Nah," he grunts and fucks his cock into my fist. "This was so worth it. I could do this any day."

I pinch the end of his dick, and he hisses, his hands coming loose and reaching up for me.

But I grab onto them and push them over his head.

"You grab onto me, and we're done. Keep them above your head."

He eyes me, not wanting to do what I say. He wants to test me, and fuck, I'm so ready for it. But instead, he exhales shakily and grabs onto the headboard.

"Good boy," I praise, pulling out a silk blindfold and placing it over his eyes.

I'm not ashamed of what I look like or who I am. That's not what this is for. This is for emotional preservation. The same goes for him touching me.

Looking him in the eyes while I fuck him could possibly wreck me. Letting him put his hands on me would be the end of me.

He's wormed his way into my life. I need to make sure that he stays out of my heart.

"Eli," Luke grumbles in protest, and I'm so tempted to give in, but I swallow it down.

"Lift your head."

He does as I say, and I tie that blindfold tightly behind his head. I push myself up and remove each piece of my clothing, letting my eyes slide across his slick, hard body. When I'm finally naked, I lower my body down on top of him. My chest is pressed against his, his cock against my groin, but not inside me.

"Oh fuck. I can feel you," he says, arching his hips into me. "You feel so good. Fuck, I want to *see* you."

"No," I say and lean up with my hands planted next to his shoulders and rock against him.

His hands clasp onto the headboard so tightly I can hear the wood creaking, and I stare at his panting mouth and want to kiss it. I want to bite down on his tongue and lick my way across his face.

"Say my name," I hiss as I move against him, our hard stomachs sliding together, and his cock twitching deliciously between my legs.

"Elliot," he pants.

"Who's fucking you?"

"You. Only you," he groans, and his acceptance only makes my heart expand.

Oh fuck, I think as our moans mix. Why does it feel so good? Why does it have to be him?

"You're going to come with me," I pant, and Luke is humping up against me roughly now, the entire bed hitting the wall with each movement.

"Yeah, Eli. Fuck, yeah. Please."

My skin is on fire. Our sweaty, writhing bodies slip and slide as we move against each other frantically.

"Now," I say and then arch into him over and over as my orgasm crests, and I tumble into the abyss. I feel his cock jerk as he unloads between us, and then there's only the sound of our breathing in the silence.

His blindfold has slipped a little, and I press my forehead against it as I pant.

"Luke," I say softly, slipping the blindfold up a little and seeing that his eyes are closed.

"Are you asleep?" I ask, trying to catch my breath.

"Wore me out, Doc. Might need a snooze."

I huff out a small laugh and then peek once more.

Yep. He's asleep.

Of course he is.

I hover over him, my eyes sliding across his face, and then gently, I run my finger over his eyebrow and down his cheek before touching his lips.

Those lips that I didn't kiss.

Regrettably.

I lean down slightly and let my mouth hover over his. I could close the gap, just let my mouth move against his, and he'd never know. It would be my little secret.

Why am I so tempted when I've never been before? It was never like this with Andrew. I'd kissed him, but the desire to do so was never this strong. There has *never* been such a pull to do something so out of character for me.

What is it about him that I'm so drawn to?

I cover his eyes with the blindfold again and push myself off the bed. I clean myself up in the bathroom, and pull on my pajamas before moving back to where he's sprawled out gloriously naked on the sheets.

I remove his blindfold and then I see the controller next to the bed and remember the plug. The sleepy bastard fell asleep with a vibrator in his ass.

I chuckle to myself as I lift his leg and gently remove it. I run a damp washcloth over his abdomen and groin, cleaning him, and he breathes steadily, never stirring. When I'm finished, I lie down next to him and pull the blanket up over us.

My mind reels from what just happened, and I wonder what the hell I was thinking. I just had unprotected sex with the man. We didn't even talk about it first. Jesus, fuck.

I've completely lost my mind. I've never done that before in my entire life.

I nudge him to ask him if he's been tested recently because I have to know or I'll ruminate on it for hours, but he doesn't wake. No, he just twists and nestles himself into me.

"Luke," I whisper, and when he refuses to wake up, I shake him.

"He's mine," he grumbles in his sleep, and I inhale sharply, my heart thumping wildly.

Well, I'll just have to ask when he wakes up.

In the meantime, I'll suffer through this snuggling he's subjecting me to.

And dammit, if I don't sleep like the dead.

LUKE

I wake up next to Elliot, my face pressed against his bicep, and damn, he smells like clean laundry and sex. I flex my hand and feel it slide against the bare skin of his stomach. Hell, yes. My hand was sneaky last night and must have slipped under his *Sesame Street* pajamas.

Hm.

He feels good. All hard, and warm, *and mine.*

My rigid dick is pressed against his thigh, and I rut against him once. Then I let my hand slide up over a dusting of soft hair until it's right over his firm pec, and I run my thumb across his nipple.

"Your hand is up my shirt," Elliot says groggily, and I freeze.

"'Course it is. I'm in your bed and you're hot as fuck."

Elliot huffs but doesn't ask me to remove it, so I take it as an invitation to stay, maybe settle in and put down roots. I move over to the other nipple and play with it a little, my dick pulsing against his firm thigh. What we did last night was the hottest thing that's ever happened to me and I need more with him. So much more.

"Have you had an STI panel recently?" Elliot asks, and it's so out of the blue that I laugh a little.

"Morning to you too, Doc?" I say and then decide he's too far away. So, I roll a little further onto him and nuzzle my face into his neck.

"Answer the question, Luke."

"Yeah, I have. I'm fine. Don't stress. Don't stress."

Elliot sighs and runs a hand through my hair. "Good. And I'm negative as well."

"I wasn't worried. I know you're too paranoid to do anything reckless."

Elliot tugs on my hair and forces my gaze to his. "Last night was reckless. I've never done that before. *Never.*"

I lean up on my elbows, now completely on top of him. Damn, I wish he was naked. I want to feel his skin against my cock.

"Yeah, I bring that out in people. Make them all crazy-like. I make you crazy too, huh?"

"Yes, you do," he says, his eyes sliding down to my lips, and I wet them.

"About that...how come you didn't kiss me last night?" I ask, and Elliot glances away quickly.

"I don't do that."

"You don't like it?"

"It's too intimate."

"Hm...one day, Eli, you'll kiss me and you'll want it. Trust," I say, sounding more confident than I feel. Because maybe this guy doesn't want his mouth on mine. But I can be convincing.

I think.

Elliot eyes my mouth again, and then he's wrapping his legs around mine and rolling until he's on top of me.

"No more talking about that," he says sternly, leaning up slightly. And then reaches down between us and grabs onto my cock.

"Hands on the headboard."

"Come on, Eli," I say. "I wanna touch you some more. It wasn't enough."

He rolls his lips between his teeth like he's really contemplating it, and then shakes his head. "Headboard now, or this isn't happening."

"Fuck, you're a monster," I grumble, placing my hands over my head, but my complaints disappear as he works me over the edge all over again.

Shit, he's good with his hands. He should have been a surgeon.

———

"You will not go back to sleep," Elliot says, and I pry my heavy eyelids open. Damn him for being so fucking hot. I'll end up in a coma if we keep at it. I keep passing out every time we fuck around and it's becoming a problem.

"Nah. Just resting my eyes."

"If you *rest your eyes*, you will go to sleep. I need to go to work," Elliot says as he moves into the bathroom. "You should leave."

"Nah. Think I'll stay right here. Can't get rid of me so easily now. I'm sticking like Gorilla Glue."

"I don't know what that is."

I peer over at him. "Oh, Eli. I'm going to teach you so much. Let me see, how do I put it in terms you'll understand?"

He eyes my chest as I smear my come into my abs.

"I've grown on you like a cyst. A benign cyst filled with joy and excitement and sexy times."

"That's a revolting analogy. And you need to clean yourself up."

"Later," I say, and Elliot looks conflicted for just a minute because I know he doesn't want to go to work when I'm right here. But he'll never admit it. Instead, he just turns and disappears behind the bathroom door. I hear the lock engage, and I think, for just a second, about using those lock picking skills Sem taught me. But then I discard it.

Elliot will come around eventually. One day he'll let me touch him while we fuck.

I'll give him time. I can be patient.

When he emerges twenty minutes later, a towel wrapped around his waist, I can't help but take him in. This is a sneak peek he's never allowed me before, and I'm already feeling my heart rate increase.

"Eli, shit. If I were you, I'd walk around naked all day."

His cheeks pinken slightly, and I push myself up and move toward him, reaching out and tracing a finger down his bicep. He's lean and not as built as me, but he's still got definition. His chest is broad and firm and I can see just the faintest line of a scar running under each pec. I move my finger to his flat stomach and slide it lower. Goosebumps erupt across his skin. I love that his body tells me how I affect him, even when he'll never admit it. I'm so hard again already.

He tracks my movement, his lips parted and his dark eyes

dilated, and then before my finger can touch the towel, he backs away out of reach.

Damn, I want to unwrap him, just peel that towel away and drop to my motherfucking knees. I wonder what he likes. I've done a little research, and let me tell you, I will not be disappointed with whatever is underneath that towel. I am one hundred percent into all of it.

"How about I bring you lunch today?" I say and lean against the door frame.

Elliot eyes me—my face, come-covered chest, and cock, and then moves into the closet.

"Fine. If you insist."

"I so fucking do."

And then he closes the closet door, and I just stare at it. He won't even give me a glimpse of that ass.

Damn him.

I hop into the shower, and when I'm done and dressed for work, I stroll into the kitchen. Elliot is already in there brewing coffee.

I move in behind him, wrap my arms around his waist, and press my face into his neck.

He stiffens for a moment before melting into me. It seems he's accepted his fate.

"There are frozen breakfast sandwiches in the freezer."

I smile against his skin. "You buy those for me?"

"I would never," he grumbles, but his cheeks are flushed again.

"Admit it. You bought me fucking food. You're keeping me."

"I just know you eat more frequently than a newborn baby and I didn't want you to expire from hunger. I don't know how to dispose of a corpse."

I snort and move away from him, throwing two breakfast sandwiches into the microwave. "Sure you do. You're the smartest person I know."

"Fine, yes, I could manage it," he mutters, then hands me a to-go mug. "Creamer is in the fridge as well."

I run my fingers into his hair and press my lips to his temple. He bristles, so I let him go and drown my coffee with the white mocha creamer he bought, just for me.

I can see him now, mulling over choices in the grocery aisle, all serious and scowling. He probably checks the ingredient labels too. I bet this is the healthiest white mocha creamer on the planet.

"Thanks, Doc," I say, lifting my mug up to my lips and taking a sip. "This is fucking delicious."

"It's nothing."

He jokes. It's not nothing. This is everything.

I know what this means.

"I gotta run," I say as I grab onto my breakfast sandwiches and my to-go mug and move toward the door. "I'll see you at lunch."

He watches me go. "Fine."

I wink at him and disappear outside, slipping into my truck, and I can't wipe the damn smile off my face.

———

I battle through traffic hell to get to his office but it's so worth it. We were finishing up at the docks today, so I just left a little early. But not before I snapped a picture of myself in my truck, legs spread, my shirt pushed up to my neck.

He likes these photos, I know he does. He'll never admit

it, but Amanda told me he zooms in on them. She's caught him looking.

Twice.

I wonder what he does in private, when no one is around to catch him. Does he look at those pictures while he gets himself off? Does he moan my name when he comes?

Me: Almost there.
Elliot: Great.
Me: Don't sound too excited.

I snort and run a hand across my mouth. He's such a grump.

My grump.

When I walk into his small office, I don't see anyone at the front desk, but I do see Elliot. He's standing, arms crossed, in the middle of the waiting room, waiting for me. He's not even talking to the two patients sitting there. One is even speaking directly to him, but Elliot isn't paying any attention. He's just anxiously looking at the door as I stroll in.

Fuck, if he isn't *so damn cute.*

"Hey, Eli," I say and wrap my arm around his shoulders and press a kiss to his temple. "Waiting for me with bated breath?"

"Absolutely not," he replies, and I chuckle as we move toward his office.

As soon as we're inside, I press myself into him.

"What are you doing?" he asks as he wraps his arms around me and squeezes.

"Giving you a hug," I reply. "You won't admit it, but I know you love it. You're a total hugger."

He sighs and presses his cheek to my chest just as Amanda barges right in. She doesn't even knock.

Elliot clears his throat and peels himself away from me.

Amanda eyes us both with a smirk, her animated eyebrows quirking up individually. They remind me of the little fuzzy, blue-haired worm dude from the movie *Labyrinth*. I sorta want to snatch one up and take him home in my pocket.

"Nice to see you again, shit-stain," she tells me.

I smile widely. "Back atcha, dick face."

Elliot's mouth lowers into a frown, and he sends a glower at Amanda. "What is happening here?"

"We're friends," I say, and Amanda smacks her gum loudly.

"What he says."

"I didn't know you had friends," Elliot tells Amanda, who just rolls her eyes in response. "Do you always call your friends such awful names?"

"Nah, only the special ones," I respond.

"And we both know Luke is *very special*, don't we?" Amanda says and arches an eyebrow at her boss.

"Damn the women in my life," Elliot mutters, and I nudge him.

"Loosen up, Doc. We're having lunch," I say and then toss Amanda the third brown paper bag. "Your favorite."

Elliot eyes us both, and after Amanda blows me a kiss, she closes the door. Then she opens it again and peeks her head in. "Lock this shit if you're going to do something naughty."

I snort a laugh, and Elliot sighs loudly.

But I nudge him and pull a sandwich out for him.

"Got it nice and healthy for you. Wheat bread, light mayo, and I even had them put on some avocados. Those little green things are expensive as fuck, yeah?"

"Thank you," he says and takes a small bite.

"Anything for you, Eli."

He munches on his sandwich, eyeing me, and I resist the urge to peel myself out of my clothes and let him use me as a tabletop. I'd even let him use my dick as a chair.

I shift in my seat and take a large bite out of my sandwich.

"So, I was thinking about Colorado, and I sent you an email of all the shit we can do. You want to be in on the final decision, or can I just pick everything?"

He nods absently, his eyes on my thighs. I spread them a little wider, and he squirms in his seat.

"Alright, I'll make the reservations," I say.

"Hm," he replies, and I lean into him a little.

"A train ride, a cave tour, and a tantric massage."

"Yes," he replies, and I nudge him with a soft laugh.

"So, the itinerary sounds good?"

"Yes." His eyes snap up, and he grimaces. "Oh hell. What did I just agree to?"

"Everything, Doc. We're getting married, having babies," I joke.

When he stutters and almost chokes, I chuckle. "Nah, just kidding. Just the itinerary for Colorado. I have it all planned out," I repeat. "I'll email you everything."

"And do your accommodations factor into it? Where will you stay?"

I shrug, hoping he lets me in. Lets me stay. "With you?"

He huffs and looks away. "Fine."

"Knew you'd let me. That was a huff of excitement."

"It was not."

I throw my legs over his and lean back, finishing my sandwich and taking a long sip of my Coke.

He grumbles but still rests his hand on my thigh while he

finishes his food. When I offer him a sip of my drink, he takes it reluctantly. He pretends to hate it, but I see the way his eyelids flutter.

He loves the damn sweets but won't let himself enjoy them.

I grin on the inside.

I'm going to love watching him enjoy the little things, and I'm sure as fuck going to enjoy him enjoying me.

CHAPTER SEVEN

ELLIOT

"Hi there. You think we could upgrade to first class?" Luke asks the woman behind the counter who looks flustered by his attention. I don't blame her.

He's been flustering me too.

For the past week, he's been everywhere—in my personal space, in my bed, and always in my thoughts.

I can't seem to exorcise him. There has to be holy water for this kind of thing. Maybe I should see a priest.

I'm worried where this will lead and how hurt I will be at the end of it all.

"I'm so sorry, but we don't have anything available," the woman says as she smiles coyly. She fluffs her hair, but it's un-fluffable. There's too much hairspray in those strands to move them. I can smell her from here.

Not a chance, lady.

I eye Luke and realize just how damn hot he really is. I can see what she sees—his dirty blond curls peeking out from under a grey beanie, his thick thighs stretching out his worn jeans and his fitted T-shirt which shows off all his muscles. He's delicious. Tack on his charming smile and his confident, out-going personality and he's like a fantasy come to life.

I pat my hair and then quickly shove my hand in my pocket.

Great. Just fucking great. I'm jealous of a woman who fluffed her hair in his general direction.

I need serious help.

"No worries," Luke says and gives her a sensual wink.

Can winks be sensual? It sure looks like they can.

Luke doesn't seem to notice my wayward thoughts as he wraps his arm around my shoulders and leads me to some chairs. I'm letting him touch me far too often. It's rattling the insides of my carefully put-together brain. The filing cabinets are falling open, and papers are scattered all over the floor. Pretty soon, a gust of wind will carry them right outside, where they'll be trampled and shat on.

Damn it all. I need to gain a little more control in these situations, but I'm helpless to do anything but just let him do what he wants. Is this what parents feel like when they have children? Do they eventually just give up and let the child run wild? Because I feel like I've lost all control when it comes to him.

He's running roughshod over the carefully crafted parts of my life.

"Guess we'll have to sit *extra close* in economy," he says, and I take a swig of my water. It'll be a long flight with him pressed against me. Not that it's going to be anything new and not that I'm really complaining.

Like the other morning when he just rolled right on top of

me and laid there. He was heavy and hot, and I fucking loved it.

He's slowly melting the cold, dark parts of my heart.

I've never met a man so open and willing to experience new things.

I've never met a man like him, period.

"Thinking about it, huh?" Luke asks and then leans over and whispers, "My ass is still sore."

Oh my god.

"Do not bring that up here," I mutter, and Luke chuckles and shifts in his seat.

"Just telling the truth. Tell me you packed that little kit of yours."

I eye him and give a clipped nod. "Yes."

"Fuck yeah."

He leans back and spreads his arms across the back of the chairs. His fingers play with the ends of my hair, and I do not lean into him. Absolutely not.

I sit there completely still and statuesque. Completely dignified.

Then he's gently massaging my earlobe, and I subconsciously tilt my head toward him. I mentally slap myself for it. I have to keep it together.

I am not lovesick.

I'm a thirty-five-year-old doctor, for fucks sake.

When we finally get seated on the plane, Luke's practically on top of me, his hand resting on my thigh as he threads his fingers through mine. He leans back and watches a movie on his phone like this is no big deal. Meanwhile, I'm feeling like a teenage kid holding hands with their crush. I'm a goddamn mess.

I order a mini vodka from the flight attendant and gulp it down.

Then I order another one.

It doesn't help, of course. The airlines don't sell alcohol that can make you act more rationally. No, quite the opposite.

By the time we get to the hotel, I'm desperate and overly eager. The alcohol only served to make me hornier.

I don't have time for this.

But I want it, nonetheless.

As soon as the hotel door shuts behind us, I'm on him. The suitcases are abandoned and roll away slowly as I roughly shove my body against him, threading my fingers through his and pressing both his hands against the wall.

"You have been very distracting," I mutter as we rut against each other, his erection against my groin. God, he's always ready and willing. This will never grow old.

"Gonna punish me, Doc?" he grunts.

"Don't have time for that. I have ten minutes," I pant and then do something so ludicrous that I will look back on this for weeks and wonder what the hell I was thinking.

But teenagers don't think things through, do they? No, they just exist in space and act on their basest needs.

That's me, needy and reduced to a primitive human. Getting off is the only thing I can think about right now. I turn my back to his chest and untuck my shirt and unbutton my pants.

I grab onto his hand and guide it below my waistband.

I feel Luke exhaling deeply against my neck as he brushes his lips against my sensitive, overheated skin. But I don't hyperfocus on his lips or the fact that his mouth is *on me*. I can't, or else I'll just burst right into flames.

"Do it like this," I instruct, almost breathless as I move

his thumb on one side of me and the pointer and middle on the other, and then I slide his fingers the short distance up to just beneath my tip and then back down.

"Oh fuck," Luke mutters, and his grip tightens. I wince.

"Not so tight."

"Oh shit," he huffs. "Sorry."

He loosens his grip a little, and then he does it again.

"Better?" he asks, his breath brushing against my neck.

"Yes. So good," I moan.

He hums under his breath and he's touching me so good. I lean back into him, my eyes squeezed shut and my legs trembling as he works me toward the edge.

"So hot. You're so hot. I can feel you, but I wanna see," he says, his cock impossibly hard against my ass as he arches into me. "You gonna let me see, Eli? Let me see you spread out naked for me? I bet you taste so good."

Oh my god.

I can't let myself fall into temptation.

But damn, if it isn't enticing.

The things he could do with his tongue, and with his dick.

His other hand moves up my shirt, sliding against my bare chest as he moves up to grasp onto my neck. His big thick hand squeezes my neck gently as he bites down lightly on the skin just below my ear. And then his fingers in my pants do a little twist right at the end of me, and I feel myself cresting. I moan loudly and come so hard my vision blacks out for a moment. My body slumps against him, feeling overly sensitive.

"No more," I grunt, and Luke slowly removes his hand from my pants.

Then he brings his fingers up to his nose and inhales deeply. It's filthy and gross, and I can't help but blush.

No one has ever smelled me before.

I like it way too much.

I pull away from him because I'll kiss him if I stay where I am. And I can't do that.

Must not do that.

"That was...nice."

"Nice," Luke snorts and then glances down at his still hard cock. "You came like you haven't had an orgasm in years."

Well, before him, I technically hadn't. Not with someone else. But me and my trusty hand have worked wonders. Throw in a few toys, and who needs a man?

Me. I need a man. Specifically, Luke. It seems I was wrong.

Luke eyes me and adjusts himself. "You gonna leave me hanging, Doc?"

"Yes, because I have to leave," I say, tucking my shirt in. "And you won't touch your dick until I get back. I'll text you instructions."

"Dammit, Eli," he grumbles, and I smile wickedly, feeling like I have the upper hand for the first time in days. Or, maybe it's the vodka giving me false confidence.

"It will be worth the wait."

I glance at my phone and curse. I'm going to be late. I'm *never* late.

I tuck my phone into my pocket, grab onto my suit jacket and shrug it on.

"Keep an eye on your phone."

"Got it. And when you're done with this little power trip of yours, we have a train to catch."

"Fine," I say and then rush out of the room, staring at my reflection in the elevator doors to straighten my wayward hair.

Damn Luke and his magical hands.

The elevator stops on the third floor, and an older gentleman steps on. I must look like a mess because he eyes me, and I can't help the lie that spills out of my mouth.

"Fell asleep on the plane. I'm running a little bit late."

I don't know why I think he needs an explanation. He doesn't know or care about me. But for some reason, it makes me feel better. It's better than admitting that I just had Luke's hand down my pants as he brought me to orgasm.

Or admitting how much I liked it.

The conference is in full swing when I sneak inside, finding a seat in the back. A few people swivel their heads to look at me, but I just meet their gaze with a stony one of my own. They wouldn't be so quick to judge if they had a Luke of their own.

They'd be late too or might not even show up at all.

My phone vibrates, and I pull it out and bite my lip because it's a picture of Luke on the bed, his dick straining up in the air and a pout on his lips.

Those lips I haven't kissed yet.

Luke: I'm in literal pain.

I glance around and then quickly reply.

Me: Do not touch it.

Then, before I can shove my phone into my pocket, it buzzes again, and Luke is saluting me with a smirk on that handsome face of his.

I bite back a grin. I fear I have a condition. My face keeps spasming.

"You were late," a familiar voice hisses in my ear, and my phone clatters to the ground. I need to buy a better case before I crack the screen entirely.

I lean down to grab it, but Andrew swipes it off the floor before I can, and being the invasive asshole he is, he glances down at the screen.

I snatch it from his palm and shove it into my pocket.

"Ah, you have a new man toy?" Andrew whispers, and I swallow. Because there he is. The man I was hoping to avoid. The guy my sisters dispelled with witchcraft. Where are their magical herbs now, huh? He looks impeccable with perfectly parted brown hair and his aristocratic nose. He's wearing a grey sweater vest and flawlessly pressed pants.

What did I ever see in him?

My tastes have completely changed.

"Yes," I lie because I am not getting into this with Andrew. He doesn't get this part of me. He had it, and then he threw it all away.

"A guy like that," he replies softly with a smug look on his face. "It doesn't bother him that you're...you?"

I just stare blankly at him. God, my sisters were right. He always made me feel like shit, about everything. I should have recognized the signs earlier and ran, but I didn't.

He'd use small, subtle digs and jabs, trying to tear down my self-esteem. To him, I was always too boring, too intro-verted, too quiet, and too grumpy. Nothing was off-limits to his ridicule, not even my body. He made sure that I felt lesser than, in every way. Looking back, I realize it was all just a fucked up effort to make me feel too insecure about myself to leave him, thinking no one else would want me. And sadly, it worked. I'd stayed for far too long.

Never again.

"Go away," I say, turning my face forward and grabbing my laptop out of my bag.

But he doesn't leave, he just looms, and not at all in a sexy way.

I don't dare check my phone to see if Luke has responded because I don't want Andrew to see. I want this part of my life to remain the way it is—private. Well, as much as it can be with my sisters involved.

Finally, the speaker announces a break, and I scramble to find a new place to sit, but Andrew's still there, eyeing me from across the room.

I resist the urge to flip him off or shout something very unprofessional in his general direction. Why can't he just leave me alone?

Maybe no one wants to sit with him because he's a dickhead with a questionable personality. Maybe all of his friends realized what an asshole he is and left him. Either way, I don't care. I stopped having feelings for this man years ago.

My phone pings, and I glance down at it and see Luke with his arm thrown around a woman I don't recognize. Immediately, my blood pressure skyrockets, and my lips turn down into a frown. Well, this day couldn't get any worse. First, Andrew and now it seems Luke has gone off and found my replacement.

Luke: Made a friend while rocking climbing.

Luke: Her name is Denise.

Luke: Look at this.

Then another picture comes in of him, obviously taken by his new friend, as he scales a steep rockface. I don't need to look hard to know it's him. I've studied that body in detail. I slide my fingers across the screen, enlarging the image.

What the hell? Is this what he's doing this morning?

I zoom in some more and ogle the muscles in his arms, clearly not paying attention to what the speaker is saying. I spent thousands to be here, and I'm not even listening because Luke looks like sex scaling that mountain. He has no business doing that. It looks dangerous.

Another picture pops up of him giving a thumbs up to the person on the ground, and I click my phone off. Then I click it on.

Then I zoom in again.

Me: That does not look safe.
Luke: Nah, Doc. I made it down just fine. Just gotta trust the rope.

I stare at his words and shift in my seat. Trust the rope? I barely trust myself, especially with the decisions I've made recently. I'm not sure I could trust a fucking rope.

Luke: You worried about me?

Absolutely not. I am not worried at all, but then visions of him on a gurney, broken and bloody, cause my breath to catch in my throat. I click my phone off and press my hands onto the armrests, squeezing my eyes shut. I need to get it together, to act like a rational, logical being, but the entire time the speaker drones on and on, I think about *him*.

When the conference is done, I rush to the hotel room and exhale when I hear that the shower is on.

I lean against the wall to catch my breath and then stand up straight and swipe a hand through my hair.

I'm fine. This is fine. He's fine.

Moving into the steamy bathroom, I see the silhouette of Luke behind the glass door, and I feel my mouth go dry. It's the Sahara in there. I need a glass of cool water. Where's the fucking oasis when I need it?

He's glorious; words can't do him justice. Water sluices down all of his thick muscles, and he swipes his hand through his wet hair and tilts his head back.

My fists bunch near my sides as his head tilts, his eyes catching mine.

He smiles, and rests a hand on the top of the shower door. He turns toward me entirely, and that enormous cock rises in acknowledgment as he just stares at me.

It is the most sexual thing I've ever experienced, his hazel eyes watching me, and I want nothing more than to get in that shower with him and run my hands across the strong planes of his body. To just *feel* him.

But I don't. I just stand there in this humid room and watch *him* watching *me*.

Then the shower door opens with a squeak, and he strides out, soaking wet, and stops directly in front of me.

He's dripping on the tile floor but doesn't reach for a towel. He just eyes me, and I can't breathe.

"Missed you, Eli. Been aching for you all day," he finally says, and my eyes slide to his heavy, straining cock.

Then I do something I absolutely shouldn't. I blame him. He has some kind of spell over me. Perhaps my sisters ordered another box, one that has a voodoo doll of me, and they're making me do this. Yeah, we'll go with that.

I drop to my knees and grasp onto his hips, my fingers digging into the smooth, taut skin.

His breath stutters, and I waste no time. I open up and pull him right inside my wanting, salivating mouth.

Luke groans deeply, his hands gently cradling my head as I take him all the way to the back of my throat.

"You're fucking brilliant," he grunts as I press my nose right into the coarse hair of his groin and swallow around him.

"Holy shit," he adds, and then I pull back and do it all over again.

He's exhaling shakily, his fingers digging into my scalp lightly as I work him toward the edge. I cannot believe I'm doing this; haven't done it in years.

I hate being vulnerable and submissive like this.

But he's so careful with me. He barely moves. He just trembles as I consume him.

I meet his hooded gaze, and he gently cups my cheek, almost reverently, as if he's worshiping me.

My heart squeezes inside my chest as I drag my tongue back over his length, sucking hard.

"Shit, Eli," he grunts, gently wrenching my head back and off his dick. "You're so good. *Too good.* I'm going to come if you keep that up."

I arch an eyebrow at him, and he tosses his head back and groans.

I take him back into my mouth and bob my head furiously until he's chanting my name. The sound of him falling apart, piece by piece, makes me suck him harder.

I want him shattered because of me.

"Fuck. Eli. Coming. Oh shit," he grumbles, and then I feel the taste of him splash on my tongue. A small moan escapes my throat as I swallow it down. I'll never admit it, I'll take this to my grave, but I *savor* it.

I let his softening length slip from my mouth, and some of his come dribbles down my chin and onto my shirt.

His eyes follow it, and he swipes a thumb over my lips.

"That was really fucking good, Eli. You've got talent," he tells me, and I pretend like that doesn't puff me up.

But it does. I'm irrationally gleeful that he enjoyed it. That he enjoyed *me*.

I pull his hands off of my head and stand up, slowly unbuttoning my shirt. Luke watches my fingers like he's about to be quizzed on it. That's how intently he's studying me.

"You want me to return the favor?" he asks softly.

I pause what I'm doing and meet his stare.

"Fine."

He moves to kneel, but I stop him.

"No," I say and step closer to him, undoing my pants. Just the button and zipper, nothing else. It's a slippery slope, and currently, I'm dangling on the precipice, holding on to a rootless weed halfway out of the soil. I'm going to fall so hard, yet still, part of me wants to just let go.

Let go. Let go.

No, not yet.

Luke inhales sharply as I remove my shirt entirely and turn to press my bare back against his chest.

Luke glances in the mirror, watching me, and our eyes lock.

We look so hot together, shirtless and disheveled, and yet my heart rate increases from the vulnerability I'm showing.

But that's all forgotten when he slips his hand below my waistband until he's right where I want him, and damn, he has a good memory. A groan escapes my parted lips.

"Look at you," Luke says hoarsely, his eyes meeting mine in the mirror and then sliding across my abdomen. "Listen to you. Those sounds."

I'm panting, small moans slipping from my mouth. I can't help it. Can't control myself.

His hand moves up my torso and his thumb traces a faded scar before moving to my nipple.

"The things I want to do to you, Eli," he mutters. "If you'd let me."

Oh god, in this moment I feel like I could. I could let him inside of me, his fingers and his cock. The thought of it, just that small vision is enough for me. I come on a low groan, grasping onto him.

And when I'm slumped against him, his strong arms holding me up, he presses a soft kiss to the top of my head.

"You're so damn hot," he mutters.

"So are you."

It's an admission that shows too much, but I don't care at the moment. He's wrecked me in the best possible way.

Luke runs the tip of his nose across my temple, and his hands flex against my chest.

"As much as I want to just chill here and do all that again, we gotta get going, so we don't miss the train," he says.

Hell, I could care less about trains or reservations right now. I'm exhausted from the trip, from feeling so out of control, but mostly from letting myself be so vulnerable with a man that I barely know. I'd gone into a relationship with Andrew quickly and look where I'd ended up.

The truth is I'm just afraid.

I glance over at Luke and that look of excitement on his face has me pushing forward and running a hand through my mussed hair. Enough of this worrying. I have to move forward.

I always have, always will.

"Give me five minutes to change. Then we can go."

———

Luke and I sit side by side in a train car as we make our way up Pike's Peak. It's the highest summit of the Rocky Mountains at fourteen thousand feet. The cog railway system we are currently on was created years ago to bring people up the mountain. It's about a three-hour round trip, stopping at the summit to see the Visitor Center and then heading back down. I didn't even know this existed until Luke led me onto the train car and we took our seats.

I don't think I would have enjoyed Colorado Springs half as much without him here with me. He's making me do things I would have never done myself. If I had come alone, I would have spent my evenings in my hotel room, reading a book or perusing the internet. Food would have been delivered to my door.

I'd never be sitting in a train car chugging up a mountainside.

He was right when we first met. My existence pre-Luke was boring. He crashed his way into my life and made it fun.

I listen absently as the guide talks over the speakers about the history of the mountain and its significance, but what I'm really focused on is Luke's hand in mine.

As soon as we sat down, he linked his fingers with mine and hasn't moved them. I'd grumbled and muttered, but he'd ignored me.

I bite back a smile at the thought.

I will not smile.

"Hey, yeah, I have a question," Luke says when the guide opens up the floor for questions. "Why don't these trains have bathrooms? Seems like that might be an issue for some passengers."

The guide grins softly. I'd smile at him like that, too, if I was someone else. He's endearing in his own way.

She briefly explains how the train can't accommodate them, but I'm only half listening. I'm just *feeling* Luke next to me. It's almost like an out-of-body experience.

Luke leans back, satisfied with her response. "Fucking interesting, huh?"

"Yes." It's not interesting, yet here I am saying that it is.

The announcer takes a few other questions from passengers and then says, "I just found out that we can't go any farther up the mountain. The tracks up ahead are frozen. We do apologize and are offering refunds back at the station...."

"Shit," Luke says, eyeing an older couple across the aisle. "Someone is going to pee their pants. Hope they brought diapers."

I pinch my lips shut, lest I laugh. "And this is what's cluttering that brain of yours?"

He nudges me. "Hell yeah. And, you know, thoughts of you."

"Hm, I rank up there with adult diapers. How very charming."

Luke pulls our entwined hands up to his mouth, biting down softly on the tip of my thumb.

"You're so funny, Eli."

I glance away from him, feeling my heart stutter a little too painfully in my chest. It's not a medical condition. I'm a doctor, so I know. No, this is far worse.

This is my heart falling a little in *like* with this man. I told myself I wouldn't ever let myself fall again. I never meant for any of this to happen.

Luke just burst into my life like a four-alarm fire and burned my sheltered hideaway to the ground.

I'm exposed now.

He leans closer to me. "When we get back to the bottom, let's get dinner downtown, and then," he presses his lips to my ear and whispers, "we can go back to the room and fuck around."

I shift in my seat, my hand still clasped in his.

"You could take out that torture kit of yours. Play with me a bit."

I bite my lip to stifle a smile. "That could be arranged."

He huffs a laugh and eyes me.

"I've got the biggest boner right now," he mutters, and I peek down and see it. "Stop looking, that just makes it worse."

I feel my cheeks heat, and I force my gaze out the window. I will not stare at his dick like a dog begging for treats. I have more self-control than that.

But all through dinner at the small, eclectic restaurant downtown, I internally squirm.

"What made you want to go into welding?" I suddenly ask, because I need to focus on something else and prove to myself I can carry on an adult conversation, dammit.

Luke grabs a piece of bruschetta and shoves it in his mouth. He licks his thumb, and I watch with rapt attention as his tongue moves across his skin and then over his bottom lip to catch a crumb. Shit, I'm going to need a lobster bib to handle all this drool if I don't pull myself together.

"I'm good at it. I like working with my hands. I've been doing it since I was eighteen. My dad bought me a welding machine and brought home some metal sheets; I've never looked back. Got all my certificates too."

He pops another piece of bread into his mouth. At this rate, we should have gone to an all-you-can-eat buffet. The bill is going to be enormous, but Luke told me he'd pay for it. He'd leaned into me and said, "I may be a blue-collar worker, Eli, but I do just fine."

As he'd driven us to this restaurant, I'd looked it up.

Yeah, Luke makes almost as much as me. Fuck, if that doesn't impress me.

"Are you a journeyman?" I ask.

"Yep. Gonna be an expert welder next year. You know why, Eli?"

The way he says my name has me focusing intently on his mouth. I wonder if he'll eat me with that mouth. I suddenly get a vivid image of his head between my legs, his stubble rubbing against my thighs....

I swallow thickly and meet his eyes.

"Why?

He leans back, and our legs bump together. "'Cause I'm good at what I do. That's where we're alike."

"I'm not so sure about that. I'm not sure I'm an excellent doctor. Mediocre at best. Good at times." I pause and see Luke eyeing me. "You look like you disagree."

"Yeah, Doc, you don't see what I see."

I arch an eyebrow at him, trying to contain myself. "And what is that?"

"That you're a damn good doctor. Amanda told me so. You think she'd put up with your shit if she didn't like you?"

"She likes how much I pay her."

"Nope," he says, hooking his foot around the leg of my

chair and pulling me closer to the table. "She told me how good you are. Her eyebrows don't lie."

I watch him as I sip my drink and then decide that it's quite noisy in here. In order to have a decent conversation, I need to sit right next to him. That's the *only* reason I push myself up from my seat and move my chair right next to his. Luke smirks at me like he knows all of my tricks and then wraps a thick arm around my shoulders, playing with my earlobe as I nibble on my food.

The proximity to him—his size, his warmth, his scent—they're doing awful things to my insides. Internally, I'm clawing to be set free, to just let go, but I'm trapped inside this fucking cage of civility and principles I've meticulously built.

By the time we're done eating, I'm ravenous and chomping at the bit, nearly frothing at the mouth. My entire body aches for him and I feel crazed.

The moment we step into our hotel room, my leash snaps and I attack him. I don't even pretend to be composed. I just plaster myself to his chest, clutch onto his shoulders, and devour his strong neck with my lips and tongue. I'm weak, so fucking weak.

Desperate.

"Eager, huh?" Luke chuckles, and I clasp onto the collar of his shirt and walk him back toward the bed. "I'm not judging. I know the feeling. Was feelin' it all through dinner. What you gonna use on me tonight?"

I can't even think. I just want to feel. "You'll see."

Having Luke in my control—a strong, larger than life man submitting and bending to my will—I've never felt more powerful and masculine than I do at this moment. He could so easily turn the tables on me, but he doesn't. He lets me do what I want. And, fuck, *I want everything.*

The back of his knees hit the mattress, and he sinks down onto it. I press my fingertips into his chest, and he falls onto his back.

"Oh, I'm going to enjoy this," I mutter and then work his jeans open.

He lifts his hips as I slide his pants down his long legs, and then I tug off his boxers, tossing them on the floor.

"Take your shirt off," I tell him, and he leans up, the muscles in his abdomen flexing as he rips the T-shirt over his head and then he's blessedly naked. I run my fingers across his inner thigh, hearing his breath stutter as I do so.

"You gonna take off all those fancy clothes for me, Eli?" he asks. I pop the top button of my shirt through the hole, watching in awe as Luke's chest rises and falls frantically as I slowly work each button open. He's getting off on this, watching me strip for him. So, I do it slower, torturing him the same way he's tortured me.

All. Fucking. Day.

When my shirt is finally gaping open, I let it slide from my shoulders, and Luke leans up on his elbows to get a better view.

"Pants," he grunts, and I tilt my head.

"You'd like that, wouldn't you?"

"Hell yeah. Come on. You've seen all of me. I want to see all of you."

I unbuckle my belt and pull it slowly through the hoops, the leather whispering through the fabric. And the entire time, I'm warring with myself. I'm not sure I should bare myself like this to him. The vulnerability makes my stomach clench.

I already feel so out of control with him, I'm not sure I can take any more.

"No. Not tonight. On your hands and knees."

Disappointment falls over his face.

"Serious?"

"Now, Luke."

He reaches his hand out toward me and I take a step back. He eyes me for a moment and huffs but then complies and turns over on the bed. A small part of me, for just a moment, wonders if I've made a mistake. But then the larger, more logical part of me overrides it. I barely know this man. I'm confident in who I am, but knowing yourself and opening yourself up to others are two very different things. I can't deny the small, hidden part of me that worries if Luke will turn out like Andrew. I'm not ready for that soul-crushing disappointment.

This is me protecting myself. I don't owe Luke anything.

"I'll like whatever I see, Eli," he says, as if reading my mind. His head is turned toward me, resting on his folded arms.

"That's not the issue, Luke."

"Then what is it?"

I pause, wondering if I should lie, and then decide against it. "This has nothing to do with my body, not really. It's the emotions that come along with it. There's an intimacy in baring myself fully to someone...and I'm not sure I'm ready."

Luke wets his lips and meets my gaze. "I'd never hurt you."

I swallow and tear my gaze away from his, and eye his tight, round ass raised in the air. "I know."

I grab onto my kit and roll it out in front of him, hoping to distract him from this conversation. It seems to work because his cheeks redden as he eyes the toys in front of him.

"What are you gonna use this time?"

"My strap on," I say and pull it out. "Think you can take it?"

Luke presses his cheek to the mattress, his pupils dilating as he eyes the pink flesh-colored dildo in my hand.

"Hell yeah. My ass was made for you."

A smile pulls my lips up, and I reach out and stroke a lock of hair from his face.

"Good boy."

He flushes crimson and I slide my thumb across his lips.

"Stay," I add and then move into the bathroom.

I tug on my boxer harness, pulling the shaft through the opening at the front, and place the bullet vibrator in the small pocket below it, against my dick. I glance down at myself and wonder what Luke will think when he sees this.

Will he like it?

I feel equal parts nervous and excited as I walk from the bathroom, and his gaze lands heavy on me.

"Oh shit," he mutters from the bed, his eyes sweeping over my body and landing on my cock. "So hot. You're so fucking sexy."

A flush spreads over my skin as I move in behind him.

"So are you," I reply as I spread his ass cheeks. My finger brushes against his hole, and he gasps.

"More," he demands, and I chuckle.

"You'll get more when I say you can," I reply, reaching over and grabbing onto the lube. I dribble some on my fingers, rimming his hole with them.

Luke grunts a little and then moans when my finger breaches him. His fists clench the sheets as I work my finger inside of him.

Fuck. Me. This sight right in front of me is everything.

I'm not going to last. I'm already halfway there and I haven't even switched on my vibrator yet.

"Come on, Eli. Give me more," he mutters as I slide two fingers in and out of him, stretching him open for me. "Give it all to me."

I hum under my breath and then add a third finger, and his breath comes out as a wheeze. "Oh shit."

"You wanted more," I say darkly as I add a fourth. He's arching back into me now, fucking my fingers because he wants this as much as I do.

Oh, he's so ready for me to fuck him.

I remove my fingers and lube up my cock, switching my vibrator on to the lowest setting, otherwise this will be over way too fast. I place myself right at the entrance of his hole.

Luke looks at me over his shoulder, and I almost come just from the vision of him—his panting lips, his reddened cheeks, his tousled hair. He looks disheveled and fucked already, and I haven't even done anything yet.

"You ready?" I ask, my voice hoarse, and my fingers digging into his muscular hips.

"Hell yeah."

I shift my hips forward, and our eyes stay connected as I slide inside him.

And god, the power I feel coursing through me, the way he takes me so good without any complaint. This is almost better than an orgasm.

"Fuck," he mutters and drops his forehead onto the sheets when I'm fully seated inside of him.

I slide my hips back, exiting him entirely, and then push my way back inside. It's slow, torturous, and meant to drive him crazy, but it's doing things to me too. I feel flushed and eager, wild and insatiable, as my heart pounds in my chest.

I have never felt this good during sex. Never.

Luke grunts as he pushes back against me.

"Harder," he says, and I tighten my hold on his hips as I pull out and ram into him, the muscled flesh of our thighs slapping together.

His whole body shifts up the mattress, and he moans as I fuck my way in and out of him.

His skin shines with sweat and exertion as his right hand feverishly jerks his cock in time with my thrusts. I lean over him so my hands and chest can feel his body thrum and tremble as I hit his prostate each time.

"Oh fuck," he growls, and I move faster in and out of him. "Tell me I can come, Eli. Tell me. I need it."

Well, look at him, asking for permission.

I wrench his hand away from his cock and replace it with my own lubed hand, stroking his thick cock as my hips arch into him. And god, I'm close, so fucking close. I need to come with him.

My thoughts are incoherent and jumbled as I feel myself nearing the brink.

"Luke. Come," I breathe.

And my words send him over the edge. The sound of his moans, the shudder of his body, and the wetness of his release covering my hand have me following moments later. I groan as my orgasm completely overtakes me.

When it's over and the intense spasms finally stop, my sweaty face presses against his broad back as his torso moves up and down in exaggerated breaths.

"Goddammit, Eli," he mumbles, his eyes closing. "Just when I think it can't be any better...."

A smile tilts my lips up, and I squeeze my arms around him just a little tighter.

"You were so good," I say, and he huffs a laugh.

"Told you my ass was made for you."

"It was, Luke. It's mine now."

———

I wake up pressed against Luke, his arms and legs wrapped around me like an octopus. Visions from last night flow fluidly through my mind as I blink my eyes open.

The way Luke stared wide-eyed and appreciatively at me as I walked from the bathroom, my strap-on cock protruding from groin.

How he panted as I slid my cock into his ass.

The feeling of him trembling beneath me as I rammed into him over and over, his fingers clutching the sheets as my hips slapped against his.

How he moaned my name as he released all over the sheets.

How he tucked me into his chest after I'd pulled out of him and cleaned up, pressing a kiss to my head and then falling fast asleep.

I'd laid there for hours analyzing this entire thing and came to one conclusion.

I like-*like* Luke van Beek.

This is very, very concerning.

An alarm goes off in the dark, and Luke reaches for it with a grumble, shutting it off and then burrowing his face into my neck.

The way his lips skim my skin makes me wriggle.

"Ticklish?" he asks, and I sigh.

"Yes. Just a little."

"Mm, love that."

He brushes his lips across my neck again, and chuckles darkly when I squirm against him.

"We better get going. I have a reservation for us to hike the incline in forty-five minutes, and we need to make sure we arrive back in time for your first session. Don't want you to be late again."

I sigh heavily. "I would rather not go. It sounds like torture. Stairs are not my friend. I prefer elevators."

"Come on, Eli. I've seen you. You're in shape. You'll be fine. Plus, it's on my bucket list and I wanna do it with you."

I preen a little at the fact he wants to experience new things with me. I reach back and thread my fingers through his hair and tug lightly.

"Fine."

He stretches, and then rolls off the bed, standing with a jump. He pops his neck and then bends over to grab onto a shirt and some athletic shorts.

"Aren't you sore?"

"A bit. Guess we'll see how I do walking up all those stairs after taking that monster up my virgin ass."

I huff a small laugh, "Oh Luke, you haven't seen anything yet." He stumbles a little and I smirk, "Do we really have to do this? Are you sure you wouldn't rather spend the morning in bed with me?"

"I see what you're trying to do, being all seductive and shit. But yeah, Eli. We gotta do this and we're going to have a great time. We've got this."

———

He lied. We don't, in fact, got this.

Why did I let him talk me into this? Oh god, who was the sadistic bastard that made this damn thing? I'd researched it as Luke drove us to our destination and balked slightly. When Luke had told me about it earlier, I'd been half listening. Now, I'm regretting my life choices. This incline has 2,744 stairs, gaining two thousand feet of elevation in less than a mile. I am fairly fit, I run and swim regularly, but this shit is on a whole other level.

My thighs burn, and the elevation as we ascend is killer. Why aren't my lungs working properly?

I glance behind me and grow suddenly dizzy. Oh fuck, that's steep. I can't see the bottom of the stairs behind me, and when I turn my gaze forward, I still can't even see the top. I turn my eyes toward Luke, who is lounging on one of the railway ties used for steps, taking a picture of himself near the step marker nailed into the wood.

"Almost there, Eli," he says with a smile, his eyes meeting mine.

I arch an eyebrow at him and swipe at my forehead.

I thought I was in good shape, but I need to up my game because Luke is making this entire thing look much too easy. He could have finished already, but he has been waiting for me every twenty steps or so. He never makes me feel like shit about how slow I'm moving though. No, he just waits patiently a few steps ahead of me, snapping pictures of himself, me, or the view.

I want to respond to his positive, encouraging words, but I can't speak. I can't breathe. I now know what Sisyphus felt like. Zeus was a vindictive asshole.

"No need to chat," Luke says and then takes a sip of water. "I get it."

"You don't need to wait for me," I say, just to prove him

wrong. I can speak, thank you very much. I just need to make sure all the words are exhaled on a single breath.

"Nah, Doc," he says as I come to a stop near him. "I want to finish this with you."

He hands me some water, and I glug it down sloppily. Some even dribbles onto my neck and down my shirt. But who cares? I'm surviving at this point. I swipe the back of my hand across my mouth.

"Ready?" Luke asks after a moment of silence.

"Yes."

Then we're moving up once again. The air is thinner up here, and patches of snow line the ground. I shiver slightly, wondering if I should have brought a sweater. Luke's not wearing one, just a long sleeve shirt and shorts which show off his ass, and every once in a while, I get a small peek at his tattoo. It almost makes this agony worth it.

After a few more minutes, I pause, inhale deeply, and then on an exhale, I say, "Tell me more about your family. Distract me from his hell."

Luke eyes me and puts his hands on his narrow hips.

"You wanna know me, Eli?"

I wave my hand in front of my face because I will not be using words to communicate. Gestures will have to do.

Luke chuckles and then says, "Uh, well, I have three brothers...well, two actual brothers and a cousin who is basically like my brother. We grew up together. Anyways, Liam is the oldest and is married to Anne. Sem, the one you met, is younger than me by a year and is married to Magnus, and Caleb, my cousin, is engaged to Whit."

Hm, so plenty of gay or bi people in that family, it seems. I wonder how they feel about trans men?

I squash that thought immediately. There is no need to

wonder because I am not getting romantically involved with this man. That is not happening.

I clear my throat and wheeze. "And your parents?"

"Yeah, they're still around. Live up in the high desert. Been married for thirty-six years this June."

I wet my mouth and then nod. I wave to the stairs in front of us, signaling that I'm ready to keep going.

Luke walks by my side and says, "You should come meet them sometime. They'd love you."

I eye him and shrug. I'm getting rather good at this. Who needs words when you can just flap your hands and wiggle your fingers?

"Yeah, that shrug isn't working for me. I'd rather it be a nod, Eli."

I pause again and then nod. Obviously, I'm having some kind of seizure and need to be checked out immediately. What is wrong with me?

I like him.

That's what's wrong.

I am doing things because I want to make him happy.

The last time I did that, my heart got wrenched from my chest and squished like a bug.

Luke doesn't know the torment I'm in because he just smiles widely and clutches the back of my sweaty neck, squeezing it lightly. Just that one slight touch propels me forward. I tell myself that it's because I want to get this over with, but really, I think it's because I want him to be proud of me.

Oh hell.

I trudge forward, finding some inner strength, and when we finally make it to the last twenty steps, I pause and inhale deeply. I don't know if my legs will carry me up to the top. I'm doomed to stay here for eternity. A helicopter will need to come to deliver me back to the hotel.

"You got this, Doc," Luke says softly, reaching a hand toward me.

I stare at it, telling myself not to do it, but, of course, my mind doesn't listen to reason. I just link my fucking fingers through his and light up inside when he squeezes them gently.

He pulls out his phone and holds it out in front of us. "Gonna document this momentous occasion."

I roll my eyes as he hits the record button but we manage to take the last twenty steps together.

"Look at us," Luke says to the camera, pulling my hand up to his lips and kissing it lightly. "We made it...smile, Eli."

I glance over, grimacing, and Luke chuckles as we crest the top. I wobble over to a bench and sink down with an audible plop.

Luke follows me and sits down next to me, our thighs brushing.

"Hell," I manage to breathe, and Luke chuckles, reaching into his bag and pulling out a beer. He pops the top, takes a long swig, and then hands it to me.

"Gotta have a celebratory drink, yeah? Packed it just for this occasion."

I eye it and then think, what the hell, but don't say it because I'm still catching my breath and cannot speak.

I take a small sip. Bitterness floods my tongue and I grimace.

"Good, huh?"

"Yeah," I wheeze, and then we sit silently for a few minutes, as I watch as other people ascend the last steps. I gape as a few actually turn around and run right back down. That cannot be safe. They're going to break their knees.

"Crazy, huh?" Luke says, leaning into me slightly.

"Yes, the more I learn about humanity, the less I understand."

Luke chuckles and fiddles with his phone. I eye it and say, "Please send me that video. The one you took of us taking the last steps together."

He swipes at his screen. "Done. Now tell me the truth, Eli. You gonna watch that video when you're all alone?"

I hand him his beer. "Never."

Luke smiles at me because he knows me too well, and then he glugs his beer down before placing the empty container back in his backpack.

"Alright, Eli, we got an hour to make it to the bottom," he says, looking at his phone, and a miserable groan escapes my mouth.

"Come on, Doc," he says, standing and stretching his legs and back. "We don't want you to be late. And we can cut our time in half if we run down the trail."

I close my eyes and breathe deeply.

I can do this.

I think.

———

I limp into the conference with a minute to spare and sit in the back. I have a feeling that tomorrow Luke is going to need to carry me around wherever we go. That burn in my legs will only compound until I can barely walk. I will be hobbling around like I'm a hundred years old in a few short hours.

But, even so, I feel the smallest kernel of pride erupting inside of me.

I did it. *I did it.*

Luke had looked at me with something I couldn't decipher as we climbed into the rental car and made our way toward the hotel. Maybe he was proud of me too, and that did something terrible to my heart.

As we drove through the small downtown on our way back to the hotel, Luke pulled the car over and placed it in park.

"Give me five minutes," he'd said and then jogged across the street, returning five minutes later with a green T-shirt that read *I Climbed the Manitou Incline.*

I'd taken it reluctantly, pretending like my heart didn't warm at his thoughtfulness. Nope, this heart is an iceberg, I'd reminded myself.

But hell, Luke is my climate change and my polar ice caps are melting. This can't be good.

"You'll wear it, yeah?" he asked me with raised eyebrows, and I'd hummed a noncommittal answer.

Because I have a secret.

I'll wear it when no one is around, stare at it, pet it, and remember every fucking thing about today. But I can't let my sisters see me in it, or else they'll know how far I've fallen.

The truth is, my fingers that have been grasping onto my bitterness are letting go one by one. Pretty soon, it's going to be a free fall.

My phone vibrates against my thigh as the speaker for this session drones on and on. I pull it out, seeing a picture of Luke wearing the exact shirt he'd bought this morning. His muscles fill it out deliciously, and I envision myself pushing that fabric up his broad chest and biting down on his pec.

Ridiculous. Utterly ridiculous.

Keep it together, Elliot.

I bite the inside of my cheek to keep myself from smiling.

I glance up and see Andrew watching me from the other side of the room. My eyes roll up to the ceiling, and I ignore him, choosing to focus on Luke instead.

Luke: You ready for tonight?

My mind is blank. I can't remember for the life of me what is happening tonight. There is no room in my head for anything other than him.

Quickly, I pull up the itinerary and see we are doing some kind of lantern tour in a cave.

What the hell am I doing?

I don't go on cave tours.

I don't tourist.

I don't people.

And yet here I am, my fingers typing before my brain can fully process what I'm doing.

Me: Yes.
Luke: I know you're super excited. I can hear it in that three-letter word. Anything you want to do before we go? We have an hour.

I drum my fingers on my thigh and focus on the speaker for a moment before typing out very detailed instructions. Oh yes. There is so much I can do in an hour.

Let's see how good he can be.

CHAPTER EIGHT

LUKE

He's late, and I'm getting restless. I glance at the clock blinking at me from the small table and blow out a breath.

I'm contemplating pulling myself up off the floor where his text messages demanded I be, when I hear the lock click, and Elliot strides in. He looks like a wet dream in his classy, professional clothes, all formal and authoritative. His glasses just add another level of appeal.

He glances at me and wets his bottom lip. Immediately my dick perks up.

Asshole.

Looking so smug.

And hot.

"You're late," I grumble, and my dick twitches in his general direction. It knows what's up. It's ready. It can't help but remember last night when he pounded into me.

Oh fuck, that was the hottest sex I've ever had. When my cousin had told me receiving anal was the way to go, I'd scoffed.

I'm not scoffing anymore.

I'm fucking hooked.

The door shuts behind him, and Elliot turns to face me. "I was held up with some colleagues."

His low voice does things to my libido. I like the sound of it too much. I shift on the dildo I'd stuck to the ground earlier and bite back a low groan. Fuck it's big, and I'm still sore from last night.

But I wasn't going to say no. I'm so into this it's insane.

Elliot runs a hand across his lightly stubbled jaw. "I see you did as I asked."

I snort. "You knew I would."

Doesn't he know already? I'm a total sucker for this guy. I'll do anything he wants.

"I'm pleased, but before we...continue, I need to shower," Elliot says, and I grumble my frustration.

"I've been kneeling with this dick up my ass for twenty minutes, Eli. I'm dying here."

I bounce on the dildo once, twice, three fucking times, and Elliot makes his way over to me.

"No more. Not until I'm done."

I sigh and sink all the way back until I'm fully impaled on it. "You're killin' me, man."

He reaches out and caresses my cheek. "Oh, but Luke, you're such a good boy. You look so sexy like this. I know you can keep it up," he says seductively.

Fuck. I can't *not* obey after he says shit like that. Seems not only do I like being told what to do but I love the praise too.

Elliot sees it, because his lips twitch as he turns and disappears into the bathroom, leaving me horny and alone.

I watch the clock. One minute. Two. I stroke my cock. He never said I couldn't pet my pathetic dick, and really, it's self-preservation. I've been sitting on this dildo for far too long, and I'm ready to go.

Who knew I'd be such a slut for it?

Fuck, I'm going to come if I keep this up. I have no stamina with this guy. I just think of him, and I almost come. I grip the base of my cock and sigh.

Asshole, making me wait.

Ten minutes later, Elliot comes out of the bathroom, a towel wrapped around his waist. Steam follows his lithe figure, and I can smell him.

Fresh. Hot. Sex. I can't help but watch him, all of that lean, slick muscle moving toward me. My fist tightens around my cock as he strides past me and lowers himself onto the couch just opposite me.

"Took your time," I grumble, and the corner of Elliot's mouth turns up as he spreads his legs slightly. But I can't see a damn thing.

Asshole, always tryin' to hide from me.

"Take it off. The towel. Off," I bite out and grip onto my thigh so tightly it hurts. I want to go to him, rip that offensive piece of shit from around his waist and straddle him. I want to press my face into his neck and grind against him. But I won't.

I can be civilized.

He thinks I can't, but I can.

This, right here, is me behaving like a fucking angel.

Elliot cocks his head, his eyes meeting mine, and then he

slowly drags that towel up his thighs. *Inch by inch* until I'm nearly wheezing in anticipation.

But that asshole stops right before I can *see* anything, and I snap my mouth closed and groan.

"Come on, Doc! What the hell!"

He smirks again and then opens that wry mouth of his. "Fuck yourself," he tells me.

I shake my head and squeeze the base of my dick to keep myself from coming. "Nah, Eli. Not until I see you."

I don't want to push, but I do anyway. He wants to show me. I know he does. I can tell. I can so fucking *tell*.

He bites his bottom lip as if in deep thought and then stands up and moves over to stand just in front of where I'm kneeling on the ground.

He's so close that I'm helpless to do anything but lean forward and press my face against his warm stomach. He smells so fresh, like soap and a rich, heady scent that is entirely his. It makes my mouth water.

Elliot's fingers curl into my scalp, tugging on the strands roughly as I run my hands up his thighs and grasp onto his bare ass—that firm ass that I haven't even seen yet but have imagined far too many times.

He arches into me as I lick my way across his stomach, biting, nibbling, my hands kneading his cheeks.

"Come on, Eli. Please," I whisper, my words whispering across his abdomen.

My eyes slide up his naked chest until I meet his dark gaze.

He swallows, his throat working as he nibbles on his bottom lip. He looks unsure, like he's debating, but there is no need. He has to see that I'm so into this.

And then he nods.

He *fucking nods*, and before he can change his mind, I'm ripping that towel from his hips and watching it fall to his feet.

I groan at the sight before me.

Muscular thighs, neatly trimmed pubic hair, and there it is. It's probably about two inches long, and fuck, if I haven't researched this to death but it's better than I imagined. I'm so gone for it.

"Oh goddamn, Eli, your dick is so hot. Can I suck it?" I say licking my lips, and then I can't even wait for a response. I shove my face right into his pelvis and clutch him to me.

"Luke," Elliot whimpers and jolts as I wrap my lips around him. Sliding my tongue over him gently, he gasps. That sound sends shockwaves through me, igniting something deep inside of me, and I reach down to pump my own dick. It's straining, leaking, and eager to come.

And fuck, I'm still on this dildo. It's shoved so far up my ass I can taste it. I want to move, but Elliot is more important. I want him to come first. I want to see him fall apart. I need to *hear* it.

I move my lips and tongue, thanking the gods for porn because I watched so much of it preparing for this. I read all the forums, and it's paying off because Elliot is moaning, his fingers pulling my hair so tightly it hurts.

"So good," he gasps, his mouth open and cheeks flushed red, and just the sight of it nearly sends me over the edge.

I do a swirl with my tongue and his eyes roll back into his head.

But I want him to look at me.

Look at me.

Me.

Only me.

Suddenly, his eyes snap open and our eyes meet. Something I can't decipher moves through those dark depths as his mouth opens in a silent moan. I slide my lips over him once more and he cries out, his entire body trembling and twitching, and then he slumps against me, his hands on my shoulders, his chest heaving

He inhales deeply as I lick and kiss my way over his thighs.

"That was...there are no words," he says softly.

I press my nose into his skin and hold him against me.

"I'm a fucking pro."

He huffs a small laugh and then pulls away, his hands shaking slightly as he strokes my cheek tenderly.

"You did so good, Luke."

My name on his lips makes my heart pound harder, and then I nearly lose my ability to breathe when he drops to his hands and knees and wraps his mouth around my cock.

————

"You didn't say this was a haunted cave," Elliot grumbles, and I grasp onto his free hand and pull him toward our tour group. Lanterns are the only thing lighting the space, which gives it an eerie feeling. Shadows bounce across the walls, and our voices echo in the cold, windy chambers.

"I didn't know it was, but fuck, it's creepy, right? All those miners who died digging this out. A few ghosts gotta be down here, yeah?"

Elliot stands a little closer to me, and I swallow my laugh.

"Why did you think the lantern tour was a good idea?"

"Dunno. Looked like a good time. You need good times in your life, Doc," I reply, and he glances around warily.

"Luke, have you noticed our guide? I think she's high on

something. If we get lost, she won't know her way out," Elliot whispers into my ear. He's almost on top of me. Seems Elliot is a bit of a scaredy-cat. Don't worry, boo. I've gotchu. I protect what's mine.

"Why do you think that?" I ask, pulling him into me.

"Just listen to her."

I turn my face toward the guide and listen intently, a smile forming on my face as she speaks.

"Yeah, I see what you mean. I'll ask her if she can hook us up after. She probably has the good stuff. Probably grows it herself in her closet."

Elliot scowls at me. "Absolutely not."

I lean over and press a kiss to his temple. He leans into it a fraction, but I still notice.

"You ever do drugs, Eli?"

"Never. And by that look on your face, you have done copious amounts."

"Not copious, but I've tried them all. Never got hooked, though. Just wasn't for me."

I am hooked on Elliot, though. Especially that mouth of his. The way he speaks to me, the filthy things he says, the way he sucks me down his throat—yeah, I have a lot of favorites when it comes to this guy, but his mouth takes the cake.

We move through more of the caverns, Elliot right by my side, my arm wrapped around him. I can't stop touching him. I want to touch him all the time.

"How are your legs?" I ask, and he glances up at me, then he looks around warily as the guide speaks in the distance.

"Fine."

I lean down and whisper in his ear, "Gonna let me massage them again later?"

"If you insist," he replies.

"Oh, I so fucking do."

Maybe he'll even let me suck his dick again.

"Watch your head, dudes," the guide says, drawing out the last word as she ducks and squeezes between two rocks. People follow her one by one, and Elliot and I wait our turn, too consumed with touching each other to rush our way through this. Nah, I like just standing here, feeling him against me.

A mom and her son walk in front of us and move through the narrow passageway, but a sudden, loud *crack* and grunt makes me look up.

The teen boy is clutching his head, wobbling slightly on his feet.

"Shit," I mutter as he teeters backward. He pulls his hand away, and I see his palm is covered in blood.

The mom is on him, her hands on his shoulders, her eyes frightened, but she doesn't need to be. Because without even thinking, Elliot hands me his lantern and strides forward, his voice clipped and loud.

"Tell that tour guide to put down the 'shrooms and get back here. We need a first aid kit and I need more light over here."

My dick twitches in my pants at his tone of voice. Apparently, I also like it when he bosses other people around.

I glance down at my dick and sigh. Should have canceled the cave tour and let him tunnel inside of me instead. A very deep excavation would be nice right about now.

Elliot moves his gaze toward me, clueless about where my mind's gone.

"Luke, help me get this boy seated."

"You got it, Doc," I say and then practically carry the

shocked teen to an outcropping of rocks. He sits down and sags against the wall as Elliot kneels down in front of him.

"What's your name?"

"David."

"David. I'm Elliot. I'm a doctor. You're fine. You'll be fine. Head wounds always bleed a lot. It's nothing more than a cut."

David nods as the tour guide comes rushing toward us, a pack clutched in her hands.

She skids to a stop when she sees us, her eyes wide.

"Whoooooaaaah," she draws out. She glances at the blood and sways on her feet a little. "Gnarly. Yeah, you know, I can't do this. I don't like blood." She breathes deeply through her nose. "Yeah, might pass out."

She goes a little pale, and Elliot rolls his eyes.

"What an absolute shock," he says dryly as he turns his gaze away from her. "Luke, please ensure that woman doesn't pass out on the floor. I don't want to deal with a panicky, hallucinating person while in a haunted cave. We don't want to disturb the ghosts."

I snort a laugh and move toward the guide, who is fanning her ashen face. I help her sit on the ground, and she puts her head between her knees and inhales deeply.

Meanwhile, Elliot is bandaging David up. He's so efficient and clear-headed that he's done in a matter of minutes. Then, I'm helping David stand, and he and his mother are being led away by another guide.

"You were awesome," the guide says, swiping at her sweaty head. "Cool beans that we had a doctor up in this house. You saved the day, man."

Elliot arches an eyebrow at her, and she shudders a little.

"Perhaps lay off the cannabis before you come to work," he snaps, and the guide jumps slightly.

I laugh and pull him back into my side. "Keep it together, Eli," I say softly. "We don't want her leaving us stranded in here."

Then to the guide, I say, "Go on. Let's get this tour over with."

I lean down and whisper in his ear. "You were good with that kid. Even made him laugh once."

"Yes, well, I worked in the ER for a few years. I can deal with high-pressure situations. This, I'm telling you, was not high pressure. He had a cut. It's nothing compared to a gunshot wound or a tree branch through a torso."

My eyes widen at that, and I stop walking.

"For real."

"Yes, unfortunately."

"Still, Eli, it was impressive. Got me all fucking hot for you, Doc."

Elliot's eyes fly to my crotch, and he quickly looks away.

"Yes, well, I'm not getting you off in here. There are too many people. You'll have to wait until we get back to our room."

I press a small kiss on his head, and we continue the tour. I'm barely listening to what is being said though, I'm too focused on Elliot walking beside me. He's all stoic and calm, like he didn't just save the fucking day.

I adjust my pants as I force my gaze away from him.

"Why didn't you stay working in the ER if you're so good at it?"

"It didn't suit me. If you haven't noticed, I'm a stress case. You should have seen me while I was working that job. I realized two years into it that I needed to take better care of myself. It's why I went into general practice."

"And how do you like it? Your practice?"

"It's fine. Stable. It was an established practice before I came along. All I did was buy the previous doctor out." He looks up at me. "My sisters loaned me the money. I owe them thousands."

"They did it because they love you."

"Of course. And I love them," he says quickly. "It was a way to help me, but really, it was a bigger fuck you to my parents."

"You gonna tell me why?"

Elliot rolls his lips between his teeth and then sighs.

"Well, you know some of what happened because my sisters can't help but blab. But my parents disowned me when I came out. They told me to hide who I was, or leave. I chose to be who I am. So, when I turned eighteen and started testosterone therapy, I left and never looked back. My sisters followed me. My parents had four children one day, and now they have none."

Goddamn. He's so brave.

"And you haven't seen your parents since?" I ask.

"No, and I don't care to. Not if they can't accept me for who I am."

I pull him in a little closer. "Good. Fuckers can stay away."

He looks up at me, and our eyes meet. "I do feel bad sometimes."

"Why?"

"Because they aren't bad people, they're just ignorant and set in their ways, and now they're all alone. And my sisters don't have parents. Because of me."

I grasp onto his chin and force him to look at me. "They

all made their own choices, Eli. You're not responsible for the choices other people make."

He blinks, wetting his lips. "Right. You're right."

My eyes flick to his lips, and I almost lean down and press my mouth to his, but I don't because Eli takes a step back, and my hand falls to my side.

"We should catch up," he says, and I nod.

Yeah, okay, Eli. I can read you. I'll just try again later. I can play this game all fucking day long.

When we finish the tour, I meander around the small gift shop because I want some souvenirs, and that's when I see Elliot holding up a shirt. He glances at it, presses it to his chest, but when he catches me looking at him, he quickly shoves it back on the rack. His cheeks are red, and he won't meet my gaze. Fucker won't let himself have fun things.

Fine. He doesn't need to twist my arm.

I'll buy it for him.

I walk over to where he's inspecting a row of snow globes and grab the shirt he'd been eyeing off the hanger.

"What are you doing?" he huffs as I stroll over to the counter. He's on my heels, hissing, "I don't need that shirt, Luke. I won't wear it."

But those words go in one ear and out the other.

Blah, blah, blah.

"That will sit in my dresser and never come out," Elliot continues. "The moths will eat it before I put that damn thing on."

But I still hand the boy behind the counter my credit card and then stuff the shirt in my bag. He thinks I can't tell how much he wants it. Well, one day, I'll catch him with it on. He'll blush and stammer, and then I'll just bend right on over and let him fuck me. Because I am just that gone for this guy.

Maybe I'll peel that shirt off of him before he does, or maybe I'll let him wear it while he pounds into me. I could go either way.

And let me tell you a secret.

Later that night, when he thinks I'm not looking, he peers into that bag, reaches in, and pulls it out. He eyes it, his lips twitching, and my heart just outright stutters in my chest.

The next morning, Elliot sleeps through his alarm. It's funny, I didn't think someone like him was even capable of that. I'd assumed when I first met him that he'd always wake up before his alarm even had a chance to go off. But he's been snoozing right through it ever since I started sleeping over.

I'm getting a big head over it. I know he's sleeping better when I'm with him.

He's probably dreaming of me too.

I press soft kisses against his bare chest. He actually slept without a shirt. His *Sesame Street* pajamas haven't left the suitcase.

I convinced him to keep them there, using my tongue.

"Eli, gotta get up," I say softly, running my hands up his neck and into his hair. He presses against me and huffs contentedly.

"You're gonna be late, Doc," I say and move further on top of him. His hands slip down my bare back, and he ruts up against me.

Love how responsive he is when he's asleep. Whatever hinders him from opening up during the day isn't present now. He's cuddly and sweet and raw.

He'd probably even let me kiss him if I tried.

I want to try.

I move my lips up his neck, and he squirms. I hover over his face, my lips impossibly close to his, and then his eyes snap open.

"What are you doing?" he mumbles, and my mouth presses against his cheek.

"Gonna kiss you," I mutter.

His chest heaves underneath me, and his fingers dig into my back.

"Don't," he whispers, and I lean back slightly, our eyes connecting in the pale grey light of the early morning.

"Why not?" I ask.

"Because," he huffs.

"Because why?"

"Because I can't with you, Luke. I just can't."

He's stiff underneath me, no longer yielding, and I roll onto my back. Disappointment weighs heavy on my chest as I stare at the ceiling and try to forget I even tried. I know he hates being vulnerable, but haven't I already shown how much I want him? What more do I have to do to prove myself?

"I'm sorry," he says softly.

"Nah, don't worry, Doc. I get it."

He shuffles around next to me and then inhales, almost like he's going to say something, but then his mouth shuts. He does it again and then sighs heavily, rolling off the bed and moving into the bathroom.

Huh. Wonder what he was going to say.

Probably nothin' good. Better to just let it sit inside him for a while longer.

————

"You got back early," I tell Elliot as I lean against the wall. I'm still sweaty from the climb with Denise earlier and haven't showered yet. Probably all smudged with dirt too. I pull my shirt over my head and drop it to the ground, and Elliot's eyes slide across my skin.

"Thought you had a session right now," I add.

Elliot unbuttons his shirt slowly, and my heartbeat accelerates.

"It wasn't important."

My fingers pop open the button on my jeans, and Elliot's eyes follow the movement.

"Not important. Huh. Interesting," I say. "Because you were going on and on about the speaker presenting today."

"Turns out they were very boring. Not worth my time," Eli says, and I scoff and move toward him.

My hands reach out, and I cup the back of his head, pulling him into me. My eyes flick to his full rosy lips, but I don't lean down. I don't take what I want.

I learned my lesson. Denise and I had a long chat about it this morning. She could see the hurt on my face and knew something was wrong. I'd tried to blow it off, like it was no big deal, but she pried it out of me. Really, she bribed me with these little snack bars she makes. They're fucking delicious.

Truth is, I want his lips on mine. I want to be the exception to his no-kissing rule.

Yeah, and maybe I'm still a little hurt over it, even though I'm trying not to be. I keep telling myself it will be worth the wait, that when Elliot finally opens up to me, it will be fucking extraordinary .

"Admit it. You missed me."

"Never," he hisses.

"You wanted to come back to me. You couldn't even wait another hour, so you left early."

He shifts on his feet, his eyes not meeting mine.

"You are ridiculous." But his cheeks are flaming, and he's fidgeting nervously.

So, I put him out of his misery.

I cup his cheek, my thumb brushing against his lips. "Where do you want me?"

His eyes snap up to mine. "Bed. Ass up."

"Hm. You got it, Doc."

CHAPTER NINE

ELLIOT

I don't know what I'm doing, but somehow my hand slipped into Luke's, and it stuck there. It's been stranded there for at least an hour, and I think there's no point in rescuing it now. No need to bother with an SOS, either.

I'm living on this island now.

My ass stings," Luke says as we walk through the Garden of the Gods National Park. Red rocks jut up from the ground around us as we navigate a hiking trail. In the distance, I can make out snowcapped mountains.

It really is beautiful out here. I glance up, and my wandering eyes catch on Luke.

Yes, very, very beautiful.

"Perhaps if you talked back less, you'd incur less of a punishment," I reply, thinking of how I spanked that ass so good earlier. When we were done, the two of us panting from our release, he'd pulled me up from the bed and insisted we go on this hike. My legs still ache from the Incline, but he'd convinced me with those sexy eyes of his. I'm completely hypnotized.

"But that's no fun," Luke says and squeezes my hand. I agree. It's much more fun this way.

"Have you been enjoying your time here?" I ask, pulling the hood of my jacket over my head with my free hand. It's starting to snow lightly, and the sharp chill in the air makes me shiver.

"Yep. Love it out here. I'd move out here if I could."

My heart sinks at that comment. It's irrational and illogical, but I still *feel* it.

"Will you move?" I ask, trying to sound casual. What if he does? What if he leaves me?

"Nah, my family is out in Cali. Gonna stay there, near them. They're my home."

My panic subsides and I let out a shaky breath.

"Would you ever move?" he asks me.

"No. My sisters are nearby. I'll stay wherever they are."

He pulls me to his side as we walk. "Totally get it."

We move around a group of tourists trying and failing to take a group shot. Luke actually stops and offers to take their picture.

For the first time since beginning this hike, our hands begin to separate, and for some reason, my fingers just clench and hold onto him tighter.

Like I said, they're stuck.

Luke gently tries to tug his hand from mine, but my fingers won't budge.

"You gotta let go, Eli."

"I'm trying," I say, and he snorts a laugh.

I arch an eyebrow at him. "You shouldn't have offered to

take someone's picture. That's what they make selfie sticks for. This is a good lesson for them that next time they should be better prepared."

He brings our clasped hands up to his mouth and presses a kiss to my knuckles. "Nah, Eli. Gotta be friendly."

And then, one by one, he pries my fingers from his.

My hand flops to my side, depressed and lonely. So, I shove it into my pocket. No one needs to see how obviously pathetic it is.

Luke snaps the picture for the family, and then my hand, like a magnet, snaps right back into his. It's appalling.

I blush and fidget, but my hand wants what it wants. There's no controlling it.

Luke doesn't remark on it. He just pulls me down the trail.

"Denise and I climbed that rockface over there yesterday," he says, pointing to his right. I eye it and then purse my lips.

"She seems like a bad influence."

"Nah, she's just a nice lady who likes to make her own granola bars."

"That may be true, but I think she's unsavory."

Luke laughs. "What the fuck are you talking about, Eli? Denise is fun, and let me tell you, those granola bars are life. Just the right amount of crunchy and chewy with nuts and chocolate. I told her she should market them, but she just said, 'Fuck the man'. Dunno."

I sigh. "It's just that you only just met her. You don't know her."

"I know her just fine," Luke replies and then eyes me. "Why are you going on about this? You jealous, Eli?"

"Absolutely not. I don't get jealous."

I get jealous. I'm a big fat liar. It's not a feeling I usually experience, but for some reason, it seems omnipresent with

Luke. I was jealous of the flight attendant fluffing her hair in his general direction. I'm jealous of granola bar Denise, and I am even jealous of those towels Luke wears around his waist after he gets out of the shower.

I'm a lunatic.

"Nah, I think you're jealous of me hanging out with Denise, but you don't need to be. She's just someone I met while climbing, just a friend. You have to know that all I see is you."

I sniff and press myself a little further into him. Fine, so maybe that placates me a little. As long as I'm *all* he can see.

When we return to the hotel, Luke and I strip out of our winter jackets and face each other. Something electric snaps in the air between us, and I plaster myself to the wall and inch along it to stay away.

I will not stick myself to this man. I have some self-restraint left in me—just a sliver, but I cling to it.

"Got a surprise for you," Luke says as I grab a water bottle from the fridge and twist the cap off. I'm trying to distract my magnet hands. They need to do something else besides trying to attach themselves to him.

I'd like to maintain some sort of dignity, despite my body rebelling at every turn.

"Is this surprise on the itinerary?"

"Nah, Amanda said to leave it off."

Oh dear god, this cannot be good. This is going to be very, very bad. I can hear her cackling at home right now, knowing exactly how this "surprise" will go down.

I'm going to fire her when I get back. Kick her to the curb.

Oh, who am I kidding? That woman won't leave. I've fired her multiple times, and she just glowers at me. I'm stuck with her for all eternity. Even when I make it to hell, she'll be down there glaring at me.

I lean against the wall and fiddle with the plastic bottle some more. My traitorous body still wants to squish itself to Luke, who is pulling his shirt off and revealing his gorgeous chest. However, I remain at a respectable distance, hoping I'll be able to resist the pull.

"I'd like to know what this surprise is," I say, and Luke smiles at me, tossing his shirt onto the couch.

"Nah, then it won't be a surprise."

"I think this is a very, very bad idea, Luke. Especially if Amanda suggested it."

"She said you'd love it."

A knock on the door has both our heads swiveling to it.

"Do not answer that, Luke."

"You gonna punish me if I do?"

I scoff and set the water bottle down. "That can be arranged."

But the promise of a spanking is too intriguing for Luke to resist. Because he pulls the door open and two young men walk inside. Both are donned in white loungewear, and the shorter one eyes Luke's chest a bit too long.

No, you cannot have him.

He's mine. I found him first.

Luke points to the middle of the living room. "You can set up here."

They both smile at him, and my stomach clenches nervously because I have a feeling I know what this is.

"Care to tell me what this is now, Luke?" I hiss, and he pulls me into him. My hand immediately plasters itself onto his skin and strokes across his pectorals. The muscles flex under my touch, and I'm momentarily distracted from what is happening around me until Luke utters the following words.

"A couples tantric massage."

My entire body stiffens, and my fingers flex against his skin.

"Excuse me?"

"A massage."

"*No*. No, you said something else. What kind of massage is this, Luke?"

"Uh, tantric? Amanda said you'd like it."

I slam my eyes shut and sigh, "I'm going to kill her."

"Nah. Don't hurt her. This is gonna be fun. She said we'd love it."

I pull Luke into the bedroom as the two men set up their tables, and oh hell, are those candles they're lighting? Incense? Management is going to be called up from the smell. We're going to burn this place down. Literally.

When the bedroom door is shut, I turn to him and grasp his biceps. "This is a sensual massage, Luke."

He mulls that over for a minute and then shrugs. "Sensual sounds nice."

I rub my temples. "That's one word for it."

A knock on the bedroom door has me jumping slightly, and Luke pulls it open.

The smaller of the massage therapists leans in. He eyes Luke's chest again and then says, "You should both shower before we begin our body-to-body massage."

"Red flag," I say dryly, but Luke just grabs onto my hand and leads me into the bathroom. He twists the shower faucet on and then turns to face me.

"I am not going to do this," I mutter, but Luke is using his fingers to undress me, and I just stand there and stroke my hands along his arms, neck, and chest. His eyes meet mine when he reaches my pants, and I sigh.

"You're determined to make me enjoy this, aren't you?" I ask.

"It came highly recommended. Got five stars on Yelp."

I touch his cheek, and his fingers hook into the waistband of my pants. "Fine. I will try this. For you. But if I say stop...."

He nods. "We stop."

He tugs my pants down, and I step out of them. His face is right there, and he leans forward and nestles his nose right against me.

My fingers thread through his hair, and he kisses my hip softly.

Then he stands, and we step under the hot spray. And I am useless. I just stand there, my hands slipping and sliding over his skin while he washes me.

"Can't stop touching me, huh?" he asks smugly. "Don't think I haven't noticed."

"It's a problem," I mutter. "I *will* find a solution to it. There has to be a medicine or something. When I get home, I'll ask the pharmaceutical reps if they have any experimental drugs they're working on."

"I sure hope not," he replies. "I like you all clingy."

I scoff and try to pry my hands away, but they don't listen. They just brush across the planes of his back as I press into him. My head rests on his chest, and I can hear the erratic pounding of his heart right beneath my ear.

His cock is growing hard against me, and I turn my face and bite down on his collarbone.

"You do things to me, Doc," he mutters.

I look up and meet his stare. My eyes flick to his mouth, and he wets his lips.

I could kiss those lips, slide my tongue into his mouth. I have never been more tempted in my life.

But no, I have to resist. This is my last holdout. If I do this, it's game over. I'll end up giving him everything then and I'm so fucking afraid of where that will lead.

"We should get out," I say, not moving an inch. I just cling to him like a barnacle.

"We should."

We stand like that for several more minutes, me peeking up at his mouth, imagining what I could do to it as he runs those big hands across my back.

But finally, Luke presses a kiss to the top of my head and says, "We better go. The masseuses are waiting."

"Masseurs," I mumble.

"I don't know German, Eli."

I snort and press a kiss to the side of his cheek.

"It's French. A masseuse is a woman, masseur is a man. But you can just call them massagists to keep it neutral."

"Huh. Learn something new every day. Did they teach you that in medical school, Doc?"

"No, I actually learned that listening to true-crime podcasts. With my luck, these guys are here to rub us down and then murder us."

Luke smiles and reaches around me to turn the water off. "Well, let's not disappoint them then, shall we?"

I sigh, and then we're stepping out of the shower and pulling towels around our waists.

When we move back into the living space, the lights are off entirely, candles casting an orange glow across the walls. Incense wafts around the space, and it's almost overwhelming. In the middle of the room, two tables are set up next to each other, and the massagists are standing on either side, watching us approach.

"Welcome," they say in unison.

"Well, that is entirely creepy," I mutter, and Luke chuckles next to me.

"Lie down on the tables, face down, shoulders touching. We will begin with your back and then move to the front," the taller one says.

I eye Luke and then my massagist. "I'll keep my towel on."

Luke glances down and then nods. "Yeah, me too."

"It's better if you are completely nude," the ogling massagist says, and I narrow my eyes at him.

"He'll keep it on," I snap. Because Luke is mine.

Mine.

No one is going to touch him without my permission.

We slide onto the tables and lie down on our stomachs, our shoulders touching, our faces just inches apart. We're so close I can see that the pupils in Luke's hazel eyes are blown out.

"This is kinda hot," he mutters as he shifts a little closer to me.

"That's the point," I reply, and he wets his mouth, and my eyes track that tongue of his.

This is becoming some kind of obsession, as is everything with Luke.

"Alright, breathe in...and now out," one says, and we do as we're told. A second later, hands are on us, and they begin kneading our sore muscles.

Luke groans deeply, his eyes fluttering, and the sounds he's making are obscene, making me hot and flushed. It reminds me of when we fuck.

Our eyes lock, and we just stare into each other's depths as hands move down our backs.

"I think this was a mistake," Luke whispers, and I snort.

"I told you, but you didn't listen."

"They're touching my ass," he mutters, glances back, and huffs. "They're not going to touch my asshole, are they? Like do a prostate massage?"

"They better not," I grumble but can't help the amused chuckle that slips from my mouth at the mortification slipping across his face.

He jumps slightly, and I chuckle.

"You laughing at me?" he asks with a smile, and I clamp my mouth shut. "You are. You're laughing. Your eyes are twinkling."

"Yes, well, you got yourself into this," I reply and then snap loudly, "Do not touch me there! Privates are to remain private."

The massagist removes his hands from my ass cheeks and moves to the back of my thighs. Good. The only person who gets to touch me there is Luke. I'm very particular about that.

They work down our legs, and I have to admit, they're doing a fantastic job. But when they tell us to turn over, Luke's eyes widen.

"I don't think I should," he whispers. "I have the biggest boner right now from just looking at you."

I snort. "This is a tantric massage. That's the whole point."

"You mean this is going to end with a happy ending?"

"I don't think so, but with the way your guy was eyeing you, I wouldn't put it past him."

Luke lowers his eyebrows. "I dunno if I like this, Eli. Don't want anyone touching my dick but you."

Welp, that's enough for me. I lean up on my elbows, glance behind me, and firmly say, "We're done here."

The two massagists look confused, and one even looks disappointed. He probably wanted to jack Luke off. I don't blame him. He probably developed magnet hands, as well, and doesn't want to tear his palms away from Luke's skin.

"We were hired for ninety minutes," one of them says. "Are you sure?"

I slip off the table and grab my credit card. "Of course. I'll still pay and tip well if you leave the oil."

They look at each other and then begin packing up. Luke moves to sit on a chair, his thighs spread out before him, a tiny towel covering his crotch. I catch myself eyeing him as the candles are blown out, leaving us cloaked in the moonlight.

When they're finally gone, I move toward Luke and pull that towel away from his groin, exposing him.

"Better," I say. "Much, much better." And I run a finger across his thick length.

"Eli," he huffs, his cock straining towards me.

"Get on the bed. Face up. You wanted a tantric massage, I'm going to give you one."

———

He's moaning, sweat dripping down his temple as I continue to stroke him. The oil is almost gone. I've used so much, bringing him close to orgasm repeatedly only to bring him back down again. He's writhing on the sheets, fisting them as he arches his hips up into my hand.

"This is supposed to be relaxing," he grunts as I slide a slick finger into his hole. I crook it, and he gasps.

"I'm relaxed," I say. "I could go for much, much longer." That's a lie, though. I'm burning up from the inside out. Pretty soon, I'll be consumed. I want to sit on him and let him slide that big wet dick right into my front hole.

But I won't. I can't.

But why I shouldn't becomes more and more unclear the longer I'm with him. God, I want him more than I've ever wanted another person and yet I can't bring myself to straddle him and take what I want.

Fear. It's there, lingering constantly. I can't seem to let it go.

I find his prostate again and run my finger over it, causing Luke to moan loudly beneath me, his hips arching off the bed as he fucks my finger.

"Please," he says on a broken exhale. "Please, Eli."

I ignore his pleas and instead bring him so close to orgasm that he's whimpering, only to bring him back down again. I can read him now. The way his jaw tightens, the way his breath stutters, how his eyes slam shut.

He's panting, has been for a while now, his thick chest heaving with each breath.

"I can't stand it," he mutters, shaking his head on the crumpled sheets. "Can't take any more."

I wet my lips and roll his balls in my hand, my other hand slipping from his cock and massaging his thighs. They bunch under my touch. I love how responsive he is, how he just takes it so good.

"You can come when the oil runs out."

He swallows roughly and groans. "Fuck. How much is left?"

I turn my eyes to the nearly empty bottle, and his eyes follow mine. He snaps his eyelids shut and curses.

"Too much left."

"You can handle it."

"Fuuuuuck," he says as I begin pumping him again.

He lasts like the good boy he is, only exploding across his chest when I give him permission, and then I move on top of him and hump myself into an orgasm. His eyes are on me the entire time, our bodies sliding against each other's, slick with come and oil. His hands knead my ass cheeks, his mouth moving across my face as I clutch onto his hair, digging my fingers into his scalp. And then, when his lips brush over mine, I lean back and come loudly.

There is no decorum here. I've just splayed myself wide open.

When we're done, we both breathe deeply, trying to steady our galloping hearts.

"Fuck, you wore me out," he says, his voice hoarse. "Why are you so good at this?"

"I'm good at this because you're so naturally submissive."

He sighs and pulls me closer to him.

"We should shower," I mutter, making no move to get off him. No, I just lie there in our mess, content and satisfied.

I haven't felt this way in...well, ever. It has *never* been this good with anyone else.

"Nah," he says, his eyelids already drooping. "Too tired. Need to rest my eyes for a bit."

I watch as his eyes close and his breathing evens out. I reach over, wipe him off with a discarded towel, and press against him.

He sighs contentedly, pulling me closer.

And once again, I sleep like the motherfucking dead.

———

When I wake in the morning, Luke is snoring softly. Instead of waking him, I decide to let him keep sleeping. He's exhausted from last night. He hasn't even moved from where we passed out eight hours ago. His body is still slick with oil, and I run a finger down his abs and then back up until it's pressed against his bottom lip.

I bite the inside of my cheek. I shouldn't do it, but damn, I want to.

And why shouldn't I? Hasn't he proven himself to be more than I ever expected?

I lean up and hover over him.

One second. Two.

I just breathe him in.

And then softly, very softly, I brush my lips against his.

CHAPTER TEN

LUKE

"Hello," a deep voice says to my right. I turn my head and see a handsome man with short brown hair and a slightly crooked smile eyeing me up and down. Yeah, this dude thinks he's charming, but I'm not interested.

Not interested in anyone but Eli.

The same Eli who snuck out of our room this morning without saying goodbye. It really put me in a mood.

"Hey," I reply, taking a sip of my beer as the man leans against the bar top. I can feel his eyes moving across my body as he sizes me up. I flex slightly to show him what I'm working with.

As in...back the fuck off, I could crush you, skinny dude.

"I uh, wanted to come over and introduce myself." He holds out a hand, and I just stare at it. "I'm Andrew."

Andrew. That name makes my ears ring as I eye this

asshole. Yeah, my bad mood just plummeted to homicidal. I know exactly who this is. Question is, how does he know me?

I don't bother shaking his dainty hand. I just let it wobble around in the space between us until he yanks it back down to his side.

"Why you talkin' to me?" I ask. "We're not friends."

Andrew clears his throat and sits down next to me. He obviously can't get a fucking clue. Nah, this asshole needs to learn the hard way.

I'm happy to teach him this particular lesson. Oh, yeah, I can be an excellent teacher.

"I just saw you sitting here all alone, and I realized that I recognized you. Elliot showed me your picture on his first day here." He leans in a little closer. "Said you were his new toy."

He says that last word like it's dirty, but I fucking loved toys growing up. I have no problem being labeled one. What I do take issue with is this dickhead talking shit about Elliot.

My Elliot.

Mine.

Even though he snuck away early this morning. Can't quite let go of the fact that he did that. He hasn't responded to my texts either. Seems like he's avoiding me, and I don't really want to think too hard about why.

"What's your point, asshole?"

Andrew clears his throat, obviously thrown that I'm not taking the bait. I'll take nothing from this dude.

"My point is that a man like you...doesn't it bother you?"

I set my beer down hard and turn to fully face him, and I really take him in. That perfectly combed hair, those bright eyes, that nice aristocratic nose. I could break all that, just smoosh it right to pieces, and make him a lot less pretty.

"Does what bother me?"

"That he's...." he gestures toward his crotch, but I refuse to look. I just stare at him blankly.

"Go on," I say, subtly setting the trap. I'm going to snap this fucker's head off. Just watch as he bleeds out.

"He's trans."

"Is that so?" I drawl.

"You didn't...oh fuck, you didn't know?" he says, then leans back and laughs a little. "I can't believe him. I didn't think he'd sink that low."

I run a hand across my jaw and eye him. "Of course I fucking knew. But that's none of your business. What's my business is that you're talking shit about *my* Elliot?"

His laugh dies in his throat, and he shakes his head, realizing I'm not playin'.

"No, of course not. I just didn't expect someone as attractive as you to be with someone like him. What do you even see in him? Or maybe it's because he still has a...." He gestures to his crotch again, and I sigh.

Alright. I was nice. Too nice. I let this go on for much too long.

I jerk my head forward and smash my forehead right into that fucker's nose.

Andrew flops back with a squeal, blood gushing from his nostrils as he grasps it. A few people turn to stare, but I don't give a fuck. Stare all you want.

Yeah, fuckers. Take a nice, *long* look. This little piggy is gonna bleed all the way home.

I reach out and grab onto Andrew's hair and tighten my fingers in the strands. His eyes widen when I get right in his face and meet his wary gaze.

"You keep talkin' shit, and we're going to have a problem." Andrew swallows and nods, and I lean a little closer. "And, Andrew, you don't want a problem with me. Trust."

He swallows roughly, and I let him go, only to glance to my right and see Elliot standing at the entrance, his face paling as he watches.

Good. Let him see what I'll do for him. I won't let anyone talk shit about him.

Even if he did sneak away like an asshole this morning.

I grab onto my beer, finish it in two swallows and then walk toward him.

Elliot's gaping mouth snaps shut as I stop in front of him, and I can't help but reach out and gently touch the side of his face.

"Hey, Doc."

His eyes snap from me to Andrew and then back to me. "Wha—what was that? What did you do, Luke?"

"Ah, that was nothing. He was running his mouth. Deserved it. Come on, let's go. Let's leave."

He shakes his head. "I...Luke, I can't do that."

"Yeah, you can. Fucker deserved it, like I said."

Elliot shakes his head. "What did he say? Tell me."

I clench my jaw. "He was talking shit about your body."

Elliot sighs and pinches the bridge of his nose. "This is just my luck." He mutters something under his breath and then meets my stare. "I have to take care of this, Luke. I don't want you getting arrested."

"No one's going to jail. They'd have to find me first."

Elliot eyes me and then says curtly, "Luke, I'm serious. Go to the room and wait for me. We will talk about this when I get back."

"I'm not leaving you with him."

"Go. I don't...I don't *want* you here. I don't *need* you here."

My heart sinks a little at his tone, and then I grab onto his chin and force his gaze to mine.

"Don't let him talk to you like you're less than. You know he's just saying that warped, demented shit to try to hurt you. You tower above him. You fucking soar, Eli."

Elliot swallows and blinks slowly.

"And you have me. *Me*. And I think you're perfect."

Elliot stares at me intently for a second, then wrenches his face from my grasp and turns his back on me.

"Room. Now."

My stomach drops, and my chest constricts. "Don't speak to me that way, Eli," I say softly. "Not after everything."

He looks over his shoulder at me, his eyebrows meeting, his eyes a little glassy, and nods. "Please, Luke. Go."

I rub the back of my neck and reluctantly move away from him. He doesn't want me here. That's okay. He can fight his own battles. He's strong, stronger than most probably give him credit for.

But as I enter the elevator and press the button to our floor, my chest clenches and worry gnaws at me.

Probably shouldn't have broken Andrew's nose.

Nah, Eli won't like that.

ELLIOT

"What in the world were you thinking, Andrew, speaking to him like that?" I ask as I meet my ex's watery gaze. He's holding a bag of ice up to his bloody nose. The space around his eyes is already starting to turn purple. Part of me is hysterically pleased with this new development, and the other part is scared shitless.

Andrew is notoriously spiteful and I wouldn't put it past him to press charges. I don't want Luke getting in trouble because of *me*.

"I thought that you had better taste. I didn't know your new toy was feral."

"Did you call him a toy to his face?" I ask and narrow my eyes at the man I thought I'd loved years ago. The man I'd bought a ring for, gotten down on one knee for.

The one who scoffed at my proposal.

"I did. Although that didn't seem to bother him. He seemed happy about it."

I fold my arms across my chest and bite down on the inside of my cheek so tightly that I taste blood. Andrew doesn't get to know these private parts of me. We aren't friends. We aren't anything. Not anymore.

"I am going to report this," Andrew says.

I arch an eyebrow. "And why would you do that?"

"Because he head-butted me in the middle of a hotel. That's assault, and it was unprovoked."

"Oh, I seriously doubt that. I'm sure you said something to set him off."

I've never seen Luke mad or act out in anger. And I know, from what little Luke told me, what Andrew had said. It was the same old shit he'd say to me when we were together.

"You were being an asshole about me being trans, weren't you? You just couldn't help yourself. You are such a prick."

He shifts on his seat, slowly losing the moral high ground.

The people next to us indiscreetly listening are hearing this too.

Fine. Let them hear.

"Were you making your usual degrading comments about me to him?"

Andrew shakes his head. "It wasn't like that. We were having a conversation, and then he just freaked out. And anyway, I was only trying to help. You two obviously can't last."

"You just can't help yourself, can you? Asshole to the core. Do yourself a favor and stay away from us. Luke doesn't need to deal with any of your shit, and neither do I."

He scoffs, and I roll my eyes, leaning toward him. "And you will not be reporting this."

"Oh yeah? And why shouldn't I?"

I have this insane urge to smash my hand against that ice pack, to listen to his nose crunch once more. To finish what Luke started.

"Don't make me call my sisters," I say, and Andrew pales, his eyes widening.

"You wouldn't."

"Oh. I would."

Andrew leans farther away from me and shakes his head. "Fine, but you keep him away from me. I don't feel safe with him lurking around this hotel."

I roll my eyes, but the following words from his mouth make my cheeks flush with anger.

"I won't report this to the police, but management is going to ask him to leave," Andrew says, almost looking proud.

Oh, fuck him.

"I'm sure they will, and they'll make *you* leave as well once I tell them what a transphobic asshole you are."

I'm bluffing. I have no idea what they'll do, and I doubt they'll side with me. But I'm furious and spouting out half-truths. I want to hurt him for hurting Luke.

I turn my back on Andrew and am met with two men from security. I speak with them even though I barely hear what they say over the roar in my ears. But I make out enough. They want Luke to leave, or they'll file a report.

Andrew hems and haws in the background like the martyr he isn't, and I clench my hands into fists, lest I slap him with one.

I shouldn't be surprised though. He's always been like this, and upon self-reflection, I'm shocked I overlooked this major character flaw for so long. He would always go along with my games in the bedroom and make me feel like shit for it later, complaining that I was too rough, or too degrading. Even though we'd discussed it, and I'd checked in with him, and we both set up safe words in advance. But he'd never used them. Instead, he chose to use my proclivities to humiliate me and make me feel disgusted with myself. There were days I'd just be consumed with shame.

Andrew liked it, seeing me so weak. He used it to *use* me. And I'd let him because I'd been afraid to be alone.

Well, I've been alone for a long time now and have made peace with it.

I'll never be with someone like this asshole ever again.

When security is satisfied that Luke and I will be leaving the hotel, I turn and flip Andrew off. He balks at my gesture, and I smirk at him.

Hope his nose stays crooked.

I return to the hotel room and when I step inside, I see

Luke sitting on the couch, his elbows on his knees, his fingers flying over his phone screen. And all the frustration I'd managed to keep bottled up earlier explodes out of me.

"What are you doing?" I snap, and those hazel eyes meet mine.

"Oh, hey, Eli," he says so casually like he isn't getting us kicked out of a hotel any minute. Like he didn't just commit assault.

"Do not *hey* me," I retort.

Luke tilts his head and watches me steadily. "You're mad."

"Of course I'm mad." Mostly at Andrew but a little at him. "I can't believe you did that. You can't go off crushing people's faces in when you get a little angry."

"Yeah, well, I did. He was an ass. Can't believe you were with that guy."

"Me either," I snap and then press my fingers against my temples. "Even so, what you did was barbaric. And I don't need you to protect me like that, Luke. I can take care of myself just fine."

Luke stands up, widening his posture. "I know, Eli, but he insulted you and kept running his mouth. And you're mine, Eli. *Mine*. I can't let people say that kind of shit about you."

My eyes blink and blink, and an ugly sound escapes my mouth. My heart accelerates, and I feel almost woozy.

"I'm not yours, Luke. Not really," I reply softly, wetting my lips. "We have never discussed any of this. Everything just moved so fast. It all just spiraled out of control."

It spiraled in the best kind of way. The two of us colliding, a mess in time and space.

But that kind of mess is scary. And I'm so very afraid of what this all means.

Luke steps toward me and runs a hand across his jaw,

oblivious to the internal nightmare I'm in. "Nah, Doc. You *are* mine. You just haven't accepted it yet. And nothing spiraled. It all fell right into place. We are exactly where we should be."

"Luke, I don't think you understand. I don't do relationships. Not anymore."

He rolls his lips between his teeth. "Not since Andrew, I assume."

I swallow and give a clipped nod. "Yes."

We just stare at each other, my stilted breaths thunderous in this silent room.

"You and me, Eli. We're gonna be a thing. You know it. I know it. Don't fucking fight it so hard. It's exhausting."

I shake my head, swallowing. "No. We aren't going to be a thing. Just because you say it, doesn't mean it becomes some kind of reality. You and I are having..." I search my head frantically for what this is and come up empty. Nothing can really describe what this is between us. So I just open my mouth and blurt out something so entirely untrue that I even wince as I utter it. "...a reciprocal relationship. This is just sex. That's all this is."

Oh no, it's so much more than that, but I can't help but push you away.

Luke freezes, leans back, and folds his arms across his chest. "You fucking with me, Doc? This some kind of game? Because this isn't just sex anymore. This is a relationship."

I shake my head. "No. It isn't. Because I don't do relationships."

Why the hell am I saying this? Why can't my mouth shut up?

"It's nothing personal," I add, only making this entire thing worse.

Luke runs a hand along his jaw, those hazel eyes assessing me. "Seems pretty personal to me."

I shake my head, my heart now in my throat. "It doesn't matter. The point is we have thirty minutes to vacate the premises. The hotel wants us to leave. Well, more specifically, they want you gone for assaulting someone in the hotel bar."

"I could give two fucks what they want. You want me to leave, Eli?"

I don't say anything. Just let my unspoken words hang between us.

Of course I don't want you to leave. I want you to stay. I just need time. Can you give me that? I need to think this through rationally. Maybe with some time apart from you, I can come to terms with what this really is.

And yet, I utter none of it. All of that just stays lodged in my brain and my mouth refuses to spit it out. My body is revolting against me. First my hands and now my mouth. What's next? My legs, my neck, my arms?

"Ah, fuck. Yeah, I gotcha," Luke mumbles and then stands up, looming over me. "It's because I hurt him, huh? You still pining over him or something? Is that why you snuck off this morning, to go see him?"

"No. Absolutely not. I left so you could sleep. And I'm not a fool. That man is a cancer."

"But you still let him eat away at you, dictating your life, your choices."

"I do not," I spit, even though I'm shrinking on the inside. Because he's right, and I don't know what to do about it. I live in so much fear from past choices that I'm nearly paralyzed by them.

"You won't choose me because of him. Because of what he did to you."

I exhale shakily and throw my hands up in the air. "What do you want from me, Luke? Huh?"

"Simple. I want *you*."

Those words make my chest constrict so tightly that I can't breathe. I can't fucking breathe.

"Well," I say on an exhale, "You can't have me. You just can't."

"Why?"

"I don't know!" I shout as I stare at his flushed face. "I don't fucking know," I say more softly.

Luke blinks slowly, his chest rising and falling evenly, and I want to lean into him and have him hold me. I want to immediately apologize, to tell him I've changed my mind. But I don't do any of it. I can't. I'm frozen. My body has completely locked down. I just stand facing him, my hands clenched into fists, my cheeks hot.

"Anything I can do to change your mind, Eli?" He asks gently.

We stare at each other. One heartbeat. Two. Three.

I don't fucking answer. I just stare at him.

He stares at me.

We. Fucking. Stare.

And then Luke moves toward the bedroom, his hands clenching and unclenching near his sides.

"What are you doing?" I ask, following him, my voice tight and clipped.

"Packing."

"Why?"

"I can read between the lines."

"What lines? There are no lines. We can leave together and stay somewhere else. Why don't I get us separate rooms at the hotel down the street?"

Luke eyes me like I've lost my mind, like I've just sprouted two new eyes. And he's justified in this. I don't really want to be separated from him, but I know that I probably should be, so I can fucking think about what this all is. Whenever he's in my space, I am just consumed by him and my mind doesn't work properly.

"Nah, Eli. It's best if I stay somewhere else tonight. Without you."

My heart thunders in my chest, and I feel a little light-headed. "What? Why?"

"Gonna give you some space, like you want," Luke says with a swallow. His Adam's apple bobs, and he rolls his lips between his teeth. "And I think you're right. I need to step away for a bit. I got this all wrong."

My jaw clenches and my eyes sting. "Fine."

Dammit. Why do I think one thing, but my mouth says another? I don't want him to go. I want him to stay.

With. Me. Always with me.

"What about tomorrow?" I ask, forcing myself not to sound so desperate but failing miserably. My voice cracks, and I can't quite figure out how to inhale.

"What about it?"

"Will you meet me here, or should I pick you up for the flight home?"

Luke runs a hand through his hair and shakes his head. "Nah, Eli. I think I'm gonna change my plans. I'm gonna stay a few days longer. I don't start on the pipeline until Wednesday."

My mouth opens and then closes, and a terrible feeling rises within me.

"But...but who will you stay with?"

"Denise."

My eyes prickle, and I give a clipped nod. Fucking Denise. That granola bitch.

"I understand. It's best this way."

It's not best. It's the worst. It's like my life is ending, and I can't do anything about it.

You can. You can. Just apologize. Tell him to stay. Why won't you work, mouth?

Despite my internal screaming, I just watch numbly as Luke finishes shoving his things into his suitcase and then grabs onto the handle. He moves toward the door, and inside I'm on my knees begging.

Stay. Stay.

But I don't move. I just stand stiff and unyielding as he opens the door. He looks over his shoulder, and our eyes meet.

"Bye, Eli."

I can't even respond. I just stand there and force air in and out of my lungs until the door clicks shut.

And then I stand there some more, and some more, until my legs ache and I'm forced to lower myself to the floor.

Is it over?

Did I ruin it?

I ruined it.

I usually ruin things.

I manage to get up and move toward the shower. I limp inside, feeling haggard, like I'm a hundred years old. I turn the water on and sink to the ground, tucking my knees into my chest.

I just sit there until my skin burns from the hot water.

When I'm done, I hear my phone ringing, over and over.

I pick it up and see that I've missed calls from *everyone*. Eliza. Jane. Kate.

But I don't answer because they'll hear it in my voice. The devastation. And I'll hear it from them. The disappointment.

So, I ignore it.

I ignore them all.

And when I go home the next day alone, the seat next to me is painfully empty.

———

My house is vacant when I arrive, but I swear I can almost smell him in the space, hear him moving about. It's depressing. I've never minded being alone until now. Now, I can feel the hollowness of my previous life.

At this moment, I realize how unhappy I'd been until he barreled his way into my space and set up shop, how much I needed someone to pull me out of my mundane, redundant existence.

I roll my suitcase into my room and just stand there, letting myself experience the feelings coursing through me. Regret, sadness, fury.

I'm so mad at myself.

Why am I like this? Why is it so hard for me to let people in, let them love me?

When I can't stand the thought of standing in my room another minute, I move into the living room and sit down at the piano. My phone lies next to me on the bench, and I glance down at it.

Don't do it.

I run a few D and F minor scales because they match my sullen mood and I'm trying desperately to keep my fingers off that screen. But I pause momentarily, and my hand is reaching for my phone.

"Don't do it," I tell myself out loud, and yet I don't listen to myself. It was a halfhearted attempt anyway. The heart wants what it wants.

Me: I made it home safely.

I glare at my phone, not sure if he will even respond.

I want him to respond.

He'll respond.

But when he doesn't, I'm sent into a tailspin. With clumsy fingers, I pull out the sheet music for Rachmaninoff's "Sad is the Night" and let the gloomy notes float around me as I press the keys. I play the song repeatedly, arching into the melody, my fingers growing numb with the effort. And I only stop when the doorbell chiming has me freezing, the piano notes just an echo in the air.

Quickly, I push myself up and swipe at my eyes, peeking out the window. A part of me thinks it's Luke.

He came back. He's here. It has to be him.

But it's not. It's just a delivery. Probably those sweatpants I'd ordered for Luke that he would look so good in.

Yep. There it is. A sad box is sitting on my front porch. I'll just shove it in my closet and never open it. I don't even have the heart to return them. Maybe I will just leave it there for a porch pirate to steal. But then I imagine some thief running around in Luke's sweats and get irrationally angry. I move to the front door, wrench it open and cradle the box in my hands.

Then I hide it behind my couch. I can't even look at it.

Fuck. This is what I've been reduced to in a matter of weeks. I'm a weak, crumbling mess. Imagine if I'd let this go on longer than a few weeks. I'd be comatose. No, it's best that I ended this. Whatever it was.

A relationship.

It's for the best.

Liar.

I sit back at the piano and play the piece once more. I don't feel any better at the end.

No. I feel worse.

CHAPTER ELEVEN

ELLIOT

"You can't fire me," Amanda says, popping her gum loudly. Her painted blue lips smirk at me, and I sigh heavily. Monday has rolled around, and I've been feeling awful. My head throbs, my chest aches, and I've repeatedly broken out in a cold sweat. I think I'm coming down with something, probably the flu. I shouldn't have come into work today. I could be contagious. It could be some kind of infection that spreads far and wide, killing off millions.

"I can. And I did."

She rolls her eyes and continues clacking on her computer.

"Whatever you say," she says to the screen but makes no move to pack up her stuff. Instead, she seems to just squish herself further into the seat, planting herself there. She's growing roots. Pretty soon, she'll be an Ent from *Lord of the Rings* and birds will be flying in here just to nest in her hair.

Well, fine, she can just stay if she wants. She never listens to me anyway.

I huff my annoyance once more, which is ignored, and move toward my office. It's cluttered and messy like my head. I should tidy up a bit, but I lack the motivation.

The only motivation I have is to check my phone obsessively. It burns a hole in my pocket; my pants are practically on fire. Because he *still* hasn't texted me, and it's been almost twenty-four hours.

My battery is hanging on for dear life because I just stare at it incessantly, and it's only early afternoon. The phone charger in my office is broken. I think Amanda cut the cord, so I'll have to suffer another four hours of patients before I can get home, plug my phone in to charge, and check my messages again. I think she did it because I hurt Luke.

She's been giving me the evil eye all day, even muttered something incoherent under her breath. She's probably hexing me.

No need, Amanda. I'm already cursed.

A small part of me wants to just cancel my appointments and go home to putter around the empty space, but then the adult part of my brain tells me that I can't call out sick to mope.

Even if I'm coming down with something awful.

I've never felt so sick in my entire life.

Not even after Andrew and I ended things.

By the end of the day, my dead phone hangs heavily in my pocket, and my inability to check my messages has caused my anxiety to peak. I'm completely worn out. After my last patient, I slump over my desk and just breathe.

I doze off for a minute and wake up with a start. When I

plod toward the exit, I see that Amanda is already gone. She's left behind a passive-aggressive post-it note on the door.

Grow a spine.

Is it passive, or is it just plain aggressive? I don't really know.

I tear it off and stuff it into my pocket.

What spine am I supposed to grow, huh? He's the one who decided to ghost me. But then again, I never gave us a chance to begin with. I made my choice, and he made his.

It's the end of something that barely even started.

I hobble to my car and slip inside, resting my head on the steering wheel. When I can't stand the throb behind my eyes a moment longer, I reach into the glove box and grab a few Advil. I pop them into my dry mouth and swallow them. They claw and scratch as they move down my throat. They obviously don't want to help relieve the pain I'm in. Even they're pissed at me.

I finally put my car in drive and make my way home slowly. I have no desire to be in that empty house all by myself. How quickly things have changed in a matter of weeks.

There is a slight desire to call my sisters and ask them to come over, just to have them fill the space. But then I think of how they'll ask me endless questions I don't want to answer, and I throw that thought in my mental trashcan.

No, it's better to sulk alone.

That way, no one can see how pathetic I've become.

When I finally arrive, I shuffle into the house and flop down on my couch, but that just reminds me of him, so I move to the guest bedroom to plug in my phone. The one room in the house he hasn't really touched.

I blink at my bright phone screen in the darkness as I lie sprawled out on the bed. I pull up the video that he'd taken of us cresting the Manitou Incline and my chest heaves. God, he'd looked so happy. So in contrast to when I'd told him this was just sex. What a lying asshole I am. It was never just sex.

That smile on his face, the way he kissed my knuckles. I can't. It hurts too much to watch it, so I click the phone off. And then I click it back on and before I can tell myself not to, I'm typing.

Me: Are you okay?

I stare at my message unblinking, but he doesn't reply. Of course, he doesn't. Why would he? He's obviously done and over me.

I'll get over him too.

In about a hundred years.

I fall asleep without eating dinner, my phone clutched to my chest.

The next morning, I wake up and feel like my entire body has been slammed into the ground. I'm achy and shaking. My mouth is dry, and my tongue sticks to the roof of my mouth. This flu is progressing. I should probably go to urgent care.

I take a long sip of water to stay hydrated but still feel completely wrung out. My heart feels funny in my chest. It positively aches.

It's probably congestive heart failure. I should just call an ambulance now and have the EMTs stick around and wait for me to keel over.

The reaper will come for me soon.

My phone pings, and I jump, stubbing my toe against the

leg of the bed. My brain kicks on, and I frantically scramble to grab it. I end up scraping my forearm along my nightstand instead. Those corners should be illegal. Who designed this thing? They should be in jail for attempted murder. I glance at my throbbing arm and note the long red stripe running across my skin.

Fuck.

My phone pings again, and all of my pain is forgotten as I dive for it. But my shitty little phone slips across the covers and falls between the wall and headboard. So, I drop to my knees and stretch for it, the tips of my fingers touching the screen as I begin to move it toward me. But then something snaps as I tilt my neck, and I flinch as pain shoots down my spine.

I clasp the phone in my hand and roll onto my back, groaning loudly.

Oh fuck. I'm falling apart.

My skeletal system is disintegrating right before my eyes.

But despite it all, I still manage to lift that phone above my face and see his messages.

He texted me.

He wrote me back.

My entire body clenches as I gasp.

Luke: I'm okay.
Luke: Made it home safe.

Quick. Think. What do I text back? Something poetic, professing how sorry I am, telling him how much I miss him.

Come back. Come home.

Me: Good

Oh fuck. That's not what I wanted to say. I didn't even add a period. It seems so unfinished. Like, I don't care that he's gone. Will he notice? Fuck. He will, won't he?

I have to fix this.

Me: Good.

I stare at my screen, groan, and slap it face down onto the floor. A sickening crack echoes around the room, and I nearly cry when I see what I've done.

My phone screen is broken to pieces.

Kind of like my heart.

And now, there is no way to respond to him with something actually meaningful.

Fuck.

I stand up slowly, hissing at the pain moving down my shoulder and up my neck, and I hobble toward the bathroom.

Even if I wanted to, I can't call out sick. I guess I could e-mail, but I can't even fathom the idea of staying home alone. What would I do with myself all the live long day?

Mope, that's what.

So instead, I shower and pull on some clothes, not really caring that my shirts haven't been ironed or that I haven't shaved my face in days. I stagger into work like I just crawled out of a gutter.

"You look like shit," Amanda says, but I just ignore her.

She's right. I'm sure I do. But I don't care enough to try any harder.

I hear a click, and Amanda is holding her phone up.

"Did you just take my picture?"

"Yep," she says, popping her gum. "I'm going to send this

to Luke so he feels sorry for your sad ass. Maybe he'll come back and make you nicer again."

"You will not send that to him. I forbid it."

She rolls her eyes, and slowly her finger descends onto her phone, smashing into the screen dramatically.

"Oops."

I sigh loudly and turn to move, but pain lances down my spine again, and I hiss.

"You going to die in your office?" Amanda asks me as I move away from her.

"God, I hope so," I mutter and slam the door.

I can do this. I can make it through another day.

One foot in front of the other, I think. And maybe, just maybe, Luke will get that picture Amanda sent and come back.

When I see myself in the mirror two hours later, I realize my shirt is inside out, and I have toothpaste on my upper lip. Why no one thought to tell me this is appalling.

I am *appalled*.

I glance down at the scrape on my forearm and notice it's lengthened. Probably some toxin got into my system, and it's heading straight toward my heart.

I'm a dead man walking.

Even though I'm on the brink, I power through. Everyone must feel sorry for me. Two of my patients don't even meet my eyes. Mrs. Melnyk shuffles around in her purse and hands me an ancient-looking candy that's seen better days, and she *never* shares. She's always stealing shit from my office—Q-tips, cotton balls, tongue depressors.

I'll do better tomorrow. I'll *be* better, I tell myself as I lock the door to the office and move into the waiting room.

"Shit," I mutter, knocking my elbow against the wall when I see someone lurking in the corner like a ghost.

A thin, young man looks over at me and rolls his eyes like he's annoyed I was afraid.

Well, excuse me for showing emotion. It seems like it's all I can do nowadays.

Upon closer inspection, the man hanging off a ladder in my waiting room looks somewhat shady. He has silver hair, piercings, and tattoos lining his skin.

"Who the hell are you?" I grumble as I rub my aching elbow.

He stares me directly in the eyes and says evenly, "Sauron."

I arch an eyebrow at him, and the man smiles widely at my annoyance.

"You're a dark lord seeking to conquer middle earth?"

"And why shouldn't I be, huh?" He hops down from the ladder and stands directly in front of me. "If you must know, because you seem like a total party pooper, Amanda called me. She told me *all* about you and I decided to do you all a favor. I'm installing cameras in here. Lex, at your service." He gives me a curtsey, which looks ridiculous because he's so lanky and tall, and he does the movement all wrong. It looks more like he's lunging for something on the ground.

My eyes slide over the tattoos lacing his skin and the piercings on his face once more. "You look like you just were released from prison," I quip.

"Oh, but what if I was? Are you going to discriminate? What if I'm just trying to get my life back on track," he snarks, and I rub at my temples. The headache that has been there all day is intensifying.

Apparently, Amanda has it out for me. Maybe she's been slowly poisoning my coffee.

My eyes flash to Lex and then to the cameras he's installing.

"Why are you installing cameras in my office again?"

"Amanda ordered them. For security. I've also upgraded your modem and router because yours were from the nineties. Didn't even know those were still around...."

I sigh heavily. "I didn't ask her to do this."

"She said you'd say that, and she told me to tell you..." He lifts his hands in air quotes. "Tough shit, boss."

I sag against the wall and rub at my neck.

"Fine. Although you don't look trustworthy."

"Oh, I am absolutely not trustworthy, but I wouldn't do Amanda wrong. She's my kind of person."

I don't know what that means, and I don't really want to know. Amanda has always been a bit of a mystery. I never asked what her deal was, and to be honest, I don't know if knowing would make anything any better. Sometimes mysteries should stay mysterious.

"How much longer will you be?" I ask because I don't want to go home yet. No, I'd much rather stay here and converse with this possible felon. That's what my life has been reduced to at the moment.

Lex glances at the ceiling and shrugs. "Meh, twenty minutes."

"Fine. I'll wait," I say, sinking into a chair and then pulling out my broken phone. I stare at the shattered screen, and Lex whistles.

"Broke that bitch *bad*, huh?"

"Yes."

"I know a guy who can fix it. He'll even give you a discount if I show up with you."

I glance at him and narrow my eyes. "Will you have him

put tracking software on my phone, and will you then stalk me with it?"

"Quite possibly," he responds, moving back to the ladder and fiddling with the wires.

Well, why the hell not? Maybe he will lurk outside my house and keep me company, so I won't have to feel so alone. "Fine."

What else do I have to lose?

Nothing, that's what. I have absolutely nothing left to lose.

I'll be dead by the weekend, anyway.

Thirty minutes later, Lex and I are walking toward the parking lot. The sun is slipping behind the horizon, and the glow on Lex's silver hair makes it almost translucent. The rings in his eyebrow and lip twinkle in the rays, and it almost hurts to look at him.

"Oooh, you have a Tesla," Lex says gleefully, eyeing my car and flipping his keys around his finger. "Can I drive this beautiful machine?"

"No."

"Well, can I at least sit in it?"

I mull it over for exactly two seconds and then mutter, "Fine."

I open the driver's side door, and Lex slips into the passenger side, touching everything.

"Do you mind?" I ask as he moves his hands onto my seat and his fingers brush my leg. I don't like him all up in my personal space. No, that's reserved for Luke and Luke only.

"Sorry, just having a tactile experience here. Never been in one of these before." He starts pressing the large touch screen. "This is very cool. Very, very cool. Now show me how it drives."

And that is exactly how I ended up driving Lex across town in my car. Apparently, my hobby is collecting strays. Will I sleep with him next?

I eye him and shudder.

No.

He does nothing for me.

It's Luke that I want.

"Take a left right here. No, not that left. This left. Your other left. Right. Yes, right here."

I roll my eyes as I finally maneuver onto a dimly lit, crowded street. There happens to be one open space between two cars, and I narrowly manage to squeeze into it.

"What is this place?" I ask. "Are you kidnapping me?" At this point, I really don't care if he is, I'm just curious.

Lex pulls his finger away from the touch screen that he's been messing with the last ten minutes and rolls his eyes.

"If I were to kidnap you, you'd know. I can guarantee you that there'd be chloroform and rope involved."

Well, that's reassuring.

Lex nods to his left. "Anywho, Diablo is down there. He knows we're coming."

"Diablo?"

"Yeah, he's a freaky fucker, so watch what you say. You don't want to offend him."

"How dreadfully exciting," I drawl and step out of the car, following Lex down some dirty concrete stairs. What the hell am I doing? I could have gone to a corner store and had my phone fixed and yet here I am. Have I lost all self-preservation? Perhaps I hope this Diablo will squish me like a bug, and just put me right out of my misery.

These thoughts are only slightly concerning.

Lex eyes me as I pinch the bridge of my nose and then knocks on the dirty door in some kind of secret code.

A second later, a small skinny kid wrenches it open.

"Lexington," the boy squeaks. His curly hair sticks up at all angles, and his wide brown eyes narrow as he takes me in.

"'Sup, Diablo," Lex replies.

"This is Diablo?" I ask, raising my eyebrow. Where is the scary gangster with a gun? I'm slightly disappointed in this new development.

Apparently, this is my life now. Interacting with tweens in dark basements.

"You bringing strangers to my house now, huh? You know the rules, asswipe," Diablo says, his gaze sliding over me once more.

Lex shrugs, pulls a sucker from his jacket and hands it to him. Diablo takes it quickly and shoves it in his pocket. "He needs his phone screen fixed. And, plus, he's a doctor. Could come in handy one day."

Okay, this is seeming less and less kosher. Perhaps Diablo is some kind of mini-mob boss. Will I be performing unsanitary surgeries using kitchen utensils in my near future? Is this my life now?

The boy narrows his eyes even further and then waves us inside. "Fine. Come in. But hands to yourself. Especially you, Doc. I don't know you."

"Is this child labor?" I ask, following Lex into the basement apartment.

"Nope, Diablo is nineteen."

"He looks like he's twelve."

Diablo huffs, "I heard that and take offense. I just happen to be small for my age. I haven't quite hit my growth spurt." He sits on a swivel chair and spins toward a slew of computer screens on a makeshift table. Is that tinfoil on the walls? Why does it smell like Cheetos?

I meet Diablo's stare and say, "I'm sorry to tell you that you'll most likely not grow any more. You're destined to be short for the foreseeable future."

"Fuck you," Diablo mutters as Lex nudges me roughly.

"Excuse him," Lex says. "He's had his heart broken. He's not thinking clearly."

I eye him. "How do you know this?"

"Amanda likes to gossip," he tells me, and I sigh heavily. Of course she told this stranger all about my sad life. I would probably do the same. It's like some kind of dramatic comedy. What's not to love about it?

Diablo meets my stare. "Fine. I'll make an exception this *one time*. Now, what can I do for you, Doctor? You said you need your screen fixed?"

I am seriously questioning my judgment, but I still hand over my phone. There's no going back now. I asked for this by engaging with a shady hooligan in my waiting room. I wouldn't be surprised if the FBI raids this place in the next ten minutes.

"Damn, how did you do this?" Diablo asks as he tilts my phone to one side and then to the other. He sets it down and grabs a set of tools from a drawer.

"By behaving like a child," I mutter as Lex leans down, his hands pressed on the table.

"So, how long will this take, man?"

"Thirty minutes."

"Make it twenty-five, and you know what I'll do for you."

Why does that sound dirty? I don't want to imagine Lex and Diablo doing filthy things. It makes my stomach hurt.

I clear my throat. "And how much will this cost me?"

Diablo is fiddling with my phone and doesn't even meet my stare. "Lex has it covered."

I eyeball Lex, who is playing with his tongue ring.

"How are you covering this?" I ask him.

"Oh, you don't want to know."

He's right. I don't.

Diablo waves his hand in front of his face. "You can have a seat. Hovering over me won't make me move any faster," he quips.

I glance around and see a dirty orange couch in the corner. I don't want to know where that thing has been. It looks like it's seen some shit. Was it originally orange to begin with, or has it slowly morphed in color over time? Perhaps that's where the Cheeto smell originates from.

"Come on. Chill, man," Lex says, flopping down on the cushions. Dust particles shoot up into the air, and I cover my face with the collar of my jacket.

"I'm not sitting there. That's probably toxic mold spores being released into the atmosphere."

Lex inhales deeply through his nose. "Ah. I love toxic mold spores. Could get high off this shit."

Oh my god.

I move farther away from him and lean against a wall that looks relatively clean.

I watch Diablo work to pass the time and ensure he doesn't do anything shifty to my phone, like install spyware. But no, he seems intent on just fixing the broken glass. He's quick and efficient; twenty minutes later, he's holding up my fixed phone.

"Done. Record time."

Lex tilts his head to the side, a sucker hanging from his

lips, his legs propped up on the couch arm, and he waggles his eyebrows.

"You're the motherfucking best."

Diablo puffs up a bit. "I am, and now *you* owe *me*."

I push off the wall and grab my phone. I turn it on and then click on my messages.

My heart falters and then sinks. A heavy sigh escapes me. No new messages from Luke. But the ones I'd sent him blink up at me like a bad premonition.

Damn.

"Why the fuck is he sighing like that?" Diablo asks. "Does he have to shit?"

"Nope. He is pining," Lex replies and then nudges me. "I can read you like a book. Come on. Let's go."

"Fine," I say and follow Lex up the steps and back to my car. We slip inside, and I stare out the windshield.

"So, what's the plan now?" Lex asks, leaning back and eyeing me.

Do not do it. Do not even think about it. You will not.

"Want to hang out?" I ask.

Lex pops his sucker from his mouth.

"Thought you'd never ask."

CHAPTER TWELVE

ELLIOT

I drive Lex to his car, which is still parked at my office, and then he follows me home. But I debate just driving by when I see my sisters hovering right outside my front door. They're watching my car approach so there's no escaping them now. Their gazes widen when they see Lex stepping out of his car and sashaying toward them.

"Who is this?" they ask in unison.

Luke's right. It's eerie.

Lex doesn't think anything of it, though. He just does his weird half curtsey-squat. "Lex, at your service."

They take him in. All of him, from his silver hair and pierced face down to his ripped jeans and black combat boots.

"And where did you two meet?" Jane asks.

Lex smiles widely. "At his office. He looked so *very* pathetic, so I took pity on him and decided to be his friend. And who are you?"

"His sisters," they say all at once.

"Ah," he replies and lifts each of their hands, pressing kisses on the back of each.

And they let him.

I roll my eyes because he should not be charming them. I already have enough crazy in my life. I don't need to invite more. I don't even know why I asked him here in the first place.

"What are you doing here?" I ask my sisters.

Eliza holds up binoculars. "We came to pick you up so we could all spy on Luke. We heard what happened."

"Can't believe you even had to ask us that," Jane mutters and then meets my gaze. "If you checked our group chat, you'd know what's going on."

"Oh my god," I grumble, shaking my head. "I am not doing this. I will not do this."

But instead of walking inside the house, locking the door, and hiding in my room, my legs move toward the minivan parked on the street. I have lost complete control over my body. Aliens have taken over. It's off to outer space now.

"Ooh, so we're spying on the ex, yeah?" Lex says.

"We were never together," I mutter as I move into the front seat. The rest pile in behind me, and Eliza slides behind the steering wheel. She barely fits, her pregnant stomach much too large.

"You should not be out and about, Eliza. You're about to pop," I tell her.

"Do not tell me what to do," she hisses. "I am not an invalid. I'm just ginormous."

I remove my glasses and dig my fingers into my eye sockets. "Fine. If we do this," I begin, making sure to speak loudly so everyone can hear, "we have to be discreet. No shenanigans. And I mean it."

Kate snorts. "He means it, guys."

"Oooh," Jane replies sarcastically. "Don't mess with El 'cause he means it."

I lean my head back against the headrest and sigh in annoyance. I don't know why I even bother. No one listens to me anyway.

Lex pipes up, "You know what? If we can distract this Luke guy, I can get inside his phone and put a tracker on it. Or on his car. Do you perchance happen to know his password?"

"Oh my god, no and we are not doing that," I say, looking over my shoulder at him. "You will *not* do that."

He stares at me and then nods. "Sure thing, Ellie-Belly. I totally *won't* do that."

But I get the feeling he will do what he wants, when he wants.

"Do not call me that."

"Ooh, but we all like it. Ellie-Belly," my sisters say.

I just close my eyes and count backward from ten.

"So where is this mysterious non-ex of yours?" Lex asks. "Where is this stakeout going to be? Hopefully near some good fast-food place because I'm a hungry bug. My tummy is a-rumblin'."

"Well, he said he'd be at..." Eliza glances down at her phone, "his brother's place."

"Wait, you've been texting him?" I ask, feeling my heart sink. Because he's not texting me. Not that I expect him to, but deep down, I'm hurt that he hasn't reached out at all.

Actually, it's more like a deep-seated ache lingering within me.

He must really hate me to ignore me like this.

"Well, sort of," Eliza says and doesn't give me any more than that, which only makes it worse.

"Anyone know where his brother's place is?" Kate asks.

And before I can tell myself that this will be humiliating, that I absolutely should not behave this way, I blurt, "I do."

They all begin talking at the same time, and then Lex hollers, *wait!* He clambers out of the van and returns a minute later with a large black duffle bag.

"What the hell is that?" I ask.

"Oh, you don't wanna know," he replies with a smirk and pulls out a laptop and...is that a listening device? Who is this guy?

"You're right. I don't," I say as I give Eliza directions.

We stop off at a burger joint, and everyone orders but me because my stomach is churning and I still feel achy all over, and I think this is a very, very bad idea.

When we finally pull into the RV park twenty minutes later, I do my best not to look.

Oh, who am I kidding? I'm pressed against the window, staring like a lovesick child. My nose breath is fogging up the glass, and my tongue is lolling out of my mouth. I can see Luke's truck parked outside and the lights in the motorhome are on.

If I was a regular, mature adult, I'd just go to the door and knock and ask to speak to him. But instead, I grab the binoculars from Eliza and adjust them to see if I can catch a glimpse of him.

"I can't see anything," I mutter in irritation.

"Hold on," Lex says as he pulls on a ski mask and wrenches the van door open. Before I can protest, he's sneaking over to the motorhome. He's very good at this and almost disappears entirely into the shadows.

"What the hell is he doing?" I mutter, and Jane bounces in her seat.

"El, don't ask questions. Just be glad this psychopath is on our side."

A minute later, Lex is back in the van, sliding some headphones on and holding the listening device up to the window.

We're all silent as he bobs his head and fiddles with some knobs, and then he wrenches one of the headphones from his ear and says, "He's just shooting the shit with someone named Sem."

"That's his brother," I explain.

"They're waiting for some chick to show up. Couldn't make out her name," Lex adds, then puts the earphones back on and bobs his head more.

"What chick?" Eliza whispers, and my heart clenches in my chest.

"I don't know."

"He didn't move on, did he?" Kate asks, and Jane nudges her roughly.

"Of course, he did not. This is Luke we're talking about," Eliza says assuredly. "He was head over heels for El."

But my mind isn't listening. I'm just envisioning Luke with someone else. Someone who isn't me, and I feel like I'm going to throw up.

A minute later, a car pulls up, parking alongside Luke's truck, and a beautiful curvy woman with long brown hair steps out.

Before she can even knock, Luke wrenches the RV door open, hops down the two steps, and envelopes her in his arms.

I remember being in those arms. How it felt.

I blink and blink and damn, my eyes sting.

"I think we should go," I mutter, and Lex pulls his earphones off again.

"He says they have a date. They're going to some art gallery."

My sisters erupt in a cacophony of spoken words that I can't make out.

I gnaw at my bottom lip and then squeeze my eyes shut.

"I want to go home," I say softly, but no one listens. I peek to my right and see Luke pressing a kiss to the side of the woman's face, and my cheeks are wet.

I swipe at them and say again, "I want to go."

But, of course, I go unnoticed. They're all talking over each other, and Kate is threatening some kind of bodily violence. Jane is physically restraining her from leaving the van, but there's no need for any of that. I've seen what I need to.

"I want to fucking go!" I erupt, and everyone snaps their mouths shut. An eerie silence settles over us.

"No need to yell," Eliza says, and I turn to look back at Luke.

Our eyes meet across the parking lot, and my entire body lights up. Then my heart stops in my chest. I'm going to need to be resuscitated.

He moves toward me, a frown on his face, and I lock the doors.

"Fuck, go. Abort! We've been spotted," Lex shouts, and Eliza puts the van in drive and peels out like she's being chased by the police. The tires skid, and rocks are thrown up against the side of the van. As we fly onto the main road, I press my fingers into my temples and inhale and exhale deeply.

Eliza reaches over and grasps my arm lightly. "I'm sorry, El."

"It's fine."

It's not fine. It's far from fine.

"I'm ordering some more herbs," Jane grumbles, pulling out her phone, but I tune them out. I just lean my head against the window and close my eyes.

I was better off not knowing.

My phone pings, and as much as I want to ignore it, my eyes are drawn to it.

Luke: Why were you at my brother's place?

I run my finger over his name and gnaw at my bottom lip.

Me: You're seeing things. I'm at home.
Luke: Nah. I clearly saw you in your sister's van.
Luke: Plus, Jane already told me to watch out. She said she was ordering another witchcraft kit.

I sigh. "Jane, seriously? You threatened Luke with witchcraft?"

She scoffs, "What? He should know why all his luscious hair is falling out."

"Oh my god," I reply, and then my phone pings again, and I swallow roughly.

Luke: Why didn't you come and say hi?

Now I'm irrationally angry. Why the hell would I do that when he's with someone else?

I type a response and then delete it. I type another and do the same thing, until I finally come to a decision.

Me: I came to say goodbye but saw that you were busy.

And then, I shut my phone off and slide it into my jacket pocket.

No more of this. I need to let this go.

I don't act like this, like some crazed stalker. I'm a doctor, for fuck's sake. I've lost my fucking mind.

"I don't feel well," I tell them. "Just drop me off at home."

But of course, they don't listen. Instead of dropping me off to wallow in my misery, they move into the house with me and refuse to leave. Jane and Kate plant themselves on the couch, pouring themselves glasses of my cheap wine, while Eliza texts her husband, Seth. Meanwhile, Lex is walking through my house, typing frantically on his phone.

He's probably scoping out the place. I wouldn't be surprised to see him breaking and entering one day. I'd probably just let him come on in, to be honest. Let him take whatever he wants, except anything that's Luke-related

No, I'll be keeping all of that.

"El, stop pacing," Jane says, holding out a glass of wine. "Drink. It will help you feel better."

Eliza grabs onto my shoulder lightly and walks me over to the couch, where I sink down between Kate and Jane. Eliza squeezes into the chair on the opposite end of the room and Lex flops onto the ground. I sip on the bitter wine and close my eyes.

I'll never admit it out loud, but it helps, just a little, having them around to keep my misery at bay.

But the truth is, I'm just fucking sad.

There is no flu. I'm not dying.

No, I'm just heartsick.

CHAPTER THIRTEEN

1 WEEK LATER

ELLIOT

"Oh god, this baby is killing me. I'm a whale. I can't move, and can't see my feet. I'm just a swollen, blubbery mess." Eliza lowers herself onto the kitchen chair, and Jane hands her a glass of water and then hands me one too.

"You need to drink, El," Kate says, reaching out and grabbing my hand.

I do as she says. I know why I hurt so much now. I've come to terms with the fact that the achy, awful feeling gnawing inside me is just me being ridiculously in love with a guy who I don't deserve and who, in the end, let me go.

I'm positively heartbroken.

Today, I called out sick for the first time since starting my practice. Amanda was silent on the other end of the line before hanging up.

I assume she's calling my patients to reschedule. Don't really care either way.

Eliza puts her hand on my forehead. "You don't have a fever."

"I know," I reply. "I'm just falling apart from the inside out."

"Have you spoken to him?" Eliza asks, sympathy on her face.

"No."

"Why not? You know that woman was his sister-in-law. He wasn't cheating. He told me so," Eliza says.

Apparently, my sisters angrily texted him the following morning demanding answers and he'd responded that it was just Anne, his sister-in-law. He was going to one of her art gallery openings that night.

For hours after learning that, I'd stared at my phone, thinking he'd text me, but he never did. He never said a fucking word to me. And, to be fair, I didn't text him either.

We are stuck in some kind of silent vortex neither of us seems to be able to escape.

"I know," I reply, but that doesn't help. Nothing seems to help anymore.

The simple fact is, I miss him terribly but I don't quite know how to go forward from here. How do I move past my insecurities and let him in? How do I reach out after everything I've done?

I don't know what to fucking do. I'm almost paralyzed with anxiety.

"It's a two-way street. He can contact me as well. But he hasn't. He's probably over it. Over me."

"Like hell he is," Kate mutters, but we all just sit in silence, mulling it over. Because it's the truth. Luke could have reached out just as easily as I could have, but neither of us is making the first move.

I'm fucking miserable.

Why is life so hard?

Why did I have to fall for this man?

"It's best for me to move on," I say, and they all start talking simultaneously. But I don't even bother asking them to stop. I just sit there and listen to them chatter, all while trying to keep it together.

It's not really working. I'm slowly unraveling.

"Oh my god, guys," Jane suddenly interrupts, shushing everyone. She stares down at her phone and swipes at it twice. "What pipeline was Luke working on?"

"Oh Jesus, I can't even think right now. That's how bad I have to pee. This baby is killing me," Eliza interrupts, pushing herself up, her hand on her stomach.

"Hold your pee, Eliza. This is important. Which pipeline?" Jane says, her eyes wide and her hand slightly shaking.

"If I see the name, I'll remember," I reply, and when Jane holds her phone up, my stomach drops.

"What is this, Jane?" I whisper, my entire body locking up.

"There was an explosion..." she begins, and I slump against the table, the entire room spinning. A roar starts in my ears and I'm finding it hard to breathe.

"Three dead, possibly more."

"Oh my god," Eliza says as I begin to hyperventilate.

Luke. Oh fuck. Oh fuck. *Fuck.*

Is he okay? I fumble with my phone and drop it on the ground. It skids across the floor, and I fall to my knees and crawl after it. With trembling fingers, I type out a message to him.

There's no response.

No response.

"Guys," Eliza cries, holding onto her stomach as she doubles over, moaning in pain. "I think that was a contraction." And then I see something trickling onto the floor and my eyes widen. "I know it's terrible timing, but I'm pretty sure my water just broke," she tacks on, shaking slightly.

My eyes snap up to where she stands, and I inhale deeply.

I swipe at my eyes and stand up, swaying slightly on my feet.

"We need to get to the hospital. We need to call Seth," I say, but my voice breaks, and I sink back down because my legs can't hold me up. "We need...." My voice trails off on a choked sob.

"I'm sure Luke's fine, El," Kate says softly, crouching beside me. But I can't stop the sobs escaping me to answer her. My chest is heaving with the pain of breathing.

If he's gone, I missed my chance.

I'd squandered it. All because of misplaced pride and fear.

Fear of loving him. Of letting him in.

Fuck.

I press my face into my hands and try to keep it together for them, but I can't.

I can't.

I'm broken and won't be put back together until I know he's okay.

"Guys, I'm so sorry, but we have to go. You know how traffic is and I just had another contraction," Eliza says, and Jane shuffles my numb body toward the van.

I sit in the back with Eliza while Jane navigates the traffic to the hospital. Eliza is grumbling in her seat, shifting uncomfortably, but she still reaches out and grabs onto my hand.

"He's okay. He's okay. I know it," she tells me, and more tears track down my cheeks. She's in incredible pain, and yet, still, she's comforting me.

They'll be there for me no matter what.

I am so fortunate to have them.

They gave it all up for me.

Eliza groans through a contraction as Jane swerves around a car and swears.

"Thanks for driving like a dickhole, bitch!" Jane yells and then drives on the shoulder of the road, passing a semi-truck. But no one says anything because Eliza's contractions are coming more frequently. I'm worried that if this continues, I'll have to deliver this baby on the side of the road.

"Seth is an asshole. Said his DnD game *had* to be today. If he misses the birth of our child, I'm getting a divorce," she grumbles.

"He won't miss it," I say and squeeze her hand, glancing down at my phone, my unanswered texts glaring back up at me.

Me: Are you safe?
Me: Tell me you're okay.

No response. Nothing.

I squeeze my eyes shut and force my mind to not think about it.

I can think about it later.

———

Two hours later, Seth arrives at the hospital, bursting through the doors like his ass is on fire.

"Oh god, I'm so sorry," Seth says, skidding on the floors and talking so quickly it's hard to make sense of anything he's saying. "The party was about to deliver the killing blow on the Soul Binder and the bard failed his stealth check and the plan fell to shambles. We narrowly avoided a TPK…."

God, Eliza is going to rip him a new one. He is a dead man.

I stare at him blankly.

"Total party kill…" he explains and Jane points to the reception desk and he jolts into action.

"You need to check in and get to her before she divorces you," Jane says and then mutters to me, "Is there a witchcraft box to cure stupid?"

I shake my head and huff. "No. The only cure is death."

Then silence looms over the two of us and I sit there, trying to think of anything other than Luke, but my eyes are glued to my phone and the news article explaining what happened.

The pipeline Luke was working on exploded, and three people were killed. There's no mention of names. It's driving me crazy. I mean, the chances of it being Luke are slim, but still, I'm conjuring up the worst. My brain can't help it.

"Jane," I say, turning to my sister, who is keeping me company in the waiting room. "I have to see if I can find out any information about Luke." I stand, and my legs ache from sitting so stiffly for hours.

"Do you want me to go with you?" she asks, and I shake my head.

"No, I'm just going down to reception to ask…" my voice

breaks, and I blink rapidly. "See if they know who the victims are, or if they can tell me anything."

She nods and says, "Call me if you need me, and I'll be there."

"I know, thanks," I say and then push through the doors. My legs are shaking as I move down to reception on the first floor.

I stand behind a few people waiting to be checked into the emergency room. After an eternity, it's my turn.

"Have you heard anything about the pipeline accident?" I ask the woman behind the counter. She doesn't even look up at me, her eyes glued to her computer. "Do you know which hospital the survivors have been taken to?"

"Memorial Care," she tells me, and I nod.

"Thank you."

I pull out my phone with trembling fingers and dial Jane. "Any news on the baby?" I ask.

"No, nothing yet."

I nod and bite my bottom lip. "Can you call Memorial Care and ask if Luke is there...I can't...I can't do it, Jane."

"Of course," she says and hangs up on me. I lean against a wall, clutching the phone, and a moment later, it vibrates.

"Yeah?" I say.

Jane blurts, "He's not there."

My heart sinks because that either means he's alive, or...he didn't make it.

"Did they release the names of the ones who...of the victims?"

"No, they couldn't tell me. HIPAA law and all that."

I understood. I did, but fuck, if I wasn't nauseous not knowing.

"Okay. Okay," I breathe.

"Think positive thoughts. He's fine. I know it," Jane says. "Luke's invincible."

I move through the double doors and repeat that over and over until it's all I can hear.

And yet, I still don't believe it. I need concrete proof to continue to exist in this life. I need to know even if he doesn't return to me.

"Jane," I ask, suddenly thinking of something. "Do you have Lex's number?"

"Whyever would I have that man's number," she replies, sounding guilty. But I know her all too well. Lex and my sisters were whispering that night after returning home from the stakeout, and I know phone numbers were exchanged.

They just can't help themselves.

They collect weirdos like they collect romance novels.

I sigh. "Give it to me. I need his help."

———

Lex shows up to my house later that night with two hardshelled cases in hand. Eliza had successfully delivered her baby girl a couple hours after Seth had arrived, and I finally got to go home after meeting baby Fiona.

I'm exhausted and aching, but my worry is keeping me up. I know I look like a mess, bloodshot eyes, rumpled clothes, hair standing every which way. But if Lex notices my dire state, he says nothing.

"Ah, so pleased to have gotten your call," he says. "I love breaking the law," he adds with a flourish, and I shush him while ushering him into my living room.

"Keep it down," I say, feeling nervous and thrilled all at

the same time. I can't believe I'm doing this and yet, here I am.

A criminal. Well, a soon-to-be criminal. If I end up in jail over this, it will be worth it. There have been no new reports on who the victims were and it's driving me crazy.

Lex hands me a case and I open it, seeing a laptop inside. I pull it out and set it on the coffee table.

"You sure you want to do this, Ellie-Belly?" he asks me, and I shake my head.

"Absolutely not. There is no way I'm going to hack into the police servers to find out if Luke's name is in there," I say, while turning the laptop on. "It's illegal and unethical and I don't condone it."

Lex rolls his eyes and shoves a green Airhead into his mouth.

"Whatever you say," he says as he chews sloppily and begins clacking away on his keyboard. My eyes don't leave the screen, even though I can't even tell what's being done. This man is scarily efficient.

"Would you like to sit on my lap while I do this? I wouldn't mind." Lex asks and I scoot a little farther away from him. I was almost on top of him, my heart racing with worry and nerves and *hope*.

Lex's fingers pause and then start up again. He pulls his lip ring into his mouth and then he's punching away at the keys again before sighing. Each movement makes my heart sputter and spin.

After what feels like an eternity, he finally stops and meets my gaze.

My heart drops and I breath out, "Tell me."

"He's alive. Or at least he's not listed as one of the deceased."

"Oh my god," I say, deflating like a balloon being pricked with a needle. "Oh my god. Thank you."

"Yes, you're welcome," Lex says, powering down his computer and shoving it back into his case. "It was eerily easy to hack into those servers. I should probably warn the police...."

But I don't hear his rambling because Luke's alive. He's not dead. I have a chance. A chance.

"Can you track him?" I blurt, interrupting something Lex was saying.

"Um, you told me you didn't want me to do that, so no."

I shake my head, feeling insane. "Never mind. That's crazy. I'm feeling crazy."

"Why don't you just call him?" Lex says, sounding ridiculously reasonable.

I stare at my phone and then, with shaking fingers, press Luke's name. It rings and rings and finally goes to an automated voicemail.

"He's not answering."

"Hm," Lex says. "Maybe he's busy."

Yes, but busy with what? With who? God, why isn't he here with me? That's where he should be. Not wherever else he is right now.

I think on this for two entire days, calling him endlessly and yet never hearing from him. I spend my time panicking and brooding.

"Okay, it's been two days since we found out Luke is alive," Lex says, putting his feet on the coffee table and leaning back. He shakes a box of Nerds into his mouth, and they crunch unattractively between his teeth. "And still, you mope."

"Yes, well, despite all my efforts, he still hasn't contacted me," I reply, stroking the hem of the shirt I'm wearing, it's the one he'd bought me after the cave tour in Colorado.

"That's very true, but maybe his phone broke. Not everyone has a Diablo at their disposal."

"Why are you here again?" I ask, nudging his feet off of my furniture.

"You're a sad human. I am here to keep you company."

"You're stealing shit from me, aren't you?" I ask, and Lex scoffs.

"You have no shit to steal," he says, then sits up a little taller. "Unless you have little gems hidden here and there. You do, don't you? Should I look behind light sockets? Or perhaps you have a false wall somewhere. Air vents?"

"Oh Jesus, you're going to snoop until you find something, aren't you? Then you're going to rob me."

He leans back and unloads more Nerds into his mouth.

Around a full mouth, he mumbles, "The only thing I've stolen is your heart."

"You have not. I barely tolerate you."

Okay, well, I don't know what's happened to me over the past couple weeks, but my life has become extremely messy. I haven't bothered to clean house either. Shit is everywhere.

"Since he isn't answering his phone, I say you show up at his brother's place again and see if you can talk to him."

"I'm slightly afraid of his brother. He will crush me. You haven't seen him up close, he's built like a tanker truck and scowls a lot."

He eyes me again. "You're very immature for a doctor."

"I know. You've said so a million times."

"It's refreshing to know that degrees don't buy common sense."

I sink down on the piano bench and glance at the phone in my lap.

Suddenly, the doorbell rings, and I just slump down and press my head against the keys. The sound of discorded notes floats through the air as I close my eyes. I'm not going to answer it. I have gotten my hopes up a thousand times, thinking it was him on my doorstep when it was just some package delivery.

I have no motivation to actually get up and look, only to be disappointed all over again.

"Oh, hello there," Lex says. "You must be Luke. I can see why Elliot has been such a mess. You are a very attractive specimen. Very fine, indeed."

I stand up so quickly that my knees knock against the lip of the piano, and I fall backward over the bench onto my ass. And then I'm scrambling toward the door, half walking, half crawling.

"Oh yes, well, I did offer to fuck him, but he turned me down. Said I wasn't his type. Now I know why. My feelings aren't even hurt about it."

"*Luke*," I shout, slamming into Lex and knocking him out of the way.

And there he is on my front porch in his torn jeans, tightly fitted grey shirt, and a beanie slung low over his forehead. God, he looks good. So fucking good, and alive.

"Hey there, Doc," he says, his hands in his pockets.

"You're here," I say, my voice cracking slightly.

Luke pulls off his hat and runs a hand through his hair. "Yeah. Your sisters told me you were worried. And you know, I got your texts." He eyes Lex and rolls his lips between his teeth. "You busy now? Or should I come back?"

"No, no, Lex was just leaving."

"Not without my Nerds, I'm not," he says and skips over to the coffee table and swipes them up. "Now I can go. Bye, Ellie-Belly. Call me sometime so we can hang out."

He waggles his fingers at me, and then he's pushing past Luke and bounding down the front steps, leaving Luke and I to face one another in this wide-open space.

"You're here," I say again because I'm apparently stuck on repeat.

"I am."

"I didn't expect you." I clear my throat and stuff my hands into my pockets. "Would you like to come in? There are still some beers in the fridge that belong to you."

"Yeah. That would be cool," Luke says, following me into the kitchen and leaning against the wall. I open the fridge and pull out the beers I couldn't bring myself to get rid of. I'd kept them, just in case he came back.

But he's not really back, is he? I don't know what he is, but he's here.

He's *here*.

My hand shakes as I hand him a bottle, and he notices because his eyebrows lower just a fraction.

"Who was that guy again?" he asks, popping the top off his bottle.

"A...friend? I don't really know how to classify him."

I don't really want to talk about Lex when Luke is standing right in front of me, wetting his lips and looking so fucking beautiful.

"Did you fuck him?"

"*God* no," I say as I run a hand through my disgusting hair. Oh, why didn't I shower today? "No, there's only been you, Luke. In so very, very long."

My voice breaks again, and I blink rapidly.

"You okay, Eli?" he asks.

And I can't find the words. They're stuck in my throat.

"I thought you were dead," I croak as I swallow down the lump in my throat.

I will not cry in front of him.

"Nah, Eli. I'm right here," he says, and then he sets his beer down and steps toward me.

Oh god, he's so close, I can smell him. I can reach out and touch him.

I tremble at the proximity, and then he gently takes my hand. He presses my palm to his chest and moves it up to his neck, right where his pulse point is.

And I feel it, the thundering of his heart.

Alive. He's alive.

"Luke," I whisper, and then my hand grasps onto his neck tightly, and I'm pulling him into me. My lips crash onto his, and he stiffens in shock.

And for one moment, one *horrendous* moment, I think he'll push me away, but he doesn't. He just groans loudly and pulls me right up against him. His tongue wastes no time sliding into my mouth, rubbing against mine, and I am helpless to do anything but melt into him.

I want him.

I want to *feel* him.

I want him on me, all around me, inside of me.

My hands grasp onto his head, my fingers threading through his hair as I tilt my face and lick my way further into his mouth. The depraved sounds we're making, they're filthy.

My hips roll against his hard cock, and I feel that pressure between my legs, and I want more. God, I've missed this, missed him.

What had I been thinking pushing him away when it could have been like this the entire time?

"Eli," he grunts as I paw at the bottom of his shirt, yanking it up. "Wait."

"No, no waiting. You've been gone so long," I mutter and pull his shirt over his head. And then my lips are back on his, and he's back to fucking my mouth as he presses me into the wall.

"Eli, wait," he says, but I cut him off, smashing my mouth to his. Now that I have him, I'm never letting him go again. There will be no more waiting, no more games.

No. There is only this. Right here.

"I thought I'd lost you—lost what's *mine*. No more waiting. Bedroom. Now," I say between kisses.

He groans his acceptance, reaches down, and hefts me up. My legs wrap around his waist as he carries me down the short hallway and into our bedroom.

Ours.

That's what it always was. I was deluding myself saying otherwise.

The moment he crashed into my life, he was mine.

He gently lowers me onto the mattress and both his hands bracket my torso as he stares down at me. Something flashes through those hazel depths. Lust, need, and an emotion I can't recognize. Because I can't even think past this insatiable hunger for him.

My hands move to his face, and I lean up and capture his mouth again, and he groans against me. I can feel the need vibrating within me.

I fumble with the shirt I'm wearing, but I'm trembling too hard to actually take it off. Who has time for clothing? Luke was right, it feels like a prison right now. I'm going to just walk around naked when he's around so I can just sit on him whenever I feel like it, without any hindrance.

"Let me," Luke says, peeling it right over my head. "I've had dreams of this," he adds. But I don't have time to really process it. I just keep kissing him, breathing his essence into me. He's so good, always so good. My hands move from his back up to his hair, and I clutch him to me.

"Please," I mutter against his mouth. "Luke. Fuck me."

"Oh shit," he whispers as he arches against me, and I let out a needy gasp.

"Need you," I tell him between kisses, my one hand fumbling with the button on his pants. He leans back, and I whimper, our lips disconnecting with a pop, but I'm placated when he rips his pants off and then mine.

"Lube," I say, managing to think clearly for just one second before my thoughts are consumed with just him.

He fumbles for it on the nightstand and then falls back onto me, his mouth melting into mine again.

"Now," I say as I push on his shoulders, rolling us over. My thighs are bracketing his, and I let my hands wander across his heaving chest. I reach for the lube, dribbling some on the tip of his straining cock, and lower my fist down his hard length, spreading the lube, and he moans, his eyelids fluttering.

And because I can't stop myself, because I'm so fucking *thirsty*, I lean down and press my mouth against his again.

"I'm going to fuck you, Luke," I say, licking my way across his lips. "You're going to fill me so good."

"Fuck," he gasps as I lower myself onto him. My front hole taking him in, inch by delicious inch.

God, it feels so good to be stuffed full like this. It's been years since I've had a cock inside of me.

And it feels so right because it's him.

He's here.

I take him all the way to the hilt and then bring myself to his very tip before impaling myself once more. He's filling me, stretching me, leaving his mark inside of me. I memorize each thrust, gasp, and moan to replay when I lie awake at night. I'm never forgetting this.

Never.

"Eli," Luke says, reaching up, his thumbs brushing against my wet cheeks. "Don't cry. Is this okay? Do you feel good?" I nod frantically and ride him harder.

"Missed you." It's all I can say. It's all that needs to be said at this moment. He has to know. He has to know how much this means to me. What I'm giving him. What he means to me. I need to tell him, but I can't think. I'll tell him when I can form words again. No more keeping things inside. I'm going to be open from here on out.

I clutch onto him, my mouth never leaving his. My tears mix with our sweat as he bends his knees and fucks into me.

"Fuck, you feel so good," he growls, running his hands over my shoulders, and down my back. He grasps onto my hips, his fingertips leaving lasting impressions on my skin.

When we crest, we do it together.

He moans into my mouth as he releases into me and I spasm around him, and then we kiss ourselves lazily off the precipice.

We don't let go, even after we're done. I just keep him inside of me, never wanting to separate from him again.

"Luke," I say, resting my forehead against his.

Those hazel eyes meet mine, and I gently cradle his face in my hands.

"Don't ever leave me again," I whisper. "I know I was wrong and that I pushed you away, but always come back. Please. I need you. Be patient with me."

He clutches me to him and pulls my lips back to his. We stay like that for ages, just eating at each other. We're hungry for it. For what this could be. For what this is.

When we finally pull apart, my lips are swollen, and my cheeks are abraded by the scruff on his face.

"Will you stay?" I ask, and Luke runs his hand up and down my back.

"If you want me to."

"I want you to," I reply, pressing my head against his chest and listening to his heartbeat.

"I'm sorry. I'm so very sorry," I say, my fingers clutching onto him.

"Me too," he replies.

"I behaved abominably," I lean up and see his eyes drooping. I push forward and press my mouth to his. "Will you ever forgive me?"

"Already did," he says and then yawns. "But we can talk more about it later. Fuck, you wore me out. How do you always manage that?"

I hover over his face, and my thumbs caress his flushed cheeks. He looks so angelic when he's sleepy.

"You're such a good boy," I whisper, and he smirks as his eyes close.

A moment later, he's snoring, and I smile and tuck myself against him.

I should clean myself up, but I don't want to. I just want to hold him a little longer.

———

I wake up on top of him, and immediately my mouth searches for his. It's like some kind of heat-seeking missile and it knows its target. Luckily, Luke doesn't seem to mind because he clutches me to him and opens for me.

"Morning," he grumbles as he grasps onto my ass and arches his hips up. He maneuvers his body and slips his cock inside of me, stretching me once more.

"Morning," I say and kiss him until we're both feverish and panting.

"Want you again," he says and I nod my acceptance.

He rolls us over, our lips never breaking contact, and he's on his forearms, fucking into me. His hard abdomen slides against mine as his tongue licks its way through each corner of my mouth. I know that usually I'm the one in control, but I love this, letting him take from me, lying here vulnerable and yet feeling so utterly safe.

"Fuck, you're so hot. I'm not going to last," he moans against my mouth, and I clutch onto him tighter as he arches into me over and over.

His grunts mix with my moans, and we come in a matter of minutes.

His forehead presses against mine as he catches his breath.

"Knew kissing you would be this good," he says, kissing me again.

He pulls out of me and falls to his back, and I feel his absence immediately. I scramble over to him and press myself against his side.

"Can't unstick yourself, huh?" he asks with a smug smile. "Knew I'd catch that mouse."

"I have accepted my fate," I say, and my hand slides over his chest.

"I gotta get showered," he says, but makes no move to get up. We lie like that for a bit longer, just lazily petting each other and sneaking in soft kisses. But even still, the reality of the past two weeks sneaks up on me.

"What did you do when you were...away from me?" I ask tentatively.

"Worked overtime," he says, running a hand across his lips. "Worked so I didn't have to think."

I press my nose into his armpit and then peek up at him. "I'm sorry."

"You said that, Eli. No need for a repeat."

"Yes, but I want you to know I mean it."

"I know you do. Everyone told me how miserable you were. Amanda sent pictures."

I sigh, feeling my cheeks redden. "Yes, Amanda made it very apparent that she was upset with me. She'd text you in front of me as some sort of torture technique."

He chuckles. "I'd rather it had been you texting me."

"I know. I messed up. I hate messing up, but I did it anyway, and I did it extraordinarily well."

He eyes me, "Nah, I like you messy."

That is not at all what I said, but he's rolling away from me, and I'm scrambling after him. I remind myself of the dog I had growing up. Marley would follow me everywhere. He would even find me in the bathroom and stare at me while I took a shit.

That's what I'm turning into, an overeager mutt.

I clutch onto the sheets, anchoring myself in place. I will not watch Luke take a shit. I have boundaries.

I hear the water turn on, and then Luke emerges in the

doorway. His arms reach up, and he grasps onto the door frame, and I just take him in.

I want to go to him, but he might want his space.

Fuck, I hope he doesn't want space. Is this some kind of quantum entanglement? No matter how far apart we are, we can't help but be drawn to each other? Oh god, let him feel the same way, this incredible pull between us.

"Can I ask you a question?" he asks, and I nod.

"Can you get pregnant?"

I wrench my eyes up to meet his. "No, I had my tubes tied. But I did have my eggs frozen. One day I'd like kids."

He wets his lips and tilts his head.

"So, we can do surrogacy?" he asks.

Oh my dear lord.

I clear my throat and nod. "Yeah, Luke. We can."

"Little Elliots grumpin' around like little Eeyores. Can't fuckin' wait."

I meet his stare because this is us discussing the future. This gives me hope that this isn't temporary. "Or little Lukes, causing chaos," I add.

He grins, and his abs flex deliciously.

"Join me in the shower, Eli," he grunts, and I rise off the bed with dignity. I do not scramble toward him like an eager child.

My foot catches on the end of the rug near the sink, and I tumble into him. We topple under the hot spray, and Luke holds me to his broad chest. We breathe heavily from the near calamity of almost smashing right through the glass, and then our mouths crash into each other. And I am insatiable.

I cannot get enough.

I'm clawing at him, licking into him with sloppy, open-mouthed kisses. Luke groans as he grabs onto my ass and lifts me up, pressing me against the wall.

My legs move around his waist, and I feel his cock right there.

"Luke," I moan as he sinks into my front hole again.

"So good," he mutters against my lips as he starts to move. "You're always *so good*."

We slip and slide against each other as he pounds into me. He's so strong, holding me up without much effort, and I am not a small person.

"How are you so perfect?" I moan against his mouth.

His hazel eyes meet mine, and his fingers grip against my ass.

"Nah, Eli. You're the one always bringing me to my knees."

My heart flutters and I smash my mouth back onto his as he rams up into me.

When we're finally done, Luke reaches for some soap and half-heartedly washes me. I just sink into him, my head against his shoulder.

I could die happy right now.

When we finally move from the shower, Luke towels me off, but it's interrupted by me pressing kisses to his mouth.

He chuckles as I chase after his lips.

"Stay with me today," I mutter. "All day. Let's do this again and again."

"Eli," he says, licking into my mouth. "I have to go home. My ma was worried."

"Oh, of course," I say, disappointment surging through me.

Luke eyes me, and his thumb brushes over my bottom lip. "Come with me."

"I have to check my calendar," I reply, but I'm already

walking into our room to pack. "Will we be staying the night?"

Luke smirks. "Thought you had to check your schedule?"

I look at him over my shoulder and then move back toward him, my hands attaching themselves to his chest and running up his neck.

"Don't listen to me. I go where you go from now on. I'm never letting you out of my sight again."

CHAPTER FOURTEEN

LUKE

Elliot is insatiable. It's like an emotional dam broke, and now he can't keep his hands off of me. Hence, the reason he suddenly pulled off the freeway. Then he tapped his fingers on the steering wheel, almost like he was debating something, before he groaned and crawled right over the console, straddling my lap.

His hands are currently in my hair, his hips grinding against mine.

Not that I'm complaining. I like this unhinged, untethered side of him. It makes me just want him more.

If that's even possible.

The past two weeks were fucking misery. I worked myself to the bone to stay away from him. My brother was worried about me and even drove out to the pipeline to make sure I was taking care of myself, that I was eating and such, but mostly just checking that I was still alive.

Nah, I was alive. I just *felt* a little dead inside.

Then the explosion happened. I'd been on break, napping in my car when I felt it—the rumble, the heat, and the shouts of panic.

Fuck, in that moment, I felt like I'd been given a second chance, because that could have been me down there.

It's why I came back to him. I wasn't ready to leave this life without fighting for something I truly want. Ever since that moment, I feel like my heart has completely reset. Everything seems...brighter and better, especially now that I have Elliot.

Although, fuck, we really should talk. We need to communicate better and come to an agreement about what this is, but it's so hard to think when his mouth is on mine.

"Let's just get a hotel," he says as he bites down on my earlobe, and hell, I'm tempted to spend the day in his arms under the blankets. But we're an hour out from my parents' place, and my ma and older brother have been texting me, waiting for my arrival. I can't put this off.

If I don't show up, they'll track me down.

When they'd heard about the pipeline accident, they were frantic. I need to show up so they can see that I'm okay. Plus, it's been a while since I've been out there, and I miss them. Just like it is for Elliot, my family is everything to me.

"Nah, Eli, I can't."

He sighs, and his bottom lip juts out.

I snort a laugh. "You pouting?"

"Absolutely not. I'm a doctor."

"So, what, now doctors can't pout, huh?"

"Not this doctor. I'm dignified and civilized, and fuck...I hate to admit it, but I just want you again. Tell me I can still have your ass, even though I've let you inside me."

I press my mouth to his again and arch my hips up.

"'Course you can, Doc. You know all you need to do is use that deep bossy voice of yours and I'm like putty in your hands. Last night didn't change anything for me. I'll still bend over for you."

He huffs. "I'm not bossy, I'm dominant. There's a distinct difference."

I just smirk at him as his hands slide across me, mapping each groove and slope of my chest and shoulders. "You're so hot. Have I told you that?"

"Yeah, once or twice," I reply, and then I flex a little so he can admire all my hard work.

He squeezes my biceps, sighs, and then slowly unpeels his hands from me. "Are you sure I can't convince you to just take a small detour?"

"Damn, Eli. I want to, but I gotta go home."

"Of course," he says and then moves over the console, showing me his tight ass through those fancy pants of his. I take a nice long look at it too.

When he's firmly planted in his seat, he turns his head toward me, and our eyes meet. Those dark fucking eyes, they get me every time. I reach down and press the heel of my palm against my aching dick.

"Do not touch it," he says, eyeing me, before sliding his eyes back to the road. It's started raining, and the pitter-patter fills the cabin as he pulls back onto the freeway.

"You gonna make me?" I ask, and he nods.

"I am."

Oh hell. Well, now I can't wait. I want inside him again. I want him inside me. I really just want to find a way to merge us into one person, so we're never apart again.

I glance down at my dick and then over at Elliot. Should

probably distract myself with other things; thinking of all the ways he could fuck me isn't helping matters.

"We should talk about where this is going, yeah?" I say, reaching out and grabbing onto his hand.

He swallows and nods. "Of course."

"So, where's this going, Doc?"

He shifts in his seat, his eyes moving from me to the road ahead of him.

"I'd like this to be a relationship. A serious, monogamous one."

"Do you?" I ask, feeling my heart rate increase.

"Yes."

That fucking word.

"You sure?"

"Yes."

I roll my eyes. "I'd like a little more than that, Doc. I'm feeling the need for romance."

He sighs. "Fine. I think you're...Luke, you're everything I didn't know I needed. You came into my life during a time that I thought I was happy being alone, but I realize now that I had no idea what happiness was before you. You constantly pull me out of my comfort zone and I'm still reeling from it all, but I don't want to go back to the way it was before. I want to stay and walk through this life with you. Only you."

"Aw, Eli. We're getting married. That's where this is going," I tell him, and he scoffs, thinking I'm joking.

I don't joke about that shit.

He shifts in his seat. "As you know, I am a little wary because of what happened with Andrew."

"I'm not that asshole," I bite out.

"I know you're not," he says. "He always made me feel less

than, but you...you've never made me feel that way. I'd like to keep you if you let me."

"I could be kept," I say with a smile. Yeah, I already hear wedding bells. I'm thinking white suits and doves. Maybe some guns and fireworks to really set the mood.

Elliot wets his lips and then glances over at me. "I like you a lot, Luke."

"Like you too, Doc."

"I'm not the easiest person to get along with."

"Duh."

He huffs. "And there's the matter of my sisters."

"Nah, they're cool. I like them."

"Andrew never liked them."

"Well, he has terrible taste."

"He does."

We sit in silence, and I press against my hard dick. Well, that conversation didn't help it go down. It's still raring to go. Asshole. Apparently, thoughts of getting married to Elliot only make it harder.

———

Thirty minutes later, we're pulling into a nearly empty Tesla charging station, and I glance at the battery life on the touch screen and snort.

Fucker is pretending like his car needs a charge when he could make it to my parents' house just fine.

"We need to charge, just in case," he says, his cheeks flushed, his breathing a little erratic.

"Do we now?" I ask, smirking at him.

"Yes," he replies as he parks at the far end of the lot where no one else is. Then he hops out, and I watch him pull the charger out and push it into the port. It's still raining, so he shields his face as he moves forward. But instead of getting back in the driver's seat, he slips into the back, his fingers already working open the buttons of his shirt.

This guy wants to fuck. But I'm going to make him ask for it. Ask for it all polite, too.

I look through the front windshield and see that the rain has made it nearly impossible for anyone to see in. It's coming down hard, pounding the sides of the car. When we get to my parents', there's going to be so much mud.

Fuck yeah.

"Get back here," Elliot snaps, pulling his shirt open and exposing his chest to me. I glance over my shoulder and take him in.

Yeah, he has a nice fucking body, gonna lick it all over later.

"You gonna ask me nicely, Eli?"

He arches an eyebrow at me. "Please, Luke. Get back here. I'd like to sit on your big fat dick."

"When you say it like that," I mutter, my cock jumping in my pants; it knows when it's being talked about. I push my door open and move to get in the back, but I'm too hasty and knock my forehead on the corner of the fancy falcon-wing door.

"Fuck," I say, plopping onto the backseat, pressing my hand against the wound. Damn, that stings.

"Seriously?" Elliot says, pushing his pants down, exposing himself to me. Everything else is suddenly forgotten.

Who fucking cares if I'm bleeding out when he's stripping for me? He's the sexiest piece of sex I've ever had sex with in my entire life.

"God, you look deranged," he says when I pull my hand

away. My fingers and palm are bloody as Elliot straddles my lap, unzips my pants, and pulls me out.

"You look like some kind of serial killer," he adds, and then that asshole smears my blood right across my cheek.

"You're so fucking horny for it," I breathe.

"It's completely unsanitary. It's barbaric," he says. His tongue darts out and wets his lips. Then he reaches over, grabs a small packet of lube from his pants pocket, and dribbles it on me.

"I am fucking civilized," he says as he sinks down onto me, "And you look just like that first day we met." He smears more blood across my face with two fingers, and hell, I'm moaning like an animal in heat. "I'll clean you up later, make you fucking respectable, but right now..." He slides up my hard length and then slams back down onto me, the car rocking beneath us. "Right now, I'm going to fuck you."

My eyes roll back in my head. "Hell yeah."

My fingers dig into the bare skin of his waist as he rides me, his tongue licking up my neck.

And hell, if this isn't the hottest thing I've ever done.

———

We make it to my parents' house an hour later than I'd expected, mostly because Elliot kept pulling over on off-ramps to plant that sly mouth right on mine.

"Is this going to be a thing forever?" I'd asked him on our last detour.

"Probably. A switch has been flipped on, and I can't turn it off. It's stuck," he sighed and then kissed me again.

"Not complaining, Doc," I'd said, and he blushed.

"Is this it, right up here?" Elliot asks, interrupting my train of thought. He drives his Tesla down the dirt road, and in the distance, my parents' two-story house makes an appearance. They own a lot of land out here, giving us the freedom to do whatever the fuck we want. On one side of the house is a large garage, and on the other are a few ATVs.

He should see all the fun shit we have inside too. I'll show him my gun safe later. Show him how to shoot one too.

Damn, that's hot.

"Yep. This is it."

He shifts in his seat, and I squeeze his hand a little.

"You nervous."

"Of course I am. This is your family. What if they don't like me? Then you'll be forced to break up with me."

"Nah, not going to happen. They'll love you."

He doesn't seem convinced. Well, he'll just have to fucking live and learn then.

I point to the left and say, "See that garage over there? I have a truck in there I built from the ground up. I want to show it to you when we're done with everything. Want to take you for a ride."

He nods, not really listening to me. Asshole is still worried. I lean over and press a kiss to his cheek, and he leans into it, just fucking melts into me. He's no longer restrained, and I love it.

When he parks in front of the house, the front door opens, and I see my ma and dad move onto the front porch. My dad is wearing some work coveralls, and my ma has a kitchen towel draped across her shoulder, her hands on her hips. A second later, my older brother, Liam, and his wife Anne step out behind them.

Elliot turns to look at me. "That's Liam?" he asks me. "And Anne?"

"Yep. The one you thought I was cheating on you with."

He flushes red at that, and I pull his lips to mine again. Can't help it.

"You're so damn cute."

He moves to kiss me again, but then Liam is knocking on our window, a crazed smile on his face. Fucker always likes to interrupt. Lives for it, in fact.

"We should get out, or he might break through the window," I joke, and Elliot's eyes widen.

A chuckle slips out of me, and I nudge him. "Come on, Eli. It'll be fine."

"We'll see," he mutters, opening his door and stepping outside.

As soon as I step foot on the gravel pathway, Liam pulls me into a hug, and we slap each other's backs.

"You've been absent for a long fucking time, bro."

"Had something to keep me occupied."

Liam eyes Elliot, a knowing gleam in his eyes. "Seems so. Now, tell me about this fancy-ass car, huh? It was so fucking quiet that it just crept up on us. Sneaky," Liam says, peering in the window and pressing his hands against the glass.

"Would you like to see inside?" Elliot says, clearing his throat.

"Hell yeah," he says and then stares at the door handles, unsure of how to open them. He presses his finger against it, and then his brows furrow.

"A fucking puzzle, this is," he mutters.

I chuckle as Elliot shows my brother how to open the door by pressing into it and pulling it out.

"Fancy," Liam says and slides in behind the wheel. He runs his hands over the steering wheel and whistles. "First Whit and now this dude. My bros sure know how to pick 'em."

I eye Elliot, and he rolls his lips between his teeth.

"You're welcome to drive it if you'd like."

"Yeah?" he says, and I cock my head at Elliot. Fucker trying to bribe his way into the family. There's no need.

"Want to meet my parents while Liam fucks around in here?" I ask Elliot and then tilt my head toward the porch where my ma and dad are whispering, their heads bent low, their eyes shifting between Elliot and me.

Elliot gives me a clipped nod. "Yes."

We leave Liam to continue fiddling with the Tesla as Elliot and I stride up the gravel walkway, our feet crunching softly. I eye Elliot and notice how his eyebrows have dropped, and his gaze has become more serious. His mouth seems to be taking in gulping breaths.

"Luke," Ma exclaims as we walk up the wooden steps to the porch. She wraps me in a hug, and I pull her into me. "I'm so glad you're here. We were so worried."

"I'm fine, Ma. Just fine. See?" I pull away and give my dad a fist bump.

"But your head."

"Just got caught on something," I explain and Elliot flushes crimson. Probably remembering what he did to me, smearing the blood around my face like an animal. He bandaged me up real nice though, all professional and shit, just like the first time.

Ma's eyes move from me to Elliot, and she smiles softly. "And who's your friend?"

"Guys, this is Elliot...or Eli as I call him. He's a doctor."

My ma turns toward him fully and grasps his hands. "Eli, so nice to meet you. Luke has been mysteriously absent, and now we know why."

Elliot swallows roughly and glances up at me. And I can't help but just smile at him.

When Ma finally lets go of Elliot's hands, he turns toward Anne, who is leaning against a porch post, and a pink blush tints his cheeks. He's probably remembering when he thought I was dating her. Like I could get over Elliot so easily.

Pfft.

"Hi, Eli. I'm Anne," my sister-in-law says, holding out her hand.

Elliot takes it tentatively and shakes it. "Nice to meet you."

She cocks her head to the side and then asks, "I'd like to paint you one day. You're gorgeous."

Elliot's cheeks darken even further, and I ruffle Anne's hair. "Back off, sis. Making him nervous."

She rolls her eyes and then sighs. "It was just an offer. If you want to give it a go, just give me a call."

Elliot nods, and my ma clears her throat.

"Well, I made cookies," she says and then looks at me pointedly. "And you will not eat them all, Luke. Save some for Elliot."

"'Course I'll save some. Sharing is caring," I tell her as we trudge inside. Liam trots in a moment later, shooting off questions about our trucks and then going on a tangent about electric cars. I do my best to listen between shoving my face with cookies. How does Ma make them so good? What kind of magic is in these? I gotta get the recipe and try to duplicate them.

A few times, I peek over at Elliot and see him talking with my parents, and even Anne, and my heart is so fucking full. He fits right in, even though he looks all stern and serious. I can tell he's still very nervous.

Our eyes meet, and I waggle my eyebrows at him. His eyes narrow back at me.

My dick twitches, and I move behind the counter to hide my erection. Damn him and that serious look he gives me.

"So that potato gun..." Liam says, interrupting my wayward train of thought. "I blasted some shit up with it the other day, and damn, bro, you should have seen it. I was thinking we could—"

"Excuse me," a voice says to my right, interrupting what Liam was about to say.

The two of us turn to face Elliot, and he blushes slightly.

"I'm sorry for interrupting, but could I speak to you, Luke."

I shove the rest of my cookie in my mouth and nod.

"Sure thing," I say, pushing up from the counter and eyeing my brother. "Hold that thought. You know I'm down to blow shit up."

Liam smirks at me as I follow Elliot down the short hallway, and when we're far enough away that no one can see us, he stops abruptly and faces me.

He straightens his shoulders and meets my gaze with a serious one of his own.

"What's up, Eli. You okay?"

"Why aren't you touching me?" he blurts, and my eyebrows meet in confusion.

"Huh? I was just eating cookies...and shooting the shit...."

"Yes, I know. I can still see the crumbs on your shirt, but you haven't put your hands on me once since arriving. Are you...are you embarrassed by me?"

"What the hell?" I ask, standing up a little taller.

His voice lowers. "Is this because I'm trans? That's it, isn't it? I knew it. Knew this would happen...."

All of that assured posturing disappears, and he literally sags under the weight of his worry.

My eyes widen at the words coming out of his mouth because what in the hell is this dude talking about? I'm so fucking confused.

"Because Andrew would do this to me too, and I can't do it again, Luke. If you're ashamed of me in front of your family—"

I grasp onto his hand, and then I do the only sensible fucking thing.

I pull him back into the middle of the kitchen where everyone is waiting for us, spin him around, and smash my lips to his. I slip my tongue into his mouth and fuck into it.

He whimpers as I hold him to me.

Asshole thinks I'm ashamed.

Nah, I'm fucking proud I bagged this dude. I know how lucky I am.

When I finally unsuction myself from his face, Elliot is flushed, his lips are swollen, and, shit, I wished I'd done this in a bedroom because my dick is ready again. You'd think it'd be tired, but it has the stamina of a superhero.

Superman hearing with a Superman dick.

Silence permeates the space, and I turn toward my parents.

"He's mine," I say, because that just about sums it up. Nothing else needs to be said.

"*Thank god*. I was hoping," my ma says, grasping onto my dad's hand.

I run my hand up to the back of Elliot's neck and squeeze gently. There, now no one has to be wondering. Especially Elliot.

"And I'm trans," he suddenly blurts, his body stiffening

against mine as if he expects blowback. Like my parents are some sort of bigoted assholes.

"Oh, is that so? How wonderful. You're perfect," Ma says, then rushes over to him and pulls him into a hug. "Welcome to the family."

Elliot freezes, his hands hanging limply at his side as Ma crushes him to her, and then slowly, so fucking slowly, he embraces her.

He blinks over at me, shock on his face. That's right, Eli. Take a nice long look. You're stuck with us now.

"Tell me you want kids," Ma says to him, pulling away and beaming up at him.

"Yes."

"Joel, he wants kids," Ma beams, and I roll my eyes.

"We're going to do surrogacy," I tell her.

She gasps and clasps her hands together. "Oh, I cannot wait. They're going to be beautiful babies."

Elliot is just wide-eyed at this, blinking rapidly.

"Excuse me for a moment," he says, his voice hoarse. He nods once and then disappears down the hallway.

Of course, I follow him and find him in the bathroom, the door open just a crack. And the sight of him nearly breaks me. His shoulders are hunched, his hands clutching onto the edge of the counter, his eyes squeezed shut as he breathes deeply.

"Eli?" I say softly.

"She said I was perfect," he says, not opening his eyes.

I reach over and press a hand to his waist, "Yeah, 'cause you are."

"No one has ever said that about me before."

"Eli, I've told you that. You must have forgotten. So, I'll

say it again. You're absolutely perfect. Perfect as you are and perfect for me."

I wrap my arms around his waist and tuck my head into his neck. His eyes flick open, and our gazes meet in the mirror.

A small sob escapes his mouth, and as he swipes his fingers under his eyes, a small smile appears. I nibble my way across his neck, and he squirms against me. Ticklish little bastard.

Hell, all this wiggling makes me want to take him right here in this little bathroom, just bend him forward and slide right in. But we don't get a chance because my brother is suddenly pounding on the door.

"Alright, dudes. Enough crying. Can we fucking go now?" Liam shouts. "This mud don't wait. We're in a drought. That dry earth is just going to suck that shit right up!"

I sigh and wrench the door open.

"Alright, bro, what's the motherfucking plan?" I ask as I pull Elliot into me. He's still swiping at his eyes, the tip of his nose a little pink.

"Elliot, my man, good to have you," Liam says as he turns his hat backward. "And as an honorary member of the family, I was thinking we could do some mudding, maybe roll some shit, and then I want to show you two that potato gun I modified. Shit, it's gonna come in handy having a doctor in the fam...."

Elliot stiffens beside me and whispers, "What does he mean by *roll some shit?*"

Ah, Eli, you'll see. You'll see.

CHAPTER FIFTEEN

ELLIOT

"You gonna spank me, Doc?" Luke asks with a smile as I grasp onto the roll cage above me. We bounce over a hill and straight into a mud puddle with a sickening crash. The truck rumbles and shakes all around us, and I wonder what the hell he put this together with? Those welds he showed me earlier won't hold if he keeps this up. This machine is going to fall apart in a matter of minutes.

"Yes," I manage to say, my teeth rattling in my mouth. Luke van Beek's ass will be so red for subjecting me to this. This entire thing is treacherous and irresponsible. I am not having fun.

I am not.

A laugh escapes me, and I bite it back. I don't want to encourage this any more than I already have.

Luke chuckles and then slows to a stop. "You think I don't

hear you laughing, Eli, but I do. Superman hearing, remember?"

I sigh, unclutching my hands from the rollbar above me.

"It was a laugh of terror and dread," I lie.

"Fucker is havin' fun, just won't admit it," he mutters. "Now, I'm going to do you a favor. See that hill over there?"

I glance through the windshield and see a steep hill that looks terribly dangerous. Vehicles should not be attempting to mount that.

"I'm going to drive up that and hopefully make it to the top. It's never worked before but I'm not a quitter. So, I'm asking you now, Eli. You wanna ride there with me or get out?"

I eye the hill again and shake my head.

"Out," I say and unbuckle my seatbelt. It takes a second because it's locked into place, and when I'm finally free, I pull his head down toward mine and lick into his delicious mouth.

"Do not end up bleeding again," I say, pressing another soft kiss to his lips.

"Never," he says with an eye roll, but I don't believe him. Because if there is anything I have learned about Luke in the past two hours it's that he's the most reckless person I know. I don't even want to know what he and his brother have planned with the potato gun later.

I don't even know what a potato gun is. I can only imagine.

I hop out of the truck, and Luke waggles his eyebrows at me.

"Alright, stand back," he says, and he's off, and I watch in horror as the truck's tires skid and roll up that mountain. For a moment, I stop breathing because this is not safe. Not at all. He's going to get seriously hurt.

My mind is still reeling when Liam pulls up alongside me in another shoddily built truck and just leans out the driver's side.

His truck has no doors. I repeat. *No doors.*

There is also no roof. It looks like he sawed it right off.

"He'll be fine. He does this shit all the time, and that's what roll cages are for," Liam says, like that's reassuring. This man is not wearing a seatbelt, and I saw what he did with his truck earlier. This man has a death wish. I do not trust a word that comes out of his mouth.

"Oh *shiiiiiiit!*" I hear hollered in front of me, and my gaze is wrenched forward. I watch in alarm as Luke's truck tilts back and somersaults down the hill. Everything seems to move in slow motion as it bounces straight toward a gulley, and all I can hear is the cacophony of crushed metal blending with whoops from Liam beside me. When his truck finally comes to a stop on its side, everything just fades to white noise in my head.

Because Luke just rolled down a fucking hill in a rickety truck that he basically glued together.

My heart stops beating in my chest as I race toward where the crumpled truck lies. Oh my god, he cannot be hurt. Not when I just got him back. I scramble through some mud to get to him, water soaking the legs of my pants, and when I reach the driver's side door, a low chuckle hits my ears.

Luke emerges from the window, a long cut on his cheek.

"That was fucking awesome," he says with a smile.

My lips turn down in a scowl as Liam jogs over and fist bumps Luke, like this is just another ordinary day. Like he didn't just almost *die*.

"Luke van Beek," I snap. "What in the hell were you

thinking?" I ask, moving toward him and sliding my hands over his body. "You could have been seriously hurt."

"Nah, Doc. I'm fine."

"He's fine," Liam says, and I shoot him a withering glare.

"Liam, mind your own business," I say, and Liam's eyebrows fly right off his forehead. Good riddance.

"We need to patch you up," I say, turning back to Luke and pulling his head down a little lower so I can get a good look at the gash. It doesn't need stitches, but he may have a scar.

"I'm fine."

"Yes, you will be fine," I say and then lean forward and add on a whisper, "But your ass won't be when I'm through with you."

He shifts on his feet.

"Promise?" he asks.

"Yes."

He turns to his brother and smirks. "Eli's gonna wreck my ass when we get back."

Liam sticks his fingers in his ears, muttering under his breath, as my cheeks heat to epic proportions.

"Do not tell people our business, Luke."

He rubs at his neck, looking sheepish. Blood trickles down his cheek as he shrugs, "Yeah, you're right, shouldn't have said that. Just got excited. Maybe my brain is a little scrambled from all that."

My fingers fly up to his eyes, and I peer into them. They look fine. I doubt he has a concussion, but Jesus, this man is going to be the death of me.

"Didn't hit my head or nothing, Eli. Don't stress. Don't stress," he says. "Just a little disoriented."

I'm placated as I walk us back over to Liam's truck and

pull out a first aid kit from the glovebox. I bandage Luke up right where he's standing, and twenty minutes later, I watch in dismay as Luke and Liam work to put Luke's truck back onto all four wheels.

When they finally manage it, I eye the crumpled hunk of metal and arch an eyebrow.

"Gonna get in?" Luke asks me, and I sigh.

"I'd rather walk back," I mutter. "The passenger side is completely caved in."

"You could ride in my lap," Luke says, and I do not entertain that. I absolutely do not. I will not ride in someone's lap like a child.

But I still plant my ass right on his thighs the rest of the way home, even steer the rickety thing a little.

I have more fun than I care to admit.

When we arrive back at the house, Luke and Liam park their trucks outside, their clothes stained with mud and oil as they high-five each other and pull out a long, white contraption.

"What is that?" I ask as they chuckle to each other, looking way too nefarious for my comfort.

Oh, this cannot be good.

"The potato gun," they say in unison.

"Oh, and what do you do with this?" I ask.

"Come on, we'll show you," Luke says. "You're gonna love this."

———

"I did not love that," I say that night, curled into bed with Luke. He rests his head on my shoulder and looks up at me.

"You so did. You even shot the thing. It made you want to

howl at the moon, huh? Rip your shirt to shreds, claw at the earth?" he says, and I roll my eyes.

"It did not. It was dangerous and a little scary."

"You can deny it all you want, Eli, but I heard you. Heard that itty bitty howl come out of your mouth, just like a were-wolf cub."

I sigh and thread my fingers through his hair, tugging on it.

"Come on. Admit it, Doc. You loved it."

I love you, I think, but I don't voice it. I should, but part of me is afraid. It's so soon. Too soon.

So, instead, I just huff, and confess. "Yes."

Luke laughs and yawns at the same time.

"Fuck, I'm pooped. That thing you did in the shower wore me out."

I tug on his hair again, and he groans.

"Did you like it?"

"Duh, you can do that to me anytime, anywhere," he says, and then his eyes slip closed.

I just lie there for a few minutes, warm and safe in his childhood bed, thinking about a future with Luke until I drift off to sleep.

CHAPTER SIXTEEN

ELLIOT

Jane: The surprise is on the kitchen counter.

Kate: Mission accomplished.

Jane: I also left you celebratory drinks, just in case.

Eliza: I'm mad I couldn't come. This baby is killing me.

Me: Eliza, you're a mother now, you can't go sneaking around at all hours like you're used to.

Eliza: That's exactly why I have a husband, so he can watch the baby while I can go sneaking around at all hours.

"Who you texting?" Luke asks, eyeing my phone. I place it in my pocket and step out of the car.

We made it home from Luke's parents' place a little later than I expected, although I'm surprised by my restraint. I only pulled off to the side of the road twice to make out with him. It was a feat of epic proportions. My entire body was literally leaning into him as I drove. It was probably very, very unsafe. I should have my license revoked.

"No one," I reply, and Luke rolls his eyes.

"You're a bad liar. You're texting your sisters, huh? What are they sayin' about me?"

"Nothing," I reply as we walk into the house.

"They still mad about me leaving you?"

I scoff. "No, they're thrilled we're back together. They want to throw a party."

"Hm, I love parties," he says as he follows me into the kitchen, and just like Jane said, there it is.

"I have something for you," I begin, feeling suddenly nervous. I take the small box and hold it out to him. "Here."

Luke eyes it as I slip it into his palm.

"Wonder what this could be," he says and then pulls the top off slowly.

His lips turn up at the corners and he smirks at me. "Knew it. I'm a fucking mind reader, like Professor X."

I shift on my feet and arch an eyebrow at him. "So...?"

He holds up the small key to my house. "You gotta ask me first, Eli. Then I'll say yes."

I huff in exasperation. "Luke, will you move in with me?"

He sets the box down and rubs a hand over his jaw, making me wait.

"Just answer, yes or no," I snap. "I can handle the rejection if you don't want to live with me."

He chuckles at my little outburst, pulls me into his arms suddenly and lifts me up, setting my ass on the counter.

"Of course, it's a yes, Eli. We're getting married, remember?"

I run my hands through his hair and pull his face toward mine. "Fine."

He grins and presses a kiss to my mouth.

"You sure about this?" he asks, and I nod.

"Yes," I say, wrapping my legs around his waist and hooking my ankles together.

"That's good enough for me."

———

1 WEEK LATER

"I finally got all my shit from my parents' house, and I'm officially moved in," Luke says, flopping down on the couch and spreading his thighs wide.

I stare at them. I thought that this insatiable need to be near him, plastered against him, would fade, but it's only grown stronger each day. I'm a needy bitch, it seems. Although, Luke never complains. He seems to like feeding the monster inside of me.

"Come here, Eli," he says. "We need to celebrate the fact that I'm officially moved in."

I huff, pretending to debate it, but my body is already moving toward his.

I sink down onto his lap and he pulls me into his chest.

"How should we celebrate?" he asks, nuzzling my neck.

"We can do whatever you want," I reply, and he sucks on my earlobe.

"How about we watch all the *Die Hard* movies since we finished all the *Lethal Weapons*."

"Fine," I reply, leaning into him.

"And we could order some pizza and then fuck."

"Fine, but only if you manage to stay awake," I reply, and he snorts, squeezing me closer to him.

"God, I love you," he mutters, and my entire body stiffens.

"What?" I breathe, my heart rate accelerating, my entire body growing warm.

"I love you," Luke says, like he's said this a thousand times before. But he hasn't. This is the first time he's uttered those three words to me.

"Do you?"

"Duh," he says matter-of-factly, like I'm an idiot for not knowing.

I eye him, my brows furrowed. "But why?"

He throws his head back and laughs, like I said something hilariously funny. It's not at all humorous. I mean it, I need to know.

"Because you're fuckin' hot and smart and you make me laugh, and I dunno, Eli, I was drawn to you from day one. Can't really explain it, I just know that I don't want to be separated from you ever again. And that's enough for me. I'm a simple dude."

I swallow, my eyes stinging. "Thank you."

"Nah, Eli, don't thank me. But you could say you love me back. You do love me, don't you?"

I see a twinge of insecurity on his face, and I sniff.

"Of course I love you. I have for a while now."

"Just too chicken to say it first, huh?" Luke says and smiles at me.

"Yes. I was a big baby about it."

"I can be your daddy," he mutters, and I elbow him.

"Do not say that. That is not my kink."

He chuckles and then says, "I do have something I want to try though. It's something we haven't done yet, but I've fantasized about."

My eyebrows rise. "What is it?"

"I want you to eat my dick while I sit on those piano keys over there. Heard you playing and it makes me super horny. I jack off to the sound of it."

My breath hitches and I feel myself instantly flooded with heat.

"Yes."

He bites his lip, and I feel his cock hardening beneath me.

"Then when we're done, you can fuck me over the top of it, yeah? With that strap on that I fucking love?"

"Yes."

I'm sliding off of him and moving toward the bedroom with a singular purpose, but then a rattling at the window has the two of us freezing.

"You have got to be kidding me," I mutter, glancing at the window and seeing three shapes hovering right outside.

Oh, I know exactly who this is. Of course, they can't just leave us alone.

I storm to the door and fling it open and see the stunned, guilty looks on Jane and Kate's faces before turning toward Lex who waggles his fingers at me.

"You three couldn't help yourselves, could you?" I sigh.

A phone hangs limply in Jane's hand and she shrugs. "We all wanted to see how everything was going and you weren't answering the group texts. And since Eliza couldn't be here... we had to record it. This is a big deal, El. Luke has finally moved in...."

I pinch the bridge of my nose, the plan to fuck Luke on my piano dissipating before my very eyes. But what did I really expect? For peace and quiet?

I've obviously lost my mind if I thought I could have *that*.

"Well, you might as well come on in then since I know you

won't leave until you do. I know Luke wants to gossip with you guys."

They look at each other and then scramble out of the bushes and make their way to the front door.

Luke catches my eye and smiles but I refuse to make light of this.

A small laugh erupts from my mouth, but I swallow it down before anyone could hear it.

"Heard that," Luke whispers.

I glower in his general direction.

"You're hearing things."

"You're happy they're here," he tells me softly. "You can eat my dick later, yeah? Let's just hang with them for a bit. Family first, yeah, Eli?"

I nod and slide my fingers through his.

And fuck, if seeing everyone in my kitchen talking loudly doesn't make my heart swell just a little in my chest.

Who would have thought that I'd end up here?

Not me, that's who.

EPILOGUE

1 YEAR LATER

LUKE

We've been together for a year and I'm getting antsy because the wedding I've planned in great detail in my head isn't happening. Not yet at least. No, Elliot dodges the question every time I bring it up, almost like he doesn't want to marry me.

But that can't be right, because he's all over me the minute we're alone. And even most of the time when we're not. That asshole can't keep his hands off of me. So, he has to want to make this official, right? Because when I brought up marriage, he didn't outright tell me 'no'.

I'm going with it. This asshole and I are forever.

Elliot steps through the door looking like sex after a long day at work. He's unbuttoning his shirt as he walks into the kitchen where I'm cooking dinner, and I salivate just a little thinking about him naked.

My dick is already ready to go.

"Hey there, Doc," I say, watching as he moves in right beside me and nuzzles me with his cheek. I lean down a bit and press my lips to the crown of his head. He shifts even closer, and I tilt his face up, kissing him deeply until he's groaning against me.

When we finally pull apart, I'm breathing heavily, and Elliot's hair is mussed.

"How was work?" I manage to ask because the dinner is burning and I'm fucking starving. Sex will have to wait.

"Amanda was a nightmare today and Lex won't leave me alone. He keeps showing up randomly and hanging out like he has nothing better to do," he grumbles.

I chuckle at his narrowed stare.

"Want me to rough him up a bit? Make him leave you alone?"

Elliot's eyebrows rise and he shakes his head. "No, eventually he'll just go away. He's made friends with some of the patients, so I can't get rid of him just yet. Plus, he makes Amanda smile...sometimes. I'd hate to kill what little joy she may have residing inside of her."

Fucker thinks I don't know that Lex and him are friends. I even like the asshole. Lex has a way of growing on people— like mold, Elliot had said one day.

He moves toward the fridge and fills a cup with wine and then sips at it. He leans against the counter as he watches me cook.

"So, I was speaking to a colleague today who works at a surrogacy center and I wanted to discuss this with you before I chicken out."

I turn off the stove and fold my arms across my chest, tilting my head as I take in what he's trying to say. Elliot's been good about not keeping things inside like he used to. It took a while, but now he's mostly an open book.

"Gotta spell it out nice and slow for me, Eli. You saying you want to discuss having kids?" I ask, feeling my stomach clench in excitement.

"Well, yes."

I run a hand along my jaw and Elliot arches an eyebrow at me.

"Do you have anything you'd like to say about it, Luke? This does involve you."

"Yeah, well here's the thing. I can't have children without being married, Eli. I need to be respectable. What will people think when they don't see a ring on my finger, and I have a baby in my arms?"

He sighs, pinching the bridge of his nose. "Fine."

I push away from the counter. "You gonna ask me or am I gonna ask you?"

He grumbles under his breath, and I feel my spirits start to sink. Does this guy really not want to marry me? I live with him for fuck's sake and we're discussing babies.

"You don't wanna marry me, Eli? Just say it, yeah?"

His eyes snap open and he gapes at me. "*Of course* I want to marry you, Luke. It was supposed to be a surprise. That's all."

My eyebrows hit my hairline. "Huh?"

"This weekend, the trip to the beach, the hotel room..." he huffs. "I was going to ask you then."

My lips curl up in a grin and I drag him close to me. "Yeah?"

"Yes of course. We wouldn't want you to feel like you're not respectable."

I press my face into the side of his neck and inhale his scent.

"We're gonna get married."

He melts into me. "Yes."

I squeeze him tightly. "We're gonna have babies."

"Yes."

I grunt and slide my hands down his pants, gripping his ass. "You're making me horny with all this commitment and responsibility talk, Doc."

Elliot snorts but arches his hips into mine and I groan.

"Forget dinner," he says, bringing my mouth down to his. "I'm going to eat you instead." Then he takes a step back from me and his voice lowers to his commanding tone, "Clothes off. On the bed. Ass in the air. Now."

And fuck, if I don't sprint to the bedroom, shedding clothes like they're on fire.

4 MONTHS LATER

ELLIOT

"I cannot believe we pulled this off in four months," Eliza says, slumping against the doorframe. "We are goddamn miracle workers is what we are."

I glance at my soon-to-be mother-in-law and she grasps onto my hands. "You look so handsome. Luke is going to bawl like a baby when he sees you waiting for him at the end of the aisle."

"That man hasn't cried a day in his life," I say and Luke's mom swipes at her eyes.

"Trust me on this."

An hour later, I'm standing at the altar in a prim tux, my hands clasped in front of me as Luke makes his way around the corner, wearing an equally prim tux and looking so damn fine that I've lost the ability to breathe.

Our eyes meet and my heart feels like it could soar right out of my chest.

He swipes at his damp eyes as he makes his way closer and when he's mere inches from me, he pulls me right into his arms and presses a kiss to my mouth. I can feel and taste the tears slipping down his cheeks as he licks his way into me.

This kiss is totally inappropriate for the moment, but I let him do it anyway. How can I not? He's mine.

All mine.

When we finally pull away, we're both gulping for air.

"You look so hot," he says softly.

"So do you."

"This tux is scratchy," he whispers, and a small laugh escapes my lips.

"Well, I can peel you out of it later," I whisper back, and Luke's smile widens.

"You got it, Doc."

He sniffs and swipes at his eyes some more, and then we take our places in front of our friends and family. It's a small gathering—my sisters, Luke's family, and a few close friends, but that's all we need. This, right here, is what's important.

Magnus, Sem's husband is leading the ceremony and I follow along as best I can, but it's hard when I'm so distracted by him. My hands keep slipping across his chest, my mouth keeps moving towards his.

And when we finally say "I do", I'm ecstatic. I've never grinned so much in my life. My face hurts. I'll have to scowl extra hard tomorrow to make up for it.

"You're my husband now," Luke murmurs in my ear, sending shivers down my spine. "No getting rid of me now."

"I never want to be rid of you," I say, leaning into him.

"Ditto."

We link hands and walk back down the aisle, past the small gathering of family and friends toward my car.

"Do you think everyone will behave?" I ask Luke and he snorts.

"Not likely. I saw a giant box in the back of Liam's car earlier. I'm pretty sure those are fireworks, the big kind. And did you notice your sisters whispering something in Lex's ear? Don't even get me started on Amanda."

"What are the chances this reception ends with the police being called?" I ask. "Really, give me a percentage."

Luke laughs loudly. "Pretty good, Eli. Pretty damn good."

He opens the car door for me, I look up into his eyes and smile.

"Well, then I'm glad I have money set aside for bail."

"I've got some of that too. A special savings account for when my brothers need it."

"Oh Jesus...." I mutter.

Luke brushes his lips over mine. "You regretting your decision to be tethered to me for all eternity?"

"Of course not. In fact, I was just thinking that I am so glad you showed up to my house uninvited that day," I reply.

"And I'm so glad you snarled at me and ran over my foot with your car."

"I do not snarl."

"You do and I love you anyways."

"Hm," I say, reaching down and cupping his erection. "Love you too."

EPILOGUE

3 YEARS LATER

ELLIOT

"I'm home," I shout, entering the house and hearing the babies screeching. It's a symphony of horrendous tones and harmonies, enough to make my ears bleed.

Oh my god, this is my life now.

I turn the corner and see Luke wearing Amelia, Noah is in his swing, and Jacob is practicing tummy time in the playpen. They're all screaming—some in happier tones than others. Except Luke, he looks surprisingly calm and unflappable, like he revels in the mayhem.

We have three fucking kids. Triplets.

Trust me, I about fainted when I found out. Our surrogate was humungous and handled it all much more gracefully than I did.

They were all born six weeks premature, and Luke and I spent hours in the NICU with each of them, as did his parents, his brothers, and my sisters.

It takes a village. I never really understood that until now. I need a whole fucking city to deal with this chaos.

"Ma just left," Luke says, bouncing on his feet, rocking Amelia slightly. "Our little girl is teething or something, because she's a total grump. Reminds me of you."

I roll my eyes and lean up, pressing a kiss to her head and then to Luke's lips.

"And the other two?"

"Just fine. Noah is always happy in that swing and Jacob likes his toys. Oh, and before I forget, Jane and Kate said they'd be over tomorrow to help out so we can go grocery shopping."

"God, I need a break."

Luke snorts. "Yeah, me too."

Who would have thought that the idea of grocery shopping would be an ideal date night for Luke and I? Not me, but god, I wouldn't trade it for anything.

"And Lex will be over later so we can just sit in the peace and quiet."

"Who knew he'd be so good with kids?" I mutter and grab Jacob off the ground, nestling him into me. I inhale the sweet baby scent lingering on the top of his head and smile. He reaches out with his small hand and grabs onto my glasses, yanking them off my face.

"Not me," Luke says with a laugh and then presses another kiss to my mouth.

"He even said he'd take them on a long walk if you want to fuck around for a bit."

"Shh," I hiss, glancing at our children. "They might hear you."

"Nah, Eli. They don't understand what we're saying. But let's take him up on the offer. I wanna fuck you," he says and then adds. "Or you can fuck me. I could go either way."

"We'll see," I say, imagining all the things I want to do with him. It hasn't grown old in the least. Just less frequent. Because...well, we have three fucking kids now.

Noah starts to cry in earnest, and Luke moves over to grab him from the swing, cradling him in his arms. I move to kiss his soft head and smile down at him before glancing back up at Luke.

"God, I love you."

Luke smirks at me, and then we all sit together on the couch for some family time.

This is my life, I think in wonder.

It's crazy and wild, and completely out of my comfort zone, but it really couldn't be any more perfect.

AFTERWORD

I hope you loved this story as much as I loved writing it. Whit is my baby, but Luke has my heart.

Up next is Lex's book....or whatever other story I conjure up in the middle of the night.

ACKNOWLEDGMENTS

Thank you to the sensitivity readers who beta read this book and gave me valuable feedback. I so appreciate your time and willingness to make sure this was authentic and true.

To Corinne Rochelle and Michelle Kardolus for alpha reading this book and pointing me in the right direction. You are both amazing.

And to my editor, Angela O'Connell, for all your hard work on this book. You always make it shine.

And last, but not least, thank you to all the readers who reached out to me with words of encouragement. They mean everything and keep me writing.

ABOUT THE AUTHOR

Cora Rose loves any kind of romance and consumes way too many books each year. She currently lives in the U.S. and spends her days daydreaming about the characters inside her head.

You can reach her on her website or email her at Cora-RoseRomance@gmail.com